AFTER DARK
WITH
ROXIE CLARK

Also by Brooke Lauren Davis

The Hollow Inside

AFTER DARK
WITH
ROXIE CLARK

BROOKE LAUREN DAVIS

BLOOMSBURY

NEW YORK LONDON OXFORD NEW DELHI SYDNEY

BLOOMSBURY YA
Bloomsbury Publishing Inc., part of Bloomsbury Publishing Plc
1385 Broadway, New York, NY 10018

BLOOMSBURY and the Diana logo are trademarks of Bloomsbury Publishing Plc

First published in the United States of America in October 2022 by Bloomsbury YA

Bloomsbury books may be purchased for business or promotional use. For information on bulk
purchases please contact Macmillan Corporate and Premium Sales Department at
specialmarkets@macmillan.com

Library of Congress Cataloging-in-Publication Data
Names: Davis, Brooke Lauren, author.
Title: After dark with Roxie Clark / by Brooke Lauren Davis.
Description: New York : Bloomsbury Children's Books, 2022.
Summary: Eighteen-year-old Roxie agrees to help her sister Skylar uncover her
boyfriend's killer, but they discover that everyone in Whistler, Indiana, is
hiding something and some ghost stories are best left untold.
Identifiers: LCCN 2022007026 (print) | LCCN 2022007027 (e-book)
ISBN 978-1-5476-0614-6 (hardcover) • ISBN 978-1-5476-0615-3 (e-book)
Subjects: CYAC: Murder—Fiction. | Sisters—Fiction. | Secrets—Fiction. |
City and town life—Fiction. | LCGFT: Novels.
Classification: LCC PZ7.1.D3575 Af 2022 (print) | LCC PZ7.1.D3575 (e-book) |
DDC [Fic]—dc23
LC record available at https://lccn.loc.gov/2022007026
LC e-book record available at https://lccn.loc.gov/2022007027

Book design by Yelena Safronova
Typeset by Westchester Publishing Services
Printed and bound in the U.S.A.
2 4 6 8 10 9 7 5 3 1

To find out more about our authors and books visit www.bloomsbury.com
and sign up for our newsletters.

To my siblings—Weston, Afton, and Aubri

AFTER DARK
WITH
ROXIE CLARK

1

"It's easy to believe in ghosts on a night like tonight, don't you think?"

Roxie Clark picked her way through the dark of the woods with the grace and ease of a dancer, like her combat boots were light as ballet slippers and the roots and crumbling leaves were as level as a stage.

Her audience trailed behind her—a tour group of eight people—and they responded with nervous coughs and laughter. Roxie's lips curled into a ghoulish smile in the middle of her skull-painted face.

The group stumbled over the forest bracken, loud enough to wake the dead. They followed the narrow beam of her flashlight, but they could have found her in the dark without it. Her long hair was so pale, it seemed to give off its own unearthly glow—a will-o'-the-wisp that might lead them into a fairy tale or might lure them to their deaths.

The air smelled like smoke and decaying leaves. The night was cold, the breeze even colder, shuddering through the body like a spirit. Roxie had always liked the cold—how awake it made her feel, prickling her cheeks, threading through her fingers, quaking up her spine.

She came to an abrupt stop. So abrupt, a woman walking behind Roxie stumbled into her back with a startled yelp, which sent the woman's teenage daughters into a fit of giggles.

Roxie held up her finger for silence. "Hear that?" she said.

The group hushed, quiet enough to make out the murmur of moving water.

Under Roxie's direction, everyone fanned out at the edge of the creek. The water unfurled under the glow of the moon, fifteen feet across, pulsing slow and sinuous like the glossy back of a snake.

Roxie took a moment to get a head count. As much as her sister liked to chalk it up to years of unfortunate coincidences, it wouldn't be the first time someone was swallowed up by these woods, never to be heard from again—and certainly not the first time it had happened to a Clark.

The group took their time shuffling into place but eventually quieted, waiting for her to begin her story. But Roxie patiently counted off another thirty seconds in her head before she spoke, because she'd learned silence unnerved people more than anything she could say. She let them listen to the murmur of the early autumn wind sieving through the shadowed trees— the scratch and hiss of dead leaves and sharp branches.

Then she shined her flashlight underneath her chin,

illuminating the skull makeup she so meticulously applied before every ghost tour. Even after so much practice, it still took her nearly an hour to get it just right. She always rushed through dinner on tour nights—every Friday and Saturday, from September 1 to October 31—usually scalding the roof of her mouth on whatever casserole her grandmother had made, just to make sure she'd have enough time. But it was worth it. Because Roxie knew good storytelling was all about the details.

"There was once a tavern on the edge of town called the Dog's Head, owned by a woman named Aurora Clark," she began, the same way she always began the tale of her great-great-aunt. "It was named for the taxidermy dog's head mounted above the bar. She told everyone who asked that she had killed it herself after it attacked her.

"Ripped it open from its belly to its chin with this knife right here, she'd say, fingering the one she always wore around her neck.

"Though that wasn't the truth. The dog had been her beloved pet when she was a girl, a German shepherd named Prince who followed her everywhere until the day he passed from old age. She couldn't stand the thought of burying him, abandoning him in the ground forever—especially those big, shiny black eyes that had looked at her with so much love.

"And besides, the head and the story she told about it served a purpose. It wasn't easy, being a young woman running a tavern all on her own. As long as everyone *believed* it was the truth, it gave her flinty stare some weight and her words extra force when she told her rowdiest customers it was time to go home."

Perhaps Roxie had inherited some of her own flair for story

from Aurora. Though it hadn't come without practice. She knew exactly how her voice sounded to her audience—equal parts inviting and ominous. She'd rehearsed the exact words of Aurora's tale over and over, recording herself and playing it back dozens of times. And then dozens more, until she stopped sounding rehearsed. She knew where to pause, where to raise her voice, where to whisper and make her rapt listeners lean in close.

"Aurora was no stranger to hard times. Her mother had been lost in a fire, and her father had been a mean man, too simple to make a point without using his fists. Living with him had made her harder and meaner herself, like a wild animal, driven through life solely by her need to survive it. It was a blessing when he ran off with a lover and left her alone to run the tavern. Things finally seemed to be looking up for her. Until the Eighteenth Amendment came along and banned the production and sale of alcohol—destroying her business in the process."

Roxie felt the eyes of the group tracking her every move as she paced along the edge of the water, and she relished their undivided attention.

"*I won't lose this, too*, Aurora thought. *Not this. This place is* mine."

But, of course, Roxie had no way of knowing exactly what was running through Aurora's head a hundred years ago. All she had to go on was what she'd found at the Whistler Public Library—an old newspaper clipping with just a few sparse lines about the incident. If anyone pressed her about it, she would admit some of the details were her invention—but with a dismissive wave of her hand, like such technicalities hardly mattered.

There'd been a grainy, black-and-white photograph of Aurora with the article. She had only been nineteen at the time, but she'd looked much older. Worn down. From the moment Roxie saw that photograph, the story came so clearly to her, it was almost as if her great-great-aunt had whispered the whole thing in her eager ear.

Maybe it was intuition. Her grandmother had always said she was attuned to people in a way that was beyond explanation. Or maybe it was just that poor Aurora had been a Clark and her story had always lived dormant in Roxie's blood, waiting for the day she would draw it out.

"So, against the law, Aurora continued selling alcohol, running her business under the table—or, rather, under the tavern, through the small cellar window. But only for people who knew just the right knock and could whisper the password. The window would slide open, an impatient hand would collect the money, and then a glass bottle would roll through before the window slammed shut again. She managed to keep the operation going for a year. But then, as it always did, Aurora's luck ran out."

Somewhere, a branch snapped. Sound was notoriously tricky in these woods, rumored to travel in ways that defied logic— maybe it had come from something small and fluffy a hundred feet off or maybe something with teeth, just a step away, breathing down their necks.

"The law had sniffed her out. She heard them when they came knocking on her door. She needed to run—but not before she jammed her pockets full of all the money in her safe then pulled the head of her beloved dog off the wall and tucked it under her arm. She hurried out the back door with her heavy pockets chiming, the sound mingling with the roar of the heavy rain that had started to fall.

"Her escape was slow, her boots sliding in the mud and the large dog head throwing off her balance. Her pursuers were hard on her heels—and they had dogs of their own.

"Aurora scurried over roots and crashed through tree branches. She fell again and again, struggling to stand more each time as her rain-soaked coat grew heavier, until she was forced to shed it, discarding every penny she owned. But she held on to the dog's head. She wouldn't leave behind her sweet Prince. He was the only friend she had left in the world. He was *hers*.

"Then she came to the creek, which had risen high, flowing over its banks and running swiftly east. She jumped into the frigid water, letting it carry her away from her pursuers.

"And it seemed her plan had worked; it didn't take long for her to get swept so far that the bloodthirsty barking became a distant echo.

"But getting back to solid ground wasn't easy—she could hardly keep her head above water, with only one free arm to swim with.

"She kicked, she clawed, putting up a vicious fight for shore.

"But in the end, it wasn't quite enough. Perhaps it would have been, if she'd let go of her dog. Instead, the only friend she'd had in life sank her like an anchor, down to her death."

When Roxie got to the end of the story, she lowered her voice ominously, gripping her flashlight with both hands as she said, "Legend has it, Aurora still lingers here, protecting her sweet Prince from anyone who dares go into the creek."

The legend had been started by Roxie herself, of course. But she didn't think that made it any less of a legend.

She motioned the tour group forward. "Maybe one of us will catch a glimpse of her tonight."

There was a moment's pause, the group members glancing at one another with more uncertain giggling and shrugging. Then they ventured to the edge of the creek, some of them bold enough to get on their knees for a better look at the black water. A few pulled pennies from their pockets and flicked them in— an offering to the dead woman underneath.

But one person from the tour group wasn't interested in looking for Aurora. He wanted to talk to Roxie instead—a man who had come with a group of his friends, all out-of-towners, stumbling and a little rowdy from time spent at the Whistler Bar & Grill before they'd come.

"Why don't you tell the one about the Riley kid?" he asked. "They found his body not far from here, right?"

Roxie blinked at him.

She'd be a hypocrite to judge him for being curious. She told stories about dead people all the time and had been fascinated by the macabre all her life. While some people wanted to distance themselves from grim realities, she had never been one to turn away from the dark.

But she narrowed her eyes at the man. "I only tell stories about my own family," she said. "That one isn't mine to tell."

Wanting to leave it at that, she started walking away from him.

But the man stopped her again when he said, "I heard your sister saw the murderer. I think that makes it a story about your family after all."

Her sister *might* have seen the murderer. There had been a series of robberies in the weeks leading up to Colin's death. One of them turned violent when the perpetrator shot and killed a teller at the bank. The last robbery had occurred at a repair shop in town, while her sister was working.

The murder had occurred later that night, close by. Possibly within a few minutes. Roxie shuddered to think what might have happened if her sister hadn't thought quickly, finding the owner's gun under the counter to scare him off.

However, the police had yet to confirm the identity of the robber or the killer, nor did they have any firm evidence that the two were the same person.

And, anyway, Roxie wasn't about to get into the finer points of Colin's case with some tipsy guy on her ghost tour.

She said slowly, so there would be no room for misunderstanding, "This is my tour, and I tell whatever stories I want to. I don't want to tell that one."

The man lifted his hands, feigning innocence as he gave a derisive laugh. "All right, lady. Your rules." Then he fished in his pocket and held out a five-dollar bill—a tip.

Which Roxie took, because cash was cash, and face paint wouldn't pay for itself. But she pointedly did not say *thank you* before the man walked away.

He'd left her feeling unsettled. She was used to talking about death. Someone bringing it up shouldn't have rattled her. But it had.

Because for Roxie, Colin wasn't a story. He was a memory—a springy head of curls the color of cinnamon. A secret tattoo of a sugar maple on his chest that she'd sworn not to tell his mom about. A devilish grin that helped him charm his way out of just about anything.

And the most vivid image of them all—the one that still made Roxie feel dizzy and sick, over a year later—

A body, torn apart by a knife and half-scorched, left to burn in a cornfield on the edge of town.

She shook her head, doing her best to clear it. She didn't have time to be distracted.

This was the last tour stop of the night, and some people had started wandering back the way they'd come, speculating on plans for the rest of the evening.

But the show wasn't over yet. Roxie had one last surprise up her sleeve. A grand finale she hoped none of them would soon forget.

She scanned the ground for something, searching frantically before she lost the attention of the tour group entirely. And then she found it, precisely where she'd left it—a glint of silver buried in the leaves. It was a metal cuff, swung open like a jaw, ready to bite.

When Roxie brought her heel down hard on the trigger at its center, it clamped shut around her ankle.

Then she threw herself on the ground and screamed.

The people in the tour group turned to stare at her, stunned as she put on a real slasher-movie performance, screeching and thrashing and digging her fingernails into the dirt as she was dragged backward, into the creek.

The cuff around her ankle was hooked to a rope, which was submerged underwater and attached to a reel mounted to a thick tree root at the bottom of the creek. The contraption was designed to reel her in like a fish whenever the cuff was closed, making it look like the ghost of Aurora Clark was dragging her to the depths.

She'd been studying ghost tours long enough to know how hard it was to actually scare anyone, because that's exactly what people on a ghost tour expect you to try to do. And that's why she wasn't offended when not a single person jumped forward to save her as her legs slipped deeper and deeper into the frigid water.

Instead, one by one, they all started to laugh.

It was a thin, uncomfortable laugh. They waited for her to cut the act—to stand and brush herself off. But their laughter got quieter, more uneasy, as she sank deeper into the creek. Her legs went under, then her hips, then her chest. Then her head.

Once she was completely submerged, Roxie stopped screaming and struggling. She reached down and pressed on a small lever at the back of the cuff, springing it open.

There was no way for Roxie to know how the group was reacting up top. She'd tested out the reel dozens of times beforehand, but this was the first time she'd used it on a tour, and she was eager to gauge the results. But, as curious as she was (and as freaking *cold* as she was), she couldn't come up just yet.

She'd heard once that Navy SEALs were trained to hold their breath for two minutes. With daily practice, Roxie had gotten up to almost two and a half.

She could just make out raised voices coming from the surface now, but through the murky water, she couldn't see anyone or make out what they were saying.

She couldn't help playing out the whole thing in her head. After a few seconds, she imagined the laughter would completely peter out. A few more seconds, and they'd be looking down the creek in both directions, waiting for her to pop up somewhere. They'd peer down into the water, trying to make out her form or the gurgle of air bubbles. Perhaps signs of a struggle?

Do you think she's okay?

Faking it. Definitely faking it.

But what if she's not? Can you hold your breath that long?

Hell no. I'd have passed out by now.

Someone should go in after her.

No, no, she's messing with us.

It looked like something was dragging her. How could she fake that?

You don't think—

What if—

Roxie wondered if anyone would call 911. She could see it on her ghost tour brochures now—*An experience so terrifying, patrons have called the police!*

She was visualizing fonts and clip art for the new promo material, just barely starting to feel the burn of oxygen deprivation, when a strong arm hooked around her waist.

She felt herself jerked backward into someone's chest, and all the air left in her lungs was forced out in a plume of bubbles.

She dug her nails into the arm, fought against the iron grip, kicking her legs and beating with her fists.

But it wouldn't let go. Her vision blurred and her lungs screamed, and the dark water swirled as she was jerked through the creek—she couldn't tell in which direction.

And all she could think, in what might be her final moments, was how the people of Whistler would respond to the news of her death. She saw them shaking their heads, trying to ward off the deep chill that passed over them, maybe even crossing themselves as they thought, *The Clark Curse always gets them in the end.*

2

Just as Roxie started to believe she was about to join the ranks of her own ghost tour, her head broke through the surface of the water, and she gasped a desperate lungful of air, only to suck down enough of the creek to set her coughing and gasping.

A heavy hand pounded between her shoulders until she stopped. And then it turned her roughly around, and Roxie froze, startled into silence.

His wet, black hair was matted to his forehead and curled against his neck. Muddy water dripped down between his eyes, which were dark and narrowed and positively murderous.

And Roxie wished, not for the first time, that her tour could be as terrifying as that look on his face.

"Hello, Tristan," she said, as though she'd just run into him in the self-checkout line at Kroger.

She was used to his lethal gaze, but when he turned it on the tour group—all of them still gathered at the edge of the creek, giving Roxie and Tristan their rapt attention—they collectively flinched.

"Tour's over," he growled. "Go."

When they hesitated, he dipped his head, just slightly, like an animal about to charge. "*Go*," he said again.

And that was all it took to send them scurrying back in the direction they'd come, lighting the way with their cell phones. Roxie watched them retreat with a twinge of annoyance. With one word, Tristan had scared them more than she'd managed to do all night.

When the last of the group was swallowed up by the trees, Tristan grabbed a root protruding from the bank and pulled himself out of the creek. Roxie climbed out behind him; he pointedly did not offer her a hand.

She pretended not to notice the slice of his stomach that showed when he wrung out his shirt. Not to mention the way it clung to his back and broad shoulders.

He waited until she was all the way back on her feet, her meticulously applied skull makeup dripping into her eyes and down her neck, before he snapped, "What the hell were you thinking?"

Roxie crossed her arms over her chest in a way that she hoped looked defiant, though she was actually shielding herself against the breeze that was whistling through the woods, making her shiver in her damp clothes. "What are you even doing here?" she snapped back.

"Your grandma asked me to walk you home."

"She *what?*"

Roxie had always felt more herself at night than during the day, and from an early age, she had developed a bad habit of sneaking out after dark to wander the streets and talk to whatever shadows she could find. She had gone through Netflix's entire catalog of horror movies before she started middle school, from the critically acclaimed to the laughably bad. She spent almost all her free time submerged in research about Whistler's dearly departed, teasing out whatever haunted threads she could find. She was the (self-proclaimed) Expert on All Things Horrifying and Creepy and Strange.

And she absolutely did *not* need an escort home.

She took a breath, ready to launch into a vicious argument when Tristan cut her off. "Take it up with Gertie. I'm just following orders."

"Do you do everything my grandma tells you to do?"

"It's a damn good thing I did this time," he snapped. "Do you know how many ways this could have gone wrong?"

"But it didn't go wrong," she reminded him, ducking behind a tree to retrieve the towel she'd hidden there before the tour started. She swiped the mess of black-and-white makeup from her eyes then tried to wring the mud from her pale hair before she held the towel out toward him—a peace offering

Tristan didn't take it. His severe look didn't crack. "Seriously, Roxie. What if the cuff malfunctioned and wouldn't release? What if you got stuck on something at the bottom of the creek? Or hit your head?"

Roxie rolled her eyes toward the star-scattered sky. "Everything was moving along flawlessly until you showed up."

"But what if—"

"What if I trip at school and impale myself on a pencil?" Roxie rubbed the towel roughly over her arms, trying to get some warmth back into her numb limbs. "What if an airplane falls from the sky and crashes through the roof while I'm sleeping?"

Tristan stared at her, his fury clouded for a moment by bewilderment. "What the hell are you talking about?

"My point is that anything could happen at any time, and I'm not going to let all the what-ifs bully me into a boring life."

In triumph, Roxie turned on her heel to walk back to the main road, pulling the damp towel tight over her shoulders.

"What about Skylar?"

Roxie stopped short when Tristan said her sister's name, like the ghost of Aurora Clark had grabbed her by the ankle after all.

Without turning around, she said, "What *about* Skylar?"

"Do you think she could take it if something happened to you?"

He came up beside her. She scowled at her boots rather than look at him.

He leaned in close to whisper, "Do you want to put her through that again? Do you think she'd survive it?"

Roxie didn't answer.

She didn't tell Tristan that Skylar hadn't said more than a few words to her in the year since Colin's death. That if something did happen to Roxie, she wasn't sure her sister would even notice.

"Promise me you're never going to pull this stunt again."

When she looked up to meet his gaze, she suspected it wasn't just Skylar who couldn't handle another tragedy—Tristan's brother had been the one murdered, after all.

Roxie's fists clenched and unclenched at her sides. She tried to come up with another argument. Anything that didn't make her sound like a complete asshole with total disregard for her own life and anyone else's feelings.

But, finally, she let go of a deep sigh and said, "Fine."

Tristan gave her a short nod in response. Then he turned back toward the creek.

"Wait," Roxie said.

He didn't respond.

She hurried after him, struggling to keep up with his long strides. "Tristan, don't you *dare*—"

"Do you want me coming back to every single one of your tours to make sure you don't drown yourself?"

That rankled Roxie down to her core—Tristan was her best friend, not her babysitter.

"Fine," she growled again. "Take it."

He kneeled on the creek bank, plunged his hands into the dark water, and hauled out the thick, dripping rope that had dragged Roxie under just a few minutes ago. He wrapped it around his forearm, and bracing his boot against a rock, he started to pull.

Roxie winced as she watched. The reel had taken her days to install. It had been a whole process, waiting for a week of dry weather, until the water was low enough that she could find a solid root near the bottom. She used extra-long screws to get the best hold, like the lady at the hardware store had recommended. There was no way Tristan would be strong enough to—

But with a little sweat and a lot of cursing, he ripped the reel free.

It was streaming mud, but Tristan coiled the rope and tucked the unwieldy thing under his arm anyway. Then he turned back in the direction of town and started walking.

Roxie chased after him. "I paid good money for that," she said.

Tristan knew exactly what she'd paid for it—he was the one who'd built it for her.

"You didn't tell me you'd be using it underwater. Or on yourself, for that matter. I specifically remember you telling me Bethel would be the one getting dragged, and I was secretly hoping she'd get destroyed in the process. She's creepy as hell."

Bethel was the name of Roxie's creepy life-size clown doll. And he was right. She *was* creepy as hell. Which was precisely what Roxie liked about her and why she didn't want to risk ruining her with this stunt. Besides—she thought a live subject would be more interesting.

"I'll give you a refund," he said.

"I don't want a refund. I'll just figure out a safer use for it."

He barked a laugh at that. "Don't bullshit me."

"I mean it!"

He stopped, giving her a hard stare. "Roxie Clark, you and I both know you don't do safe."

She opened her mouth to argue. But then she closed it.

This was the boy who had watched her climb all the way to the top of Devil's Peak last year, walking out to the edge of the highest cliff, her arms flung out for balance, just so she could get the best view of the lights in Whistler at night.

He'd been there when she was fourteen and she attempted to jump across a collapsed bridge on her bike, simply because an annoying boy from school dared her to do it.

He'd watched, horrified, when she was twelve and she'd found a black widow spider on a branch and tried to coax it into crawling onto her hand so she could get a better look at its lovely red spots.

And he'd also been there when she'd been rushed to the emergency room after all three of those stunts had gone horribly wrong.

Refusing to admit out loud that she saw his point, she asked instead, "So, when do I get the reel back, then?"

Tristan started walking away again. "How about when you're mature enough to handle it?"

Roxie gasped audibly. "How *dare* you—"

He cast a glance over his shoulder at her, a devilish slant to his lips, and gave her a sly wink—he was taunting her on purpose now.

With a growl, she lunged toward him, and he took off running. He usually had no problem outpacing her, from the time they were kids and they used to race each other home from school, but the reel slowed him down. She jumped onto his back, wrapping her arms tight around his neck and snarling into his ear, "You messed with the wrong girl, Riley."

He reached around behind him and jabbed her in the ribs, in the exact spot where she was most ticklish, and she yelped, letting him go.

She chased him all the way back home, making darting grabs for the back of his shirt, but he twisted deftly away every time. Their laughter echoed through the dark woods and down the deserted streets of Whistler.

The shops and restaurants were closed up for the night, everyone else safe in their homes, tucking into bed, their lights starting to go out one by one.

Roxie and Tristan were alone, but in Whistler, it was impossible to ever quite feel that way.

Everyone who lived in the town believed it was haunted. That was Roxie's expert opinion. As the proprietor of the best ghost tour in Indiana (according to the reviews on her website), it was her business to be attuned to the fears, doubts, and superstitions of everyone around her. But she'd never bothered to ask anyone about it directly, because she was sure most of them would lie through their teeth. They wouldn't want to be called things like *paranoid, weird, gruesome, dark, unnerving,* or *strange.* The kinds of words people were always whispering about her.

Or better yet, shouting at her from across the cafeteria while she gave them the finger, showing off her black manicure, filed into points as sharp as claws.

Whatever they said, there was no way they didn't feel the place's uniquely ominous quality. Almost like a cloud had settled over it. Lingering.

Roxie had been to plenty of other places, and none of them

felt quite like this one. All you had to do was walk down any street in Whistler, any time of day, to find out what she meant. Like every breath she drew was shared with someone else.

It's just something you have to experience for yourself, the home page of her ghost-tour website read. *And if you need a guide, come find me.*

3

Roxie had seen three dead bodies in her life.

The first was her aunt Violet's, collapsed on the kitchen floor, her cheek resting in a congealed pool of blood and her blue eyes popped open in surprise.

Roxie was six years old and fast asleep in the top bunk of the guest bedroom that Aunt Violet kept just for her nieces. She would have stayed asleep for hours more if her older sister hadn't come to wake her at dawn, sobbing hysterically.

Even at seven years old, Skylar Clark was not one for wasting daylight, and she always woke before the sun did. She'd padded into the kitchen in her pajamas that morning, hoping Aunt Violet would be up soon to make them chocolate-chip pancakes, the way she always did when the girls stayed with her while Grandma worked a night shift at the hospital.

But Aunt Violet had never gone to bed—nor would she ever be making them chocolate-chip pancakes again. Neither of the girls had woken when the woman tripped over a stool left out in the kitchen and hit her head on the sharp corner of the countertop.

Skylar had been the one to call 911. She'd sat on the couch with her eyes squeezed shut until the police came.

Roxie cried, too. But she sat next to the body instead, holding her aunt Violet's cold hand. Even when Skylar screamed at her to stop, that she shouldn't touch it, Roxie snapped back, *It's Aunt Violet!* And she didn't let go until her grandmother came.

From that day on, Skylar was meticulous about keeping their house clean and uncluttered, as though it were a matter of life or death—because, in Aunt Violet's case, it had been. The way she looked at it, a knife left out on the counter was bound to end up in someone's eye, and a pair of boots thrown near the top of the stairs was a one-way ticket to breaking your neck, and a stray sock left on the floor was certain to end with you slipping right into the burning fireplace.

She seemed to think that as long as she kept everything in its place, nothing like what had happened to Aunt Violet would ever happen again.

Roxie, however, was far too busy to worry about keeping her room tidy, let alone concern herself with the state of the rest of the house. She spent all her free time learning more about the kind woman who took them in so many nights while their grandma was working late. Who looked so like their mother but hardly spoke of the woman who had abandoned them. Roxie went through boxes of old photographs and newspaper clippings from when Violet made it to the state swimming competition and a decade later, when she won Indiana's award for teacher of the year. She found old love notes shoved into a copy of *Pride and Prejudice*, signed by a boy named Joey.

Skylar called her morbid. She refused to look at the photos, or touch anything that had belonged to Aunt Violet, or even say her name—as though any proximity to the dead woman might bring death upon herself. As though tragedy were somehow contagious.

But learning about her aunt Violet made Roxie feel the opposite—like Aunt Violet became more alive the more Roxie remembered her.

On a rainy afternoon, she was turning through the pages of one of her aunt's old yearbooks from Whistler High School, studying the signatures. Amidst all the scribbled wishes for a great summer and entreaties to never change, someone had doodled a pair of devil horns in red ink and written in big, bold letters underneath,

HOPE THE CLARK CURSE DOESN'T GET YOU
THIS SUMMER.

⌣

The second dead body that Roxie had ever seen was her mother's.

This time there was no blood. There were also no tears. Roxie was thirteen and Skylar was fourteen, and they stood in an eggshell-blue room at the crematorium while their grandmother stood behind them, squeezing them both by the shoulders.

None of them had seen the woman on the table in almost a decade. That's how long ago Katherine Clark had taken off, her engine revving in the dead of night, letting everyone in Whistler know she'd finally done what she'd been threatening to do since she was a child—running away from home to become a musician.

She'd always wanted to live loud, banging on her drum set in the garage until the neighbors called to complain, listening to the stereo so high the walls shook, taking lessons on an acoustic guitar at the music shop down the street until she'd squirreled away enough of her allowance to buy an electric one behind her mother's back. She did not want to strum sweet melodies and sing in a whisper—she would wail and screech over a thunder of her own making.

Until she'd gotten pregnant with Skylar. And then she'd tried to learn to be quiet.

She did not take to motherhood, like everyone said she would. It required patience she didn't have. Wisdom she didn't understand. Steadfastness she didn't feel. And it'd taken so much time, tending to Skylar hour after hour, and Roxie, too, when she'd come along. Time she'd still craved to have for herself—time that was whittled away even more when her boyfriend, the girls' father, had left her alone.

Most of all, she hated singing lullabies in a quiet nursery when all she wanted to do was howl into a microphone over the roar of a packed house.

Katherine had a single-minded, knife-sharp focus—a trademark the Clark women were known for. The longer she'd stayed, the more she'd felt like she only delayed the inevitable.

And so, she'd taken off, fulfilling the fate she'd wanted for herself but breaking her heart too as she left her girls behind.

Or at least that's how Roxie imagined her mother must have felt. Grandma hadn't been very forthcoming with any details of Katherine's life or what her thoughts might have been, so Roxie had pieced the story together herself.

Her research into the life of Aunt Violet had quickly spiraled into something much more, her interest spreading to the rest of the mysterious Clarks. She'd started digging through Grandma's family albums and keepsake chests and attic boxes, pawing through moldy journals and musty clothes, even trying on some garments that hadn't known the touch of flesh for decades.

Once she'd run out of material at the house, and Grandma had run through all the family stories she could remember at least three times, Roxie had moved on to the public library, going through local history books and scouring the newspaper archives.

She'd learned that the Clark women had more in common with one another than headstrong natures. And that common thread was tragedy.

There had been accidental drownings. Unexplained fires. Terrible car crashes and stabbings and shootings. Mysterious disappearances. Unlucky falls.

It hadn't taken long for the pattern to emerge. Not all the Clark women died young, of course, but the ones who hadn't seemed to be the exceptions rather than the rule. In fact, it had appeared that other than Skylar, Katherine, Grandma, and Roxie herself, there were no Clark women left.

Roxie had tried to show her sister, tried to explain to her what had to be obvious to anyone looking at the evidence. *Don't you see what this means? We're doomed! We could die at any moment.*

Skylar had rolled her eyes, used to Roxie's melodramatics. *Why are you telling me this?*

Isn't it obvious? So we can start living *like we could die at any moment!*

Truthfully, to Roxie, the realization had been somewhat liberating. What reason did they have to be careful when death was bound to come knocking anyway? Why not live the rest of her inevitably short life exactly how she wanted to?

But Skylar wouldn't listen. *There's no such thing as curses*, she'd said.

Then they'd gotten the news a few weeks later that their mother had died in an accident, crashing her car while driving drunk down Santa Monica Boulevard. But if Skylar saw it as a sign that Roxie might be right, she never said so.

Studying the woman on the table, Roxie had been struck by how much their mother looked like Skylar—chestnut curls, bright-blue eyes, and sharp chin. Right down to the little indent in their noses. Maybe that'd been why Skylar could hardly stand to look at her now. She probably thought no one noticed the way she'd focused her gaze on the edge of the table rather than at the woman lying on it. But her sister did.

Roxie had inherited her father's pale-blond hair and gray eyes. But it was Roxie that everyone in town compared with Katherine. Every time she got in trouble at school or hopelessly scraped up her elbows playing too rough at the park or talked back to an adult in a spit of anger, people always shook their heads and said, *You're just like your mother.*

Some of them added in a mutter they thought she couldn't hear: *God help you.*

Maybe that was why Grandma had seemed to be speaking to Roxie directly when she'd said, her voice thick, *Katherine lit her candle at both ends. And it burned her right up.*

Without taking her gaze from the edge of the table, Skylar had squeezed Roxie's wrist. Hard.

We won't be like her, she'd said.

On their way out, Roxie could have sworn she heard one of the crematory technicians whisper to another, *The curse always gets them in the end.*

⌣

The third body Roxie ever saw was not a Clark.

It had been almost midnight, the summer before Roxie turned seventeen, and she hadn't gone to sleep yet. She'd been busy putting the finishing touches on her new website. It was all part of a project she'd been working tirelessly on for the past six months—a ghost tour with stories that spanned hundreds of years, weaving together the harrowing and tragic lives of all the Clark women before her.

Her interest in her ancestors had become less of a hobby and more of an all-consuming obsession.

The more she learned about them, the more alive they became to her. There was a photograph she kept by her bedside of her great-great-grandmother, her head thrown back in laughter, and though Roxie had been born years after the woman died, she imagined she could hear its exact pitch echoing through the halls of the house. A half-finished diary from a second cousin revealed a love affair between her and a prominent pastor's daughter, and Roxie found wrinkled spots in the final pages that she swore had to be tearstains. There was a grainy home video of a great-aunt baking a pie, sticking her tongue out between her teeth while she kneaded the dough, and watching it always made Roxie smile—even though the woman had died a few days after the video was taken when her kitchen caught fire.

That's the same face you make when you're concentrating, she'd once told Skylar. *The* exact *same one.*

But Skylar would hardly glance at the video. *God*, she'd muttered instead. *Why are you so morbid? Get your head out of the attic and go . . . I don't know, contribute to society or something.*

Dwelling with ghosts was a waste of time, in Skylar's opinion. And Skylar Clark did *not* waste time. Her days were filled with studying heavy biology tomes and quizzing herself with a constant rotation of flash cards—a set of habits that had earned her early admission to Yale University, which she was supposed to be leaving for in just a few days.

Skylar was on track for medical school once she got through undergrad—a goal she'd had since she was twelve. Roxie didn't have the slightest idea what she planned to do after high school, too busy looking backward, her preoccupation with the past eclipsing any concern for the future. Skylar was fascinated by life and all the ways she could preserve it. Roxie was gripped by death and determined to memorialize it.

Truthfully, they probably would have drifted apart years ago if it hadn't been for the Riley brothers.

The Rileys came to Whistler the autumn Roxie turned eleven, Skylar was thirteen, and the boys were both twelve. They were renting the house next door to the Clarks, and Grandma Gertie was their landlord—it was the house she'd inherited from Aunt Violet when she died.

Colin had been the first to make contact between the families, knocking on the Clarks' door one afternoon and shoving his hand in Skylar's face the moment she opened it. "Check out this frog!"

He'd meant to scare her. But Skylar hadn't flinched—only wrinkled her nose slightly at his crassness. Then she'd taken the creature from his hand and informed him, *It's not a frog. It's a toad. You can tell by its short legs.*

She'd released the toad into the flower bed, as though to spare the creature this boy's ignorance, then went back into the house and shut the door in his face without another word.

From that day forward, it'd been clear to everyone in town that Colin was enamored with Skylar, following her around like a puppy without a leash, talking about her any chance he got to anyone who would listen—how smart she was, how witty, how completely, unbelievably beautiful.

He'd turned up almost every day to sit at the Clarks' kitchen table while she'd studied and he pretended to but mostly just stole glances at her from under his unkempt red-brown curls and tried to distract her with life's big philosophical questions, like, *Do you think bugs have dreams?* or, *What's your favorite letter of the alphabet?*

Which Roxie thought must've annoyed the hell out of her,

but Skylar had answered all his questions patiently without ever taking her eyes from whatever she was working on. And she'd kept asking him to come over to study every night.

By Skylar's sophomore year, they'd been officially dating. By junior year, he'd given her a promise ring while she told him, *The odds of high school romances working out are not in your favor,* all while she blushed and smiled uncontrollably.

Then there was the other Riley brother, Tristan, who wasn't half as charming. He towered over almost everyone at school. His curls were black, his shoulders wide and powerful where Colin's were wiry, his gaze guarded where Colin's was warm. Rumors had swirled around him from the day he arrived in Whistler, the most popular one being that they'd had to move in the first place because Tristan couldn't control his temper— hence the crooked nose that had clearly been broken at some point. That, and a severe case of resting bitch face, had solidified his status as an outcast.

It was natural, Roxie thought, for the two people Whistler was most afraid of to drift toward each other. It turned out that talking about dead people all the time was not the best method for making friends. She'd also taken to wearing almost exclusively black, adding heavy eyeliner, dark lipstick, and spiked jewelry for good measure.

It had started slowly at first—taking the empty seat next to each other on the bus and volunteering to be each other's lab partners when no one else would. Before long, they were sneaking out almost every night together to wander the deserted sidewalks and wooded paths on their bikes.

But the night Roxie had been up late working on her

website, Tristan wasn't home. He'd been out of town, staying with a cousin. So when she'd heard the sirens outside her window—first from a fire truck, followed by two more, an ambulance, and a horde of police cruisers—he wasn't there to sneak out with her and investigate. So Roxie had tiptoed across the hallway to her sister's room instead, trying not to wake Grandma on the third floor.

Skylar had already been sitting up in bed. *What's happening?* she'd whispered.

Let's go find out, Roxie had said.

They'd made their way down Poplar Avenue without a word to each other, Roxie in her rumpled clothes from the day before and a pair of unlaced combat boots and Skylar in her pajamas, her sneakers silent against the asphalt. Roxie had thought she could smell smoke as they approached the crowd quickly gathering by the cornfield at the edge of town.

Their expressions had been a mixture of tension, fear, and deep, deep sadness. A few of their faces had been streaked with tears, reflecting the lights of the emergency vehicles.

Skylar had grabbed the first person they saw—Linda, who used to give them piano lessons—and demanded, *What's going on?*

Linda had looked pained, pressing her lips together and shaking her head. *Maybe you girls should—*

Tell me what happened, Skylar had said again, her tone making it clear she wasn't leaving without an answer.

A boy has died.

Who?

After another moment's hesitation, Linda said, *One of the Rileys.*

Roxie felt a surge of panic in her chest at the words. She watched the blood drain from her sister's face.

Skylar asked, *Which one?*

When Linda hadn't answered right away, Skylar had taken off suddenly, charging under the police tape, slipping through the fingers of the officer who reached for her, ignoring Roxie, who'd chased behind her and begged, *Wait.*

They didn't have to venture far to find him, sprawled out on the ground between two rows of cornstalks that had been burned to blackened husks, what was left of them hissing with the breeze. His eyes had stared blankly up at the night sky.

Roxie thought she knew death. But this time was different. Because the third dead body she ever saw wasn't there because of an accident.

His body had been partially burned but not enough to completely hide his wounds. There had been holes all over him, cut through his T-shirt and staining the white fabric red. A gaping chasm in his side where he must have been stabbed again and again, the flesh hanging open and the pink of his insides spilling out.

If there had been any doubt, the knife left lodged in his chest put it to rest.

Murdered. Colin Riley had been murdered.

4

On the morning of Roxie's eighteenth birthday, Grandma was in the kitchen, humming like she knew a secret her granddaughter didn't.

This was a woman who, standing at four feet and eleven inches, had been going toe to toe with the Clark Curse for eighty-three years. Just under her wispy cap of white hair was a pale scar that ran from her temple to her jaw—the result of a car accident that killed her sister. Then there was the cancer that took her left eye, which she'd replaced with a glass one. She'd lost two daughters in the last decade, one to a freak accident and the other to recklessness. After all she'd been through, it was miraculous she found anything to hum about at all.

But rather than admiring her resilience, Roxie regarded Grandma suspiciously, her mouth stretching into a wide yawn as she plopped down at the kitchen table.

The old floorboards creaked as Grandma moved in her pink

slippers between the fridge and the stovetop and the sink. The kitchen was cramped, but Roxie loved it just as much of the rest of the old Victorian house, with its faded wallpaper and drafty windows. The peaked roof, ornate trim, and the spire on the west side where Grandma's bedroom was gave it the potential to look absolutely gothic, though Grandma had softened it with a cheerful yellow paint on the exterior and floral curtains in all the windows.

Roxie was still enchanted by it nonetheless—mostly because of the secrets her home sometimes revealed. The house had been in the Clark family for many generations, and Roxie had been delighted to find remnants from the previous inhabitants, like the initials carved into the banister, and the toy soldiers she'd found hidden in a vent, and the door to the backyard, where children long grown and gone had marked their heights.

When Grandma came to the table, instead of presenting Roxie with the usual plate of eggs, she set down a cake in front of her, little candied bats sprinkled in the white icing.

"You know," Grandma said as Roxie yawned again, "you would have had more time to sleep in if you'd skipped the makeup."

Roxie leveled her eyes at her. They both knew she absolutely could not skip the makeup.

She'd been putting on her liquid eyeliner that morning, her vision still blurry from sleep, and she'd accidentally made the wings too long. Instead of bothering to wipe them off and start over, she'd drawn the lines out, branching and threading them until she'd painted two little spiderwebs on her temples. She'd added a haze of dark eye shadow and finished off the look with velvety black lipstick—black like her tulle skirt and sweater and fingernail polish and everything else she wore. The only splash of color she had on was a pair of shiny red platform boots, inherited from her mother.

A teacher would probably make her wipe off the spiderweb eyeliner before second period, but Roxie still decided it was worth it. After all, she had the unsavory reputation as the town freak to uphold.

No rest for the wicked. Especially on her birthday.

"Skylar!" Grandma called up the stairs once she'd finished sticking eighteen candles in the cake and lighting them all.

They both listened for an answer or the creak of the stairs. But there was nothing.

"Skylar!" she said again.

The candles started to melt. They both waited as long as they could, until the wax started dripping onto the icing and Grandma said with a sigh, her fingers knitting together uneasily, "Go ahead."

Roxie blew out the candles in one breath.

She started scarfing down her slice of cake immediately, glancing at the clock, but Grandma said, "Slow down before you choke, dear. I already called the school to let them know you'd be late."

She started the dishes while Roxie finished eating. But they both kept looking over their shoulders at the empty staircase.

On her sixteenth birthday—the last one before Colin died— Roxie had come into the kitchen to find Skylar already seated at the table, wearing a pale-pink sweater with her hair pulled back into a neat ponytail. She'd been eating a bowl of granola while she went over her notes for a test.

She'd taken one look at whatever over-the-top ensemble Roxie had chosen that day, raised her eyebrow, and said, *How many more birthdays until you learn to dress like an adult?*

And Roxie had been ready to fire back her own insult, but then Skylar had handed her an envelope with four tickets to see *The Exorcist* at the Emerald Theater that night—enough for the two of them and Colin and Tristan to go together—and peace was restored.

Roxie's relationship with Skylar had been a lot like a game of tug-of-war in those days. Sometimes they'd taken turns yanking each other down on their faces. Other times they were balanced, perfectly poised over the center line, neither of them struggling against the other, but neither of them giving an inch either.

Maintaining that balance—or destroying it— used to take up a lot of Roxie's bandwidth. But these days, whenever she tugged on that rope, it came up limp in her hand. No one was holding on to the other side anymore.

Skylar hadn't been the same since she'd seen Colin's body. Roxie hadn't either—his murder had been brutal. Horrific. The image would never leave her head, even on the off chance she lived to be a hundred.

But it had been a little over a year ago, and Skylar still couldn't be counted on to get out of bed most days.

By the time Roxie was finished with her cake, Skylar still

hadn't come out of her room. So, with one last glance at the stairs, Roxie grabbed her backpack and walked out the front door.

And promptly dropped her bag on the porch.

Pens and papers fell out of an unzipped pocket and scattered around her feet, but she didn't even notice. She was too busy staring, open-mouthed, at the bus parked in front of her house.

A bus unlike any other bus. A bus that had been painted pitch-black. And stenciled in white letters along the side were the words *After Dark with Roxie Clark.* The name of her ghost tour.

She ran straight into the side of the monster of a vehicle, her arms flung wide, trying her damnedest to give it a hug. She felt the tears coming, but she lifted her eyes to the gray sky, trying to keep them in—she didn't want to smear her spiderweb eyeliner.

She turned her head when she heard soft laughter, and she found Tristan leaning against the hood. His hair was still damp from a shower. He wore a red flannel thrown over his white T-shirt and a pair of mud-stiff boots. His work clothes.

Roxie pointed an accusatory finger at him. "You did this."

He put a hand to his chest like she'd wounded him. "And what makes you think I'd want to do something nice for you?"

"Because this is the same bus from the lot behind the church. I've shown it to you a hundred times."

He shrugged, craning his neck to look the bus over like he was seeing it for the first time. "Could be."

"Pastor Nichols told me it hasn't run in ten years. Which means *you* must have fixed it for me."

"Hmm. I've worked on a lot of buses, so I can't say for sure."

He finally smiled when she shoved him. "Don't read too much into it," he said. "I got the thing for free. Pastor Nichols just wanted that eyesore out of—"

He caught Roxie when she launched herself at him, rocking back on his heels. Her arms were wrapped around his neck, her feet dangling well off the ground.

She felt the breath of his laugh stir against her neck. "You're welcome," he whispered, squeezing her firmly around the waist.

She hoped he didn't hear the hitch in her breath.

He put her down abruptly when they both heard someone clearing their throat behind them.

Roxie's grandmother stood on the front porch, her arms crossed over her chest, a stern look on her face.

Roxie made a break for her before she could utter a word, dropping to her knees in front of the porch steps. "Grandma, listen, I'll be *so, so, so* careful, and—"

And that's when Grandma's serious expression broke into a grin, and Roxie gasped. "You were in on this?"

Grandma walked down the porch steps, right past Roxie and over to Tristan, and patted his arm. They made an odd-looking team—Grandma's head well below his shoulder and her floral dress contrasting with his work clothes. But, together, they'd pulled off the greatest gift anyone had ever given her.

"I wouldn't trust anyone else with the job," Grandma said. "It was all his idea—he just wanted my blessing."

Roxie climbed to her feet, brushing the mud off her knees. "You don't think it's too dangerous?"

Grandma shrugged. "The state of Indiana seems to think it's all right—you only need a commercial driver's license if a vehicle carries over sixteen people, according to Google. This is only for twelve passengers. You're also an adult in the eyes of the law, as of today. So there's not much I can do about it now, is there?" Her smile had just a touch of weariness to it when she said, "I know better than to try and tell a Clark woman what she can't do."

It was her turn for a hug from Roxie. "Thank you, thank you, thank you," she chanted while Grandma patted her back and laughed. But over the old woman's shoulder, Roxie watched Tristan's gaze travel back to the porch, and a pained look passed over his face.

"What's going on?"

Roxie turned and saw Skylar standing just outside the open front door. She was staring at the bus, looking bewildered.

Her voice had cracked when she spoke, like her insides had rusted from disuse and it was an effort to even set the necessary parts for speech into motion. She held her hand up against the weak sunlight, wincing. She was too thin, too pale, her pajamas wrinkled and hanging loose on her body.

Roxie and her grandmother exchanged an uneasy look. Tristan coughed and put his hands in his pockets, suddenly very interested in kicking the dirt off his boots.

Hesitantly, Roxie said, "Well . . . it's my present."

Skylar frowned. "Present?"

There was a long, uncomfortable pause.

"For my birthday," Roxie clarified.

Skylar shook her head. "But your birthday is October 2."

"Right," Roxie said, rubbing the back of her neck. "That's today."

This was Skylar, who'd learned to recite the periodic table from memory in the summer between fifth and sixth grade. Skylar, who could tell you the name of every Nobel Prize winner and every woman who *should* have been a Nobel Prize winner. Skylar, who could tell you every single bone in the human body.

Skylar, who had so thoroughly lost track of the world that she didn't have the slightest idea what day it was.

But there was one thing that hadn't changed about Skylar— she hated nothing more than she hated being embarrassed. Her cheeks blazed red, and her eyes filled with frustrated tears before she muttered, "Sorry," and hurried back into the house before slamming the door behind her.

Roxie took a step toward the house, like she would chase after her. She wanted to tell her it was okay—she didn't care that she'd forgotten her birthday. But something made her stop short.

Grandma squeezed her shoulder. "I'll speak with her, sweetheart," she said. "Get to school."

Roxie nodded and watched numbly while Grandma walked inside.

When she turned back toward the bus, Tristan was still standing there, his quiet, thoughtful gaze on her.

Roxie shook herself, trying to rewind to a few minutes ago. Everything else aside, this was still the best gift she'd ever gotten.

"Thank you," she told him again. And even though it was harder now for her to muster a grin, she hoped he knew that she meant it.

Tristan nodded, and the smile he gave back to her was almost what she would have called *shy*.

He could look scary when he wanted to—*and* when he didn't want to. But the boy she knew never failed to help Grandma Gertie carry in her groceries. He gave thoughtful gifts. He spoke little to strangers, and when he did, he always kept his deep voice as soft as he could, like he didn't want them to startle away from him like a flock of birds.

If anyone would listen to her, she would have told them that they were wrong about him. But then again, Roxie was known for running straight *toward* what everyone else ran away *from*, so she doubted she'd be asked to give a character reference anytime soon.

"You better get going," Tristan said, glancing down at his watch.

"We should," she agreed. "I'll drop you off at work."

"You're joking."

Despite the mess of feelings tangled in her stomach, she still felt her lips curl into a wicked smile. "You wish."

5

As much as Roxie liked telling other people's stories on her ghost tours, there was nothing she relished more than being in the leading role of her own. Anyone in town could attest to it, especially those watching as she careened through the quiet streets of Whistler in her pitch-black tour bus, her name stenciled large above the windshield and music screaming from the speakers. Not to mention the scowling boy sitting behind her on one of the benches, gritting his teeth while he kept an iron grasp on the edges of his seat.

She was more than a little disappointed when she screeched to a stop in the school parking lot and no one was outside to witness her triumph. After dropping off Tristan at work, she was over an hour late.

When she walked into her biology class long after the bell rang, everyone looked up at once, taking in her makeup and outfit for the day—most of them staring openly, like she was an abstract painting on the wall. They tilted their heads this way and that and scrunched up their eyebrows, trying to puzzle out what it all meant.

She'd been going to school with most of them since kindergarten, but they had never seemed to get quite used to her. The worst of them called her names and pulled on her ponytail during class and taunted her about how the curse was going to get her. The others kept their distance. They weren't willing to talk *to* her, but they had made talking *about* her one of Whistler High School's most cherished pastime.

But then there was another, not insignificant group—the ones who were frightened of her.

Tina Maxwell made fun of Roxie's combat boots once then immediately tripped over her own shoelaces a moment later, and fell down a flight of stairs. She told everyone afterward that Roxie had made it happen somehow, as if the curse had jumped from her to Tina like some kind of infectious disease. There was another story circulating that she'd been seen wandering naked through the woods once, probably looking for some small animals to sacrifice to the Devil. In actuality, she had gone to the creek to research the story of Aurora Clark and, on impulse (the way she made most of her decisions), decided to get in and see if it helped her feel a deeper connection with her long-dead ancestor somehow. She'd only stripped down to her bra and underwear, but to be fair, they were beige and probably not distinguishable from a distance.

Whether they were mean to her, afraid of her, or completely indifferent—none of the above were very helpful when it came to picking a lab partner. After Mr. Shaffer told her to join whichever group she wanted, there was a collective shuffling in the room as everyone averted their gazes at once and huddled in their own groups, effectively shutting her out.

Things like that used to bother her, until Tristan moved to town to partner up with her on every school project and sit with her at lunch. He'd graduated last year, but still, she didn't mind working alone anymore. She did it all the time.

She grabbed a worksheet from Mr. Shaffer and took an empty seat by the window. But, as she dug around the bottom of her backpack for a pencil, she was surprised to hear the sound of someone scooting their desk toward hers.

Jackson Mowery settled in beside her, giving her barely a glance before he huddled over his worksheet. "Number one is *cytokinesis*," he said.

Roxie wrote it down. She knew Jackson was right, because Jackson was always right. The bastard.

"You spelled it wrong," he said, voice clipped with impatience.

Roxie shot him a glare.

"What? You did."

Roxie didn't dislike Jackson because he was smart. Skylar was smart, and that had never bothered her (much). She disliked him because he made everyone around him feel like they were so unintelligent, he was surprised they even had the brain capacity to remember to breathe.

They worked in almost complete silence for a few minutes, Roxie skimming her textbook for answers while Jackson watched, looking cynical, until he got exasperated enough to just tell her what to write.

They finished long before everyone else, and she expected Jackson to move his desk away the moment they were done. But instead, he sat there quietly for a moment until Roxie looked up at him.

"How's Sky?" he asked finally.

Roxie cringed at the nickname.

Nobody called her *Sky*. Not even Grandma. Skylar had made it very clear from a young age that she wouldn't tolerate being called anything but her name.

The only exception, of course, being Colin. He'd always called her *Bulldog* after Yale's mascot, long before she ever got her acceptance letter. Anytime she argued that he was going to jinx her and that she wouldn't get in, he'd flash her his dimpled smile and say, *You're too smart to say ridiculous things like that.*

But Jackson Mowery was the furthest thing from Colin you could get.

He knew he had no claim to Skylar after years of asking her out and getting turned down every time. Yet he insisted on calling her something no one else did, creating a sense of forced, uncomfortable intimacy.

On top of that, Roxie was pretty sure the only reason Jackson was so infatuated with Skylar was because she was the only person in Whistler as intelligent as he was—in other words, the only person worthy of him.

Dick.

But, despite all that, Skylar had always felt sorry for Jackson.

She used to say he showed off the way he did because of his own insecurities. That his parents and teachers had been telling him all his life how brilliant he was, had come to expect excellence from him. That had to be a lot to live up to.

Roxie harbored no such pity, but for Skylar's sake, she ignored the nickname and plastered on a pleasant smile when she lied, "She's doing fine, thanks for asking."

He opened his mouth to say something else but closed it immediately when Roxie's eyes widened. Because she had just noticed Jackson was missing a tooth.

Since they were in elementary school, Jackson had made a point of looking immaculate. His dark hair was always combed and slicked back, his face clean-shaven, his button-up shirts ironed and tucked in. Five years of braces had ensured that his teeth were perfectly straight, and he popped breath mints like an addict.

Basically, he looked like he expected someone to spring a job interview on him at any moment, and he'd be damned if they caught him unprepared.

Jackson had no patience for imperfection in anyone else and *definitely* not in himself. He was uncomfortable under Roxie's gaze, covering his mouth with his hand and turning away from her. If it bothered him so much, she wondered, why hadn't he gotten a fake? His mother was a dentist.

And then Roxie was uncomfortable, too. Because, all at once, she realized what must have knocked out his tooth.

Or, rather, *who*.

Everyone had heard about how Tristan beat the shit out of

Jackson last September. A few people had even told Roxie that he nearly killed Jackson. At the time, Roxie had rolled her eyes, assuming they were being dramatic—Jackson was annoying and condescending, and she was certain Tristan wasn't the only person who'd ever had the urge to punch him. It had happened a week after Tristan's brother was murdered, so he'd understandably been on edge. Jackson must have said something snarky to him, he lost his cool for a second, and then it was over.

She had been sure it was just Tristan's reputation that made people talk about it that way. The reputation she'd always thought was wrong.

But this was the first time she'd seen Jackson up close since the fight. She saw the white scar above his eyebrow and another on his cheek. And you'd have to hit someone pretty damn hard to knock out a tooth.

Jackson's parents had wanted to press charges, but Roxie's grandmother had gone over to their house every day for a week to advocate on Tristan's behalf, and eventually, he'd gotten off with a letter of apology. *In light of recent events,* Jackson's mother had said, *we're willing to show some compassion.*

Which translated roughly to, *Your brother is dead, so we'll cut you some slack. This time.*

The Tristan that Roxie knew intimidated people, whether he meant to or not. But she never would have thought her friend capable of really hurting anyone. Definitely not enough to reduce someone as sure of himself as Jackson had always been into the boy beside her now—fiddling nervously with the collar of his shirt, his knee bouncing erratically under his desk, heat rising on his face.

"Tell Sky I'm thinking about her," Jackson said tersely, refusing to make eye contact with Roxie.

And then he shoved his desk back into place and ignored her for the rest of class.

6

When Roxie got home from school that afternoon, she crept quietly through the front door and into the kitchen, peering around to make sure the coast was clear.

Technically, she'd just come from cross-country practice. And she had shown up, sporting a pair of knee-high black-and-white striped socks, a T-shirt with her tour's logo, and a pair of black gym shorts. But instead of running the course the coach had mapped out on his dry-erase map of the school, Roxie had ducked behind the bleachers after the first quarter mile and watched *Psycho* on her phone. She'd seen it dozens of times, but she was making her way through Alfred Hitchcock's entire filmography again, and it was too good to skip.

Joining the cross-country team had been Grandma's idea—it had been one of her conditions for allowing Roxie to do the ghost tour, that she dedicate some time to exercise and outdoor activities. (*While the sun is still up*, she'd been careful to clarify.)

When she didn't see anyone in the kitchen, Roxie hurried to the sink to dampen her face, hair, neck, and armpits with water. If anyone was going to believe she ran five miles today—though she seriously doubted anyone really believed that—she at least needed to look sweaty.

She paused when she heard something coming from the living room—Skylar and Grandma, speaking softly.

Roxie allowed herself a small smile.

In the year since Colin's death, Skylar would make rare appearances in the mornings but always spent the rest of the day locked in her room with the lights off and the blinds closed, no music or TV on to interrupt the silence she wrapped herself in. Roxie and her grandmother would tiptoe around downstairs, careful not to disturb her, only knocking tentatively on her door every couple of hours to see if they could coax her into eating anything.

Roxie had been certain that, after their rough morning, they wouldn't be seeing Skylar for at least a few days. But she wasn't in her room now. And she was *talking*. That had to be a good sign.

When Roxie walked into the living room, she found Grandma sitting on the couch. Usually she'd have dinner in the Crock-Pot by now, all her other chores done for the day, and she'd be relaxing with a Stephen King novel or TV show. But she didn't look relaxed now. She was perched on the edge of her seat, elbows braced on her knees and her head in her hands.

Roxie's smile slipped. "What's going on?"

Not more bad news. Nobody in this house could handle more bad news.

Skylar turned slowly, calmly, to look at Roxie. She had her hands clasped in her lap. Grandma's eyes were red, like she'd been rubbing at them, but Skylar looked calm, her features set. For a moment, she looked to Roxie like the old Skylar—no room for nonsense.

But then she realized that wasn't quite what was in Skylar's expression now. There was none of the ambition or determination that used to prop her up. No. This was resignation. This was giving up. This was a door slammed shut.

"I'm not going back to Yale," she announced.

Too stunned to do much else, Roxie lowered herself into the love seat by the window. She opened her mouth, though she couldn't say a word.

Yale. How many times had Roxie heard her sister say that word? It had become part of Skylar's vocabulary some time in elementary school, when one of her teachers told her Yale was only for the brightest, most ambitious students in the country and that less than 5 percent of applicants were accepted. She had come home that day and proclaimed she was going to be in that 5 percent. Roxie remembered the moment vividly—she'd been busy watching *Scooby-Doo,* wiping Cheeto dust on her shirt and wondering why anyone would want to go to a hard school on purpose.

From that day on, Yale wasn't what Roxie would call a *dream* of Skylar's. It was more like the finish line at the end of a marathon—one that was too far ahead to even see most of the time, but she kept her eyes doggedly on the horizon as she ran, never letting up the pace. Even when it had left her exhausted and miserable, hurrying between one extracurricular and the next, staying up all night studying to ensure a perfect score on the next day's test, and doing tedious research on FAFSA and scholarships and student loans so she'd be able to pay her way once she got there.

She'd read the *Yale Daily News* religiously. She had the campus map memorized by her freshman year of high school and had already picked out the dorm she wanted to live in. For her fifteenth birthday, she'd begged Grandma to visit the campus, and they had driven fourteen hours so she could see the libraries and landmarks, sit down in the dining hall, get a glimpse of her future classrooms.

She'd cried when she got the acceptance letter. Then she had run next door to tell Colin the news.

Colin had never planned on going to college at all—school wasn't his strong suit. He had his sights set on the construction business instead; he'd spent his summers building roof trellises and learning how to install drywall. But he'd known how much this meant to Skylar. That's why, after she told him the news, he'd thrown her over his shoulder and run with her down Poplar Avenue, yelling at all the confused people sitting on their front porches, *She did it! She did it!* while Skylar had covered her face in embarrassment, laughing through her fingers.

He'd known better than anyone how much Skylar had sacrificed to get there. How many parties and movie nights and dinners she'd skipped out on. She had almost no friends to speak of aside from the Rileys. She'd essentially traded away all her teenage years in exchange for that coveted spot at Yale, which was sure to lead to medical school and then a long career as a doctor.

But now, with just a few words, she was giving it all up.

"Honey," Grandma started, her hands knitting anxiously in her lap. "I explained the situation to the school. They're going to keep your spot open for you until at least next year. You don't even have to think about Yale for the next eleven months. There's no sense in making that kind of decision now. You'll feel differently—"

Skylar shook her head. "I can't do it. Not in a year. Not in two. I can't. I already know I can't."

Grandma scrubbed her hands over her face again, blinking rapidly. Roxie could tell she was trying not to say, *Why the hell not?* She looked as bewildered as Roxie felt.

Instead, Grandma told her, "I just don't understand."

Skylar shrugged, looking tired all at once. "I don't expect you to."

And that was that. Without another word of explanation, Skylar got up to leave. She was going to lock herself in her room and never talk about it again. Like all those years of ACT prep courses, debate team practices, late-night study sessions, and over-the-top science fair projects could be thrown away as easily as old toys.

Grandma jumped to her feet and stopped Skylar with a hand on her elbow. "Now wait a minute. We're going to talk about this. You've worked too hard for too long to let this go. You were so happy when you got in. You—"

Skylar calmly pulled her elbow free from Grandma's grasp. "That's what you don't get. The Skylar who got that acceptance letter isn't me anymore."

Roxie's stomach twisted.

Grandma could only stare for a moment. And then she asked, her voice unsteady, "Then who are you?"

"I don't know," Skylar said, speaking to the floor. "The kind of girl who can't make herself give a shit about stupid things like school anymore. The kind of girl who can't make herself give a shit about almost anything anymore."

And then she walked out of the living room and through the kitchen, toward the stairs. Roxie hurried after her.

In the last year, she'd hardly said anything to Skylar about what happened. Mostly because she didn't know *what* to say. Colin's death was unthinkably terrible. She had no silver linings to offer her.

But Skylar's room was just below hers, and Roxie had heard her crying so many nights through the floorboards, moaning softly under the weight of all that pain. And Roxie had wanted desperately to go to her, knock on the door, hug her.

She hadn't. She didn't feel like she had the right to. They were family, but they'd never been as close as Grandma wanted them to be. They disagreed about everything. Fought over nothing. Roxie was certain that if they weren't blood, she and Skylar wouldn't even be friends.

But she had to say something now. She couldn't just let her sister throw her whole life away without a word of protest.

"Wait, Skylar," she said before Skylar could disappear to her room again. "Do you really think this is what Colin would have wanted for you? Don't you think he would—"

Skylar stopped cold, her foot frozen on the first stair. Her hand tightened on the banister.

She turned to look at Roxie. And before she even spoke, Roxie knew she'd said the wrong thing.

"Don't," was all Skylar said.

Jaw clenched, she held Roxie's gaze. And there was no denying it—the change. This wasn't the girl who had gotten into Yale. She wasn't the same person who used to share her collection of *Goosebumps* books with Roxie or who'd told her the first ghost stories she'd ever heard while they camped out in the backyard.

Roxie remembered the day of the funeral. How Skylar had insisted on staying to see Colin's body buried. How she'd flinched, every time a shovelful of dirt hit the casket. And when it was over, she'd gone so pale and still. Like everything she was had pulled away from her and burrowed into that freshly turned earth.

Roxie's sister was not the person standing in front of her now. No, that girl had been buried in Rose Hill Cemetery. With Colin.

Skylar turned and ran up the stairs before slamming her bedroom door behind her.

7

Roxie lay down in the middle of Pike Street the next afternoon, her head resting at the center of the painted yellow lines. She stared up at the pale sky and listened to the rustle of corn in the fields around her and felt the cool asphalt against the back of her neck.

She'd done her research about the death of Becca Clark. But a story never fully came together for her until she experienced the place it happened for herself.

Not much had changed about Pike Street since 1975. According to old maps Roxie had studied at the library, there had never been any businesses or houses lining it. Both sides were owned by the Moore family, farmed generation after generation, never broken up or sold, even under pressure from developers. They were determined to keep it the same as it always had been—a tradition of uneventfulness.

But that tradition had been shattered when it came toe to toe with the Clark Curse.

Becca Clark had been beautiful, as her high school year-book photos could attest. She was an older cousin of Roxie's mother and seemed to be a softer version of her, with blushing cheeks and delicate curls.

The newspapers called her *tragically young*. They quoted class-mates who said she was *sweet* and *caring*. A teacher went so far as to use the word *angelic*.

But a letter from one great-aunt to another that Roxie had found tucked away in the attic called her *a little viper. A snake in the weeds. One to watch out for.*

Was the great-aunt bitter and jealous? Or was Becca good at playing innocent when she wanted to? That was the biogra-pher's dilemma, one Roxie was familiar with—deciding which story to tell.

The moment she closed her eyes, she could smell the exhaust fumes and hear the jeering crowd, and the blue sky had changed to starry black.

Two cars faced each other at opposite ends of Pike Street, a hundred yards apart, their engines spitting smoke. One was a slick, orange '71 Barracuda, all muscle and power. The other was a mud-splattered truck with too-large wheels, lofting it up above the gathered audience.

Under Pike Street's single streetlight stood a girl, ruby lips and black hair flashing where she stood dead center between the cars, her hands on her hips as she spun in a lazy circle, sur-veying the two vehicles.

Prom was one week away. She'd been asked to the dance by six different boys. It hadn't been easy, but she'd managed to narrow it down to two—Harlan from her woodshop class, or Max from the football team.

Work it out amongst yourselves, she had told them, according to one eyewitness account.

You're going to have to fight for me, she said, according to another.

It had been decided between the boys that they'd play a game of chicken. The rules were simple—drive their cars right at each other, going top speed. Whoever got scared enough to turn off the road first was the loser. The braver man would get the girl.

Someone must have said something to Becca. Tried to warn her against being involved in something so reckless. The curse was already embedded in town lore by then. It was all so obviously fated to end in disaster—she had to have seen it coming.

But Becca Clark ignored the advice, if it was ever given. Because what she desired most in that moment was the thrill of being so desperately wanted. The prize at the center of their dangerous game.

Roxie seemed to feel every emotion that must have roiled through Becca as it all happened. She couldn't explain how and certainly couldn't verify what had really been going through the girl's head that night. But whatever it was seemed so much stronger than a hunch. It was more like a knowing. An embodiment.

First, there was the excitement coursing through her as the boys revved their engines. She could feel the rumble through the soles of her feet, reverberating in her bones.

Then, the moment of complete control as she lifted her hands in the air, her delicate arms silhouetted like a dancer's in the streetlights. She held the pose longer than she needed to, drawing it out, relishing their eagerness to prove themselves to her. Then she brought them down, giving them the signal to go. And they did, slamming their pedals to the floor, tires screeching underneath them as they shot off like bullets through the night. Headed straight for her.

Then came the giddy anticipation as she squealed and ran to get out of the way.

Then, the shock as her foot caught in the underbrush of the ditch lining the road. She fell beyond the reach of the streetlight.

Then, the panic as she struggled to stand, only seeming to get more tangled the more she fought fate.

Then came the fear, seizing up her heart as she screamed for help, but the crowd of onlookers was yelling too loudly, egging her suitors on, drowning her out.

And finally, that very last moment, when Max veered away, giving in first, driving his truck straight into the ditch.

When Becca saw the headlights plunging toward her, just before the huge car crushed her, the terror must have been all-consuming. Horrible. Roxie felt her lungs fill with it, the scream rising in her throat—

"Car."

Roxie's eyes snapped open, and she blinked up at a blue sky once more.

Before she could react, Tristan had grabbed her by the hand and hauled her to her feet, pulling her out of the way as a mini-van approached.

Pike Street was a straight shot for miles, and they still had at least an hour of daylight left—Roxie had known that if anyone was coming, Tristan would see them a long way off and warn her. She had trusted he would.

But that wasn't the only reason they'd come while the sun was still up. Rumor had it, this stretch of road wasn't always so quiet after dark.

There had been various reports of strange happenings. The thunder of revving engines when no cars were in sight. A piercing scream from a girl no one could find. And once, a man had wrecked his car when he claimed a '71 Barracuda had shown up out of nowhere and almost hit him head on.

Roxie would have loved to come by at night to *really* get in touch with the spirit of this place, but Tristan had staunchly refused.

Are you scared? Roxie had taunted him. And he'd replied without an ounce of shame—*Shitless.*

They stood and watched the van go by. He still gripped her lightly by the elbow, and she leaned into him slightly as a breeze blew her hair across her face. The month before had been warm, hovering around eighty degrees all the way to the end of September. But in true Midwestern fashion, the weather had shifted overnight, dropping more than twenty degrees.

Roxie had worn her favorite jacket—black, faux leather, and covered with a collection of patches, mostly skulls, snakes, and band logos. But as much as the aesthetic pleased her, it wasn't enough to keep her warm. She shivered again, blinking up at Tristan expectantly, stealing a glance at his black hoodie.

With a sigh, he pulled it over his head, a slice of his stomach showing before he handed it over.

Roxie took it gratefully, pulling it over her head, loving the way it engulfed her hands and reached almost down to her knees. Loving even more that it held the heat of him. Not to mention his scent—strong coffee mixed with something else, something indefinably him.

Roxie stepped out into the street again and watched it stretch away for miles and miles. The terrain in this region of the state was almost entirely flat and featureless, aside from the seas of corn rippling like waves in the breeze. Not the most exciting view. *Boring*, she might call it. The kind of blankness that might just drive people to make trouble where there wasn't any before, just to keep things interesting.

It reminded Roxie of a saying she'd heard once—*Idle hands are the Devil's playground.*

"I think I've got enough of the story to go on," she said.

Tristan blinked, shaking his head. His gaze had been on her, but he didn't seem to see her until just now. Like his thoughts had been somewhere else. "What?"

"Becca Clark. I'm going to add her to the tour. You know"—she elbowed him, offering him a smile—"now that I've got my bus."

Her tour groups wouldn't have to go everywhere on foot anymore, which meant she could take them to spots in Whistler that had been too far before. She'd have time to squeeze in more stops and more stories.

He followed her to the bus now, parked in an inlet just down the road, and climbed in as Roxie settled behind the wheel. There was no passenger seat, so he had to slide onto one of the benches behind her—none of which had any seat belts.

As the engine rumbled to life, Roxie turned to bat her eyelashes at him. "Don't worry. I'll go slow."

"There's a first time for everything," he said. But the way he braced his hands on the back of her seat made it clear that he didn't think this would be that time.

But she was careful when she eased onto Pike Street. He'd been so kind as to distract her for the past couple of hours—the least she could do was get him home safely.

His surprise had been evident when she'd called him at work last night and told him the news about Skylar not going back to Yale. He'd been around long enough to know how much it had meant to her. He'd certainly been around long enough to know how unsettled Roxie was by the whole thing—and that the best way to lift her mood was to immerse herself in ghost-tour planning. So he'd offered to tag along with her for a little while today.

But he'd seemed distracted for most of that time, teasing her less than he usually did. Roxie, just grateful to have him with her, didn't push him or ask too many questions.

She'd always been an open book, but when she met Tristan, he may as well have had his pages glued together. Getting to know him had been a long process, and there were still times where she felt there were parts of himself he kept hidden, even from her. Especially since Colin had died.

He'd cried in front of her only once, the day after the body was discovered. He'd texted her, *Come over*, and she had, right away, running across the short stretch of lawn between their houses.

He'd been waiting for her on the porch, and she had crashed into him, wrapping her arms around him as hard as she could.

His face had already been wet. She could feel it, pressed against her neck, his whole body quaking, like it would break apart if she loosened her grip even a little bit. He sank down with her on the porch steps, and they'd stayed that way until long after the sky had gone dark.

But ever since, he hadn't talked about his grief. At least, not to her. He'd only taken a week off work, and then had gone right back to it, as determined to throw himself into his old life as Skylar had been to abandon hers.

When Roxie pulled the bus up outside the Riley house and cut the engine, they both sat in silence for a few moments. Roxie knew he needed to leave for work soon, or he'd be late. But without her even turning to look at him, even as distracted as he'd been all afternoon, he seemed to sense she had something to say. So he waited.

She had a lot on her mind. Of course, she'd been thinking of Skylar. But something else had been nagging at her since yesterday.

"Why did you beat up Jackson Mowery?" she blurted.

It clearly wasn't what he'd been expecting her to say, and taken off guard, his response seemed to come like a reflex, without any conscious thought: "Because Jackson Mowery is a piece of shit," he snapped.

Roxie stared at Colin's closed bedroom door. Before Tristan had left for work, he'd given her permission to come here alone. But now that she'd arrived, she couldn't quite bring herself to go in.

There were black scuff marks at the door's bottom left corner. She imagined Colin must have kicked it open when he got home from school every day. Right before he dropped his backpack on the floor, kicked off his shoes, and flopped on the bed.

She could almost hear his mother calling, *The knob is there for a reason! You're ruining the paint!*

And Colin mumbling something like, *Sorry, Mom*, before he rolled over and took a nap or started texting Skylar, only to do it all over again the next day.

After he was gone, no one had bothered to paint over the scuffs. Or bothered to clean up his room, for that matter. When Roxie finally worked up the nerve to open the door, the bed was unmade. Sneakers, hoodies, jeans, and hats littered the floor.

Tristan had warned her it would be messy. *After the cops searched it, Suzanna insisted they put everything back exactly how they found it. She told me not to touch anything. And after she left . . . well, I just haven't worked up to it.*

Roxie had never been a fan of Suzanna Riley. Colin was her biological son. Tristan was her stepson—the result of an affair their father had, which she hadn't known a thing about until the woman showed up on their doorstep, an infant in her arms, and unceremoniously shoved him into Suzanna's hands. *If Luke won't pay child support, I can't afford to keep his kid. I know he's got the money. Just because the government doesn't know about it doesn't mean he doesn't have it.*

Luke Riley's nefarious means of procuring cash—a combination of stealing and dealing, as far as Roxie could gather from Tristan—had landed him in jail when the boys were in middle school, forcing Suzanna to sell their house in Ohio and move to Whistler for a nursing job at the hospital. She was left to raise two boys alone, working long hours. Roxie knew it couldn't be easy. But that didn't make it okay to make it so obvious how much she favored Colin.

She hadn't made a secret of it, devoting all her patience to helping him with homework, her leftover cash to buying him every Christmas present he asked for, and her time off to sitting in the stands at his baseball games.

But Tristan—well, her husband wasn't around to blame, and Tristan seemed to become the stand-in for all the anger she had toward Luke. A representation of all the ways he had wronged her. Every time Roxie had seen them in the same room, the woman was either talking down to him, yelling at him, or ignoring him altogether.

She'd skipped town shortly after Colin had died, on the pretense of taking an extended vacation to clear her head. But no one was surprised when she never came back. Without Colin, there was nothing to keep her in Whistler—certainly not Tristan.

Roxie asked him occasionally if he'd been in contact with her, and he'd shrug. *Talked to her a couple of weeks ago. Sounds like she's still in Florida, staying with a friend.*

Wherever the hell she was, Roxie was certain he was better off without her.

Tristan told Roxie not to bother putting things back where she found them—he planned to get around to donating everything soon anyway. So she rolled up her sleeves and started looking for what she came to find.

It was something that Roxie wasn't even sure existed. Colin had *said* he was going to buy it, but he wasn't exactly known for following through. He was charmingly forgetful at his best and infuriatingly unreliable at his worst. But even though he'd been in the ground for a year now, Roxie was counting on him.

She'd thought and thought about ways to help Skylar, and this was all she could come up with—her only hope.

She checked all his dresser drawers, his closet, and the cubbies in his desk. She poked her head under the bed and shuffled through two boxes, one full of old Pokémon cards and the other brimming with photographs—some from his baseball games or award ceremonies that his mom had wanted him to keep, but mostly they were of him and Skylar, his arm around her shoulders, pulling her close and beaming like he couldn't believe his luck.

So far, Roxie was coming up empty. She'd been worried about that. She'd described what she was looking for to Tristan, and he said he hadn't seen it.

But there was one place he might not have thought to look. This house used to belong to her aunt Violet, after all. And this was the room where she and Skylar had always stayed. The house was smaller than their grandmother's, but still old enough to have outlasted many owners, and when Roxie was a kid, she'd been determined to root out any secrets they might have left behind. And that's how she'd discovered the hidden compartment.

Lifting the edge of a large, round area rug, Roxie peeled it aside and started knocking on the floorboards. When she found the hollow one, she maneuvered her fingers into the crease and pried the board up slowly.

It made sense that Colin would want to hide it. It was a gift for Skylar, so he wouldn't have wanted her to spot it when she came over.

Apparently, this was a hiding spot only Colin and Roxie knew about—everything inside appeared untouched. Including a little bit of cash, a dusty bottle of Fireball, and a small stash of weed.

And at the bottom—a box the size of her palm and an envelope with Skylar's name written on the front in Colin's handwriting.

The box was wrapped in red paper with little Christmas trees all over it, which made Roxie laugh. It had been nowhere near Christmas when he bought it—more like the middle of August, a couple of weeks before he died. He must have taken the paper from his mom's stash, either deciding the holiday theme didn't matter or not even noticing the pattern in the first place.

Roxie remembered the day last summer when he'd knocked on the Clarks' door and she'd answered it in her pj's—preferring the chilly, long nights of autumn and winter, she generally avoided the outdoors from May to September, and she had to squint against the daylight, fighting the urge to hiss like a possum caught in the high beams.

Skylar's not home, she'd said when she saw it was Colin. *Shopping for dorm supplies.*

Eager to send him away so she could retreat to the cool dark of her bedroom and *Supernatural* reruns, Roxie started to swing the door shut, but Colin stopped it with his foot. *I came to see you. I wanted to ask you about something.*

Roxie closed her eyes so he wouldn't see them rolling as she let him inside. She knew what he wanted—her opinion on Skylar.

They'd had English class with Mr. Keller together the year before. He'd sat right in front of her, even though it wasn't his assigned seat. Colin had a talent for getting away with things, charming just about every teacher into his pocket—but never quite enough to earn him better grades. He might have done better in English if he hadn't spent the whole period pestering Roxie, stealing her textbook to scribble cartoon ghosts in the margins, passing her notes to share the cringiest puns he could think of, and—whenever Mr. Keller was done lecturing— talking endlessly about her sister.

He was constantly asking her what she thought Skylar would think of certain things, like what movie she'd want to see that weekend or what candy he should surprise her with.

Roxie had told him, over and over again, *You know her better than I do.* But that never stopped him from asking.

Sure enough, when the door closed behind him, he'd told her, *I want to give Skylar a gift before she leaves for Yale.*

He'd pulled out his phone and started flipping through pictures of necklaces on display at one of the local shops, Genevieve's Jewelry.

Roxie had whistled. *Genevieve's is pricey.*

He had shrugged. *I can swing it. I want it to be special—it's not every day your girlfriend gets into an Ivy League. And besides,* he added with a lopsided grin, *I can't have her forgetting about me while she's hanging out with all those geniuses.*

She'd been about to tell him for the millionth time that she had no idea what Skylar would like when he got to a picture of a necklace with a delicate silver chain holding a pendant in the shape of a daisy.

That one, she'd said.

You're sure?

She'd nodded. *Daisies are her favorite flower.*

His eyebrows had furrowed. *They are?*

You didn't know that?

He'd shaken his head. *She just doesn't seem like somebody who would be into flowers. She's never mentioned it. How did you know?*

Roxie had shrugged. She couldn't remember having a specific conversation with Skylar about it. It seemed like something she'd been born knowing. She was, after all, good at picking up details about people. Especially Clarks.

She'll love it, she'd told Colin. *And for the record, she'd never forget about you.*

In response, he'd grinned and said, *Looks like you know her better than you thought.*

For her sister's sake, Roxie hoped he was right.

Her plan was to give Skylar the necklace that Colin had intended to give her as a going-away present. She wanted it to remind Skylar of how proud he had been of her. The one person who had always been able to get through to her was gone, but maybe this would be enough to remind her how much he'd wanted this for her. And then maybe she'd start wanting it for herself again.

Roxie gave the box a shake. She heard a metallic rattle inside. And Colin had written Skylar's name with a Sharpie across the wrapping paper. But just to make sure it was what she came for, she carefully undid the wrapping just enough to peek inside and see the words *Genevieve's Jewelry* embossed in gold foil on the box's lid.

But the envelope addressed to her sister—that, she hadn't been expecting. He must have gotten her a card to go with the necklace.

Roxie could have laughed, she was so grateful to him in that moment. This was perfect. Now her sister would get the actual words straight from him. She was certain the card would be full of all kinds of mushy things, about how he loved her and couldn't wait to see all that she would become when she went off to school.

She tucked the box and the envelope into her jacket pocket, replaced the floorboard, then put the carpet back before she left Colin's room.

She called Tristan as she locked up his house on her way out, using the spare key hidden under a flowerpot by the door. He'd probably just gotten to work, so she wasn't sure if he'd answer, but he picked up on the third ring.

"I found it," she said, a little breathless as she crossed the yard between his house and hers.

"Cool," Tristan said. Then, after a pause, "Are you sure you want to give it to her? Aren't you afraid it could . . . you know, make things worse?"

Roxie had thought of that, too. It was possible the gift from Colin would completely backfire. Instead of being a sweet reminder that would make her feel better, it might just cause more pain.

But Roxie told him, "I might as well give it a shot. Things have gotten so bad, I don't think we can make them worse."

At least she really, really hoped not.

She was about to let him go when he said suddenly, "Can I ask you something?"

"Sure."

"Why do you want to help her so badly?"

The question baffled her for a moment. "What do you mean? She's my sister."

"Yeah, but . . . you guys have never exactly gotten along."

"I know."

"She always called you a gremlin when we were kids."

And still did, up until Colin died and she stopped speaking to me, Roxie thought but didn't say so to Tristan.

"And what was it you always called her?"

"Plucky," Roxie said, with more than a little shame. That had been after the time Skylar accidentally overplucked her eyebrows right before school picture day, and it made her look noticeably stunned in her photo, like she'd been watching the photographer strip naked while he was taking it.

"And there was that time she told your grandma on you for trying to smuggle in a pet tarantula."

"Not the point—"

"And then you got back at her by throwing all her chemistry notes in the fireplace."

"I don't think—"

"And then she cut holes in the crotch of all your jeans—"

"She's still my sister," Roxie said firmly. "If I think there's a chance I can help her, I need to do it. I just know that's my responsibility and that, if our roles were reversed, Skylar would do the same for me. I don't know how else to explain it."

Tristan paused for a long moment. Until finally, he said, "Yeah. I get it."

Roxie remembered one of the pictures she'd found in the box under the bed—Tristan and Colin posing with Little League trophies, laughing at the camera, looking like they'd just conquered the world together.

And she knew Tristan had to understand better than anyone.

9

That night, Roxie sat down to dinner with Grandma and shoveled down too-hot pot roast while Grandma alternated between poking at her food with her fork and expressing her absolute disbelief about Skylar.

"I just don't *understand*."

"Me neefer," Roxie mumbled around a mouthful.

"I mean, she wanted it so *badly*. Didn't she? She skipped out early on her own birthday party to go to a debate team practice. And all those nights I drove her over to that little shithead's house just so they could quiz each other—what's his name?"

"Jackson Mowery," Roxie answered without hesitation.

"Yeah, that one. Couldn't *pay* me to hang out with that know-it-all little brat."

Roxie nodded as she took another bite.

"I've lost people before," Grandma said, rubbing at her jaw. "I lost my mother very young. And my sister. Then there was your aunt Violet, all of a sudden like that. And your mom—I was a complete mess after that. Wanted to curl up and die. But I couldn't. I had you girls to worry about. But it almost seems like Skylar thinks she's got nothing left to live for. She—Roxie, dear, if you don't slow down, you're going to choke."

Roxie put her fork down, chewed deliberately, then chased the salty beef with a sugary swig of lemonade.

"Do you have somewhere to be?"

"No."

"So what do you think?"

"About what?"

"Skylar, sweetheart. How do we help her?"

Roxie shrugged, pretending to place her hands in her lap. But she slid one into her pocket, squeezing the present from Colin to make sure it was still there. She considered telling Grandma about it. But she was afraid the woman would only tell her it was a horrible idea.

"I don't know," she said instead.

"Maybe you could try getting through to her? You know, an old-fashioned sisterly heart-to-heart."

Roxie almost spit up her next sip of lemonade. "I'm sorry, you must have gotten us mixed up with those girls from *Full House*."

"I'm serious! She might be more inclined to listen to you than her grandma. My sister and I talked about everything." She took a sip of her evening tea, looking wistful. "There was a tree right next to her bedroom window, and she'd always help me sneak out to go see your grandfather. We covered for each other all the time. Got into a lot of trouble together, too."

"But there's no tree next to Skylar's window."

"Not my point."

"*My* point is, she doesn't want to talk to me. Never has. I don't know if you've noticed, but we don't exactly have much in common."

Grandma shook her head, even though there was no way in hell she hadn't noticed. "Oh, you stop that. You have lots in common."

"She's never even liked me, Grandma," Roxie said, picking her fork back up to push food around her plate. "She thinks I'm a freak."

"That is absolutely not true," Grandma said, immediately launching into mantras she must have pulled straight from a parenting blog, about how all sisters are born with a healthy sense of competition, and they all struggle to connect sometimes, and they'll look back fondly on their childhood together when they're older.

But Grandma hadn't seen that look in Skylar's eyes earlier, when Roxie had tried to talk to her. The one that said, *I would hate you, if I cared enough to.*

"I don't think anything I could say would help Skylar," she said. "I think the only one who'd know how to get through to her would be Colin himself."

Which was exactly why Roxie was so eager to try out her plan. She stood abruptly from the dinner table before taking her plate to the sink.

When she turned back to Grandma, the woman looked at her like she was seeing her for the first time all afternoon.

"What?" she said.

Grandma leaned back in her chair with a slight curve to her lips. "You wouldn't be rushing through dinner to go see Tristan, would you?"

"No," Roxie said. "I already saw him today."

"You two have been spending a lot of time together."

"We've always spent a lot of time together."

Grandma went on as though she hadn't spoken, "And the gift he gave you for your birthday was very . . . generous."

Roxie didn't like the knowing tone in her voice. "Yes. It was."

Grandma let the smile loose now. She might as well have winked.

"Cut to the chase," Roxie demanded.

Grandma huffed at that, Roxie's bluntness ruining her fun. "I'm just saying that I don't think a boy who's only interested in being your friend would have gone to all that trouble to repair a bus for you."

Roxie shook her head. "He doesn't like me that way, if that's what you're implying."

"What makes you think that? He's probably just shy. If you asked him about it, maybe talked to him about how *you* feel . . ."

"Maybe," Roxie said, turning back to the sink and scrubbing at her plate to hide the redness rising on her cheeks.

Because she already *had* told Tristan how she felt.

But she didn't say that. Because the only thing more embarrassing than getting rejected by your best friend after admitting you've been in love with him for years was probably recounting the whole thing to your grandmother. And even Roxie wasn't brave enough to try that.

Her feelings for Tristan hadn't emerged all at once. Aside from the fact that he wasn't exactly the easiest person to get to know, Roxie had always kept herself busy with her research— whether that was raiding the attic or taking up residence in the library for hours or scouring Whistler's most decrepit buildings with an EMF reader she got off eBay until someone inevitably chased her off. She'd had more important things to worry about than crushes.

At least, that was what she'd thought. But truthfully, Tristan had been working his way into her heart in a million little ways without her even realizing it—like when he'd cleaned her knee after a bike wreck, gently wiping away the blood and gravel with the edge of his T-shirt while she bit her lip to keep from crying. Or when he let her pick out his costume for Halloween every year, sitting patiently in the chair in front of her bedroom mirror while she dabbed on fake blood or attached fangs to his teeth.

Then there was when she walked him through her ghost tour for the first time. She was still adding the finishing touches, not ready to show anyone else yet. They got to the end, and she held out her arms with a *ta-da*, hoping the face paint hid her nerves while she waited to hear what he thought.

And then he'd smiled wide and told her, *You just might have been born for this, Clark.*

That was also the first time he'd hugged her. Or maybe he'd done it before, but this was the first time she could remember really *feeling* it. The way his body had pressed against hers. The way her head had been tucked perfectly into the hollow between his chin and shoulder. How his hand had found its way into her hair and she'd leaned into it, closing her eyes.

Then her eyes had snapped open—because that was the exact moment she'd realized she was in trouble.

After that, she'd found any excuse she could to touch him. She'd pressed her knee against his when they went out for coffee, grabbed his hands whenever she had a new idea to tell him about, leaned her head on his shoulder during the early morning bus rides.

He'd never pulled away or seemed uncomfortable at her touch. In fact, he'd seemed to be finding his own ways of being in constant contact with her, brushing her hair out of her face or tracing the lines of her intricate ghost-tour makeup, sometimes pressing his palm to her neck as he turned her head this way and that to get a better look, their skin heating against each other, breath mingling, the tension mounting more and more each time they were together, until one of them would finally have the guts to break it with the confession they were both longing to hear.

At least, that's what Roxie had thought was going on. But she had a penchant for making up stories, even when it came to her own life. And reality had come crashing down on prom night.

They'd gone together—his idea. Though his promposal hadn't exactly been romantic. *Gertie says I have to go,* he'd said. *And if I have to suffer through it, so should you.*

But Roxie had seen it as the perfect opportunity to end this game of cat and mouse between them. She'd always known she'd have to be the one to confess first. He was too shy to ever be honest without her prompting.

So she'd put together a dress better than any costume she'd ever concocted—black (obviously) with spidery lace sleeves and a gauzy cape that made her look like the vampire mistress of a Transylvanian castle. It went perfectly with her spiked, glittery black heels—another inheritance from her mother.

They'd spent most of the night on the fringes of the gym, raiding the refreshment table while Roxie had ranted about the lackluster decorations and generic playlist, and Tristan had agreed that Zombie Contagion would have made a much more interesting prom theme than Disco Fever.

He'd seemed off most of the night. Roxie thought maybe it was because he was thinking about how his brother should have been there. If he'd still been alive, it would have been his senior prom, too. Skylar would have come home from Yale for the occasion, and all four of them would have gone out to Steak 'n Shake afterward to eat burgers in their fancy clothes until the early hours of the morning.

Or maybe it was because he'd sensed the same thing she did—that the attraction simmering between them for years was ready to boil.

Then the last slow song of the night had come on, and Roxie had grabbed his hand and towed him out onto the gym floor. She had put her arms around his neck. She'd thought he might be awkward, unpracticed, but he'd seemed to know what to do, letting his hands settle on her waist, gathering her to him as they swayed with the rhythm of the song.

She'd had a speech prepared—a declaration of everything she'd been feeling and everything she was certain he was feeling, too. She'd tipped her head back to look up at him, her lips parting as she prepared to give it. But, at the last moment, she'd abandoned it in favor of something more spontaneous.

Lifting on her tiptoes, she'd pressed her lips to his.

She'd waited for his mouth to respond. And for a moment, it did. She swore his grip tightened on her, pulling her in closer, deepening the kiss in a way that made her dizzy.

But then, he'd broken away, and the air had seemed to turn frigid between them.

He squeezed his eyes shut for a moment then shook his head. *I just—I can't, Rox. I can't.*

Roxie had been too stunned to respond for a moment.

She'd been so *sure*. But it was impossible to misinterpret the hard look on his face. This wasn't what he'd wanted.

Roxie had nodded. She'd thought she'd abandoned embarrassment a long time ago, but her cheeks had blazed with it, and she couldn't meet his gaze. "Okay," she'd said.

He'd stood there for a few moments, like he wanted to say something else. Roxie had never seen him so flustered. In the end, all he could do was shake his head again and walk away, slipping through the doors at the back of the gym and out into the cold night.

He'd texted her almost immediately after, saying he could still drive her home, but she told him no. She'd rather walk.

And that's what she'd started to do, sticking to the sidewalk and wrapping her cape tight around her, ignoring all the other cars that whizzed past full of her classmates hanging out the windows, music blaring, as they went to continue the party elsewhere.

But Tristan must have called her grandmother, because her old minivan had pulled up to the curb before stopping and waiting for Roxie to get in. As hurt and rejected as she'd felt, she was grateful—her feet had been killing her in her heels.

She'd gotten into the passenger seat but was surprised to find that it wasn't her grandmother driving—it was Skylar.

At this point, Colin had been gone for almost nine months, and Roxie had hardly seen her sister at all. But she'd said, by way of explanation, "Grandma was already asleep. I answered her phone."

"Thanks," was the only reply Roxie had given.

They'd made the whole ride in almost complete silence, Skylar gripping the wheel firmly at ten and two, Roxie pressing her forehead against the cold passenger side window and doing her best not to die of embarrassment. Tristan probably hadn't told her sister exactly what happened, but they'd gone together and left separately. Skylar had probably figured out the gist.

It wasn't until they pulled up in front of the house that Skylar had patted her knee awkwardly and said, *Well . . . you looked great tonight.*

Roxie had given a bitter laugh and gotten out of the car, certain her sister was mocking her. But Skylar caught up with her on the steps of the front porch and squeezed her hand and said, *I mean it.*

For some reason, that was the moment that made Roxie dissolve into tears.

Skylar had bitten her lip, clearly unsure of how to respond, aside from taking a tissue from her pocket and wiping at the mascara running down her sister's face. Roxie blubbered unintelligibly, *I thought he liked me. Why wouldn't he like me? I'm great! He should like me!*

Roxie had felt ridiculous the next day. The boy her sister loved was *dead*, and Roxie had completely lost it over a little rejection. But Skylar never brought it up again and apparently hadn't even told Grandma.

Roxie and Tristan hadn't spoken for a few days after that. But eventually, Tristan had shown up at her door, rubbing sheepishly at the back of his neck. *I'm sorry*, he'd told her.

You don't need to apologize, she'd said. *I shouldn't have just . . . assumed that you would be into me.* I'm *sorry.*

It's not—I just have a lot going on right now. I'm just not ready to—

Roxie had shaken her head. *You don't need to make up excuses. It's okay. I'll be okay. I promise.*

He'd opened his mouth, as though he would argue further, but Roxie had grabbed her coat and cut him off. *They're hosting a* Scream *marathon at the Emerald tonight. You coming with me or not?*

For a moment, he'd looked conflicted, like he had something else to say but wasn't sure if he should. But finally, he'd nodded. They'd walked together to the movie theater, neither speaking a word about the incident—and they hadn't talked about it since.

Roxie, of course, didn't tell her grandmother any of this. She only said, "We're friends. I'm happy being his friend."

Grandma gave her another sly grin, not believing her for a second.

10

After they finished eating, Roxie watched Grandma dish out a plate of roast beef, mashed potatoes, and green beans for Skylar. Grandma brought her a meal every night. Though Skylar usually only took a few bites—just barely enough to keep Grandma from worrying about her starving.

But tonight, Roxie reached out for the plate before Grandma turned toward the stairs. "I'll take it to her."

Grandma raised an eyebrow but didn't protest. Roxie restrained herself from taking the steps two at a time.

She paused outside her sister's bedroom door, listening. But no noise came from inside. She knocked softly, but there was no response. Usually, Grandma left the plate outside her door, but Roxie announced, "I'm coming in," and pushed it open.

The TV flickered with *Grey's Anatomy* reruns, the sound turned off. Skylar was sitting up in bed, her back against the headboard and her knees drawn up to her chest. Her eyes were open, but she didn't seem to be following what was on the screen.

She blinked when she noticed Roxie in the doorway. "What?" she snapped.

Roxie hesitated in the doorway. She supposed she should have come up with some sort of speech—a delicate segue into a difficult topic. She cursed her lack of planning. But then again, she wasn't sure there *was* an easy way to broach this subject.

So she dove right in, setting the plate on the dresser before sitting on the edge of Skylar's bed, not even pausing to take a steadying breath.

"Colin bought a gift for you before he died," Roxie said plainly. "I thought you should have it."

She took the little box from her pocket and held it out to her sister.

Skylar stared like Roxie had just dumped a bucket of cold water over her head. She didn't move or speak for so long that Roxie started to repeat herself, but Skylar said, "I heard you the first time."

Finally, she reached for the box and grabbed it delicately with the tips of her fingers, as though it were made of glass. She held it in both hands for a moment.

"Was it a Christmas present?" she asked, tracing one of the little Christmas trees on the wrapping paper.

"Oh no," Roxie said. "Not even close. It was a going-away present he was going to give you before you left for Yale."

To Roxie's surprise and delight, that made her sister smile. Something Roxie hadn't seen her do in a year. And she was glad she'd decided to leave the wrapping paper intact.

With just a slight tremble to her hands, Skylar pulled off the tape, careful not to rip the paper, and pulled out the box.

She smiled again when she opened it, though her eyes filled with tears at the same time. "Oh," was all she could say. She touched the pendant of the daisy necklace with the tip of her finger.

She was quiet for a long time, just looking at it. Until finally, the spell broke, and she glanced at Roxie, clearly a little embarrassed by how emotional the gift had made her. "Daisies are my favorite. I—I can't believe he remembered."

Roxie refrained from saying, *I know they are.* And she sure as hell wasn't going to tell her that *she'd* been the one to tell Colin that Skylar loved daisies in the first place.

"He was so proud of you," she said instead.

Skylar nodded. "I know he was."

The silence stretched between them again as Skylar gazed at the necklace. Roxie considered saying more but decided not to press it. The gift spoke for itself. It was a congratulations for all the hard work Skylar had put in, and everything she had achieved, and everything she was still meant to achieve. And the message was coming from the one person Skylar would listen to.

"Do you want me to put it on for you?" Roxie asked.

Skylar nodded. She pulled the necklace out of the box before handing it over and then pulling her hair aside as Roxie did the clasp.

"Oh," Roxie said, "Almost forgot. There's a card, too."

She pulled the envelope from her pocket and watched with anticipation as her sister took it, turning it over to tear the seal. She opened it almost reverently—the last words she would ever have from the boy she loved.

Roxie watched her expression carefully as she read. Maybe Tristan was right about Skylar never being exactly who she was again. But still, Roxie held her breath as she waited for some semblance of the old Skylar to bloom on her sister's face.

But all at once, that tentatively reemerging smile vanished.

For a moment, Skylar didn't speak. She only stared at the note, as though she were reading the words over and over again.

Finally, she looked up at Roxie and said, "Is this some kind of joke?"

Roxie blinked. "What?"

Skylar began to tremble all over. Her skin heated to a boiling red. Her breath came quick and shallow as she clutched the note in her hand.

"Skylar? What's wrong?"

"This is a joke," she muttered, tears streaming down her face as her breathing grew more frantic. "This is a fucking joke."

"Skylar." Roxie grabbed her shoulders, trying to get her sister to look at her. "Tell me what's wrong. Was it something in the card?"

"Get the hell out," Skylar said.

Roxie tried to stand her ground. There was something very, very wrong. "What did the card—"

Skylar shoved it into her hand. But before she could read it, Skylar grabbed her by the arm, and with a strength Roxie wouldn't have thought her withered body capable of, she pushed Roxie out of the room and slammed the door shut in her face.

Roxie stood outside a while, listening. But she couldn't hear a thing. Not even crying. Even when she pressed her ear to the door, the other side was so silent, it might as well have been empty.

She had considered that the gift might upset Skylar. But the necklace hadn't been what set her off. What could Colin have possibly said to make her so upset?

She tried to turn the knob, but Skylar must have locked the door when she kicked her out. She knocked and called, "Please talk to me. Tell me you're okay."

No response.

And then she looked at the card in her hands—which Skylar had crumpled up like trash.

Tentatively, Roxie smoothed out the paper and read.

Dear Skylar,

There's no good way to tell you this. I've tried to figure out some way to say it so it won't hurt your feelings. But it's going to hurt you, and I'm sorry for that.

I want to break up.

I'm a coward for not saying it to your face. You deserve someone who isn't a coward. You deserve the best, and that isn't me.

Colin

11

Roxie called Tristan. Again and again, she called him, pacing the hallway outside Skylar's room, and growling into his voice mail, "We need to talk. *Now.*"

She realized he was probably still at work, deep in some project. She huffed in frustration, shoving her phone in her back pocket before she put her ear to Skylar's door again.

Nothing. She was nervous about leaving Skylar alone after seeing how upset she'd gotten—Roxie couldn't exactly blame her for losing her shit after getting broken up with from beyond the grave.

She waited a while longer. But once the silence had persisted for more than half an hour, she decided there was nothing she could do for Skylar now—she'd already made things bad enough. Horribly, catastrophically bad.

After another failed call to Tristan, she hurried down the stairs and pulled on her boots. She was thankful Grandma's hearing was going. She was watching a *Twilight Zone* episode on the couch, seemingly oblivious to all the shouting that had just been going on. And she didn't notice as Roxie slipped out the kitchen door and headed into the night, avoiding any questions or knowing smiles about who she might be going to see.

She decided to walk instead of taking her tour bus—the rumble of the engine was loud enough to wake the whole block, and being outside in the cold and the dark usually helped her clear her head.

She didn't know what she would say to Tristan when she saw him beyond, *What the hell?*

Roxie was sure there was plenty about Skylar and Colin's relationship she wasn't privy to, but he'd seemed hopelessly in love with her from day one. Skylar herself had certainly seemed blindsided by the breakup note.

But Colin *must* have said something to Tristan if he was planning on breaking up with Skylar. The brothers' relationship wasn't like the Clarks'. They shared everything with each other. In fact, Roxie usually only learned about whatever Colin and her sister had been up to secondhand—when Colin told Tristan and Tristan told her.

Roxie pulled her jacket tighter against the breeze. It usually took her ten minutes to get to the repair shop on foot, but this time, she made it in six, blazing a path under the intermittent streetlights. She saw the neon glow of the sign as she approached, like a lighthouse in the night—*The Resurrection Emporium: Where the Old Becomes New!*

The Resurrection Emporium used to be an auto repair garage, and sometimes, it still was. But just fixing cars was far too limited for a restless soul like Gertie Clark's.

People brought all sorts of things to the Emporium that needed fixing or repurposing—like leaky kayaks to be patched, bookshelves that needed a paint job, swivel chairs that didn't swivel anymore, and old TVs that had lost their spark.

It had been Grandma's passion project for a while. She was in love with the idea of taking broken and discarded things and putting them to good use again. The doors of the shop had been open now for more than thirty years. About a decade ago, Grandma had been able to retire from nursing and focus on it full-time.

Roxie, Skylar, and Colin had all picked up shifts there, though not on a consistent basis—Roxie because she was too busy with the ghost tour, Skylar because she was too preoccupied with school, and Colin because he was too fond of afterschool naps. But Tristan had been a dedicated employee since he was twelve years old, when Gertie paid him under the table to sweep the floors and mow the grass.

He'd been given much more responsibility over the years and became a full-time employee after graduation. Now it was his job to fix whatever was brought to him, whether he knew how to or not. No matter what it was, he had a knack for figuring it out, whether that meant watching YouTube tutorials, flipping through dusty manuals, or just taking the damn thing apart completely to uncover where it had gone wrong.

It was fitting, she thought. He'd been stepping in to help Roxie fix her screwups for years now and had been doing the same for Colin for years before that.

As Roxie drew closer, she could see one of the Emporium's three garage doors was thrown open to the night, florescent light spilling out. Tristan was working under the harsh glow, the sleeves of his flannel rolled up, a dirty rag hanging from his back pocket. There was something black smeared across his brow, probably where he'd swiped his forearm to clear away the sweat. He was bent over the open hood of a grill, tinkering with something.

The space around him was crowded with all his other projects from that day—a pair of roller skates with shiny new wheels, a motorcycle that probably coughed and sputtered when it had come in but purred like a cat now, and a pile of odds and ends he hadn't gotten to yet. Maybe things Grandma Gertie had fished from the dumpsters in town that she wanted him to find a use for, which Tristan told Roxie she did regularly. She'd give him her ideas on how to cobble them together into something new.

Tristan is like my own Dr. Frankenstein, Grandma had told Roxie once. *Sewing things together that don't go together, shooting them up with sparks, bringing them back to life. Although,* she'd added, *maybe he's more like Igor. He acts enough like a surly henchman.* Tristan had scowled at that comment, which had made Roxie shriek with laughter, because it made him look even more like a surly henchman.

Tristan had swung the hood on the grill closed and was peering out into the dark. He must have spotted her. She started to step forward, all the questions she had about Colin's card ready to spill out.

But she froze when someone else beat her to it.

"So?" a shadowed figure said, just before he stepped into the light.

The look on Tristan's face when he met the man's gaze made Roxie pull farther back into the shadows.

Was that anger? Fear? A trick of the light?

Whatever it was, it made the man chuckle. "I take it you haven't found it yet."

Tristan shook his head. "No."

"And how many more times do you think I'm going to accept that answer?"

The man was tall and broad-shouldered, and Roxie guessed he was around fifty. He had black hair brushed back from a handsome face—square jaw, dark eyes, and a smile that held no humor. He wore a faded leather jacket, a packet of cigarettes peeking out from one pocket.

He looked familiar, but Roxie couldn't place him.

"I'm still looking," Tristan said.

He spoke like he was bracing himself, which didn't make sense to Roxie. The man was large, but Tristan was larger. Strong enough to knock out Jackson's tooth, as much as it disturbed her to think of. He should have no problem defending himself if he needed to.

"You wouldn't be lying to me," the man said. "Would you?"

He took a step closer.

"Because you know where that will get you."

A threat. It made Roxie's skin bristle. She wanted to step out and defend him, as unwise as she knew that would be. Besides, Tristan was plenty capable of being intimidating all by himself.

But instead of turning on his usual scowl, he just gritted his teeth before he said, "I'll let you know as soon as I find it. I swear."

The man shook his head again, another bitter laugh filling the narrow space between them. "Making promises actually means something in this family, Tristan. Especially now that it's just the two of us."

Family.

Roxie remembered where she had seen him before. She'd never actually met him—only seen pictures of him around Tristan's house.

Luke Riley. Tristan's father. And the last Roxie had heard, he was in jail.

"Just the two of us," Tristan repeated with a smirk. "And whose fault is that?"

This time, his father didn't laugh. He took another step toward him.

And that's when Roxie sprang out of the shadows and said with false brightness, like she hadn't heard any of their conversation, "Tristan! There you are. Glad I caught you before you left."

She took a pointed step between father and son, giving Tristan a quick hug that he was too stunned to return. But once she let go, he kept his hand on her back, as though he were ready to push her out of the way. Why he felt the need to, Roxie could only guess. Luke had taken a step back, and his hands were in his pockets.

"What are you doing here?" Tristan asked, his voice almost a growl. He clearly wasn't happy to see her.

"Just wanted to talk to you about something," she said.

Tristan blinked, shaking his head before he turned back to his father. "Uh—this is—"

"Luke Riley," Roxie said, sticking out a hand. "Your dad. I recognized you from the pictures."

Luke raised an eyebrow but shook her hand. "Pleasure."

"And I'm—" Roxie started to say.

But Luke cut her off with an amused quirk of his mouth, "The one and only Roxie Clark."

It was Roxie's turn to look surprised. "Tristan told you about me?"

"Oh, no. Boy hasn't written or visited me the whole time I was in the slammer. Can you believe it? Now that I'm out, he still can't seem to make time for dear, old dad. But I still find ways to keep track of him. And his little friends."

He winked at Roxie in a way that somehow made her feel so violated, he may as well have grabbed her hand and licked it.

"Okay," she said. "Well, I hate to interrupt. But I was supposed to meet Tristan to talk about something he's going to build me for my ghost tour. He can make almost anything. You should be proud." *Instead of talking down to him like he's your incompetent lackey,* she didn't say, but she hoped her hard eyes conveyed the same meaning.

Luke nodded slowly. "Well, Riley men have always been handy. And Tristan is a Riley man, whether he likes it or not."

Roxie felt Tristan's hand tense on her back, but he said nothing. A heavy silence followed.

Finally, Luke scuffed his boot against the concrete floor and said, "I'll leave you to it." But before he turned to go, he surprised Roxie by wrapping his son in a hug, patting his back.

Tristan kept his arms stiff at his sides.

"Remember what we talked about," Roxie heard Luke say in his ear. He added, "Love you, son." Then he let go and walked away without another glance at her, melting into the shadows.

Roxie and Tristan both stared after him until his footsteps faded in the dark.

"You didn't tell me he was out," Roxie said.

"He wasn't supposed to be," Tristan said. Then he added, with a bitter twist to his mouth, "Good behavior, I guess."

"Is he staying with you?"

"Hell no. He's been renting somewhere, I think. But he won't be in town much longer if I can help it."

Roxie waited for him to elaborate further or to mention anything about the conversation they'd been having that she wouldn't admit she'd eavesdropped on. But instead, he went to the sink to scrub the grime from his hands and asked, "What are you *really* doing here?"

Right. The shock of meeting Tristan's dad had almost completely made her forget the shock that had made her rush over in the first place. She was about to sit heavily on a stool by the workbench when Tristan grabbed her elbow and said, "Not that one," nodding down at a splintered leg that would have broken and sent her tumbling to the floor.

He pulled out an old rocker instead. "Already fixed this one," he said, pointing to one of the rungs along the back, a slightly different color from the others, that he must have replaced.

Roxie collapsed into it, feeling it sway underneath her for a moment while she tried to think of where to even begin.

She decided, as she usually did, to be direct. "Why the hell would Colin want to break up with my sister?"

Tristan, who had been sorting through his toolbox, promptly dropped the hammer he was holding, just barely missing his foot. "What are you talking about?"

Roxie fished in her jacket pocket and pulled out Colin's card. "When I found Colin's gift to Skylar under the floorboards, this was with it, too. I thought they went together, but . . . I guess not."

Tristan grabbed it and scanned the words, brow furrowed. And then his face settled into an expression she'd become all too familiar with—exasperation. "*Goddammit, Colin*," he muttered.

"You didn't know anything about this?"

"No," Tristan said, handing the card back.

"Do you have any idea what would make him do this? Had they been fighting or anything?"

Tristan sighed. "Not that I know of."

Roxie wracked her hands through her hair. "This doesn't make any sense. He was nuts about her. Wasn't he?"

Tristan nodded. "He was. But . . ."

Roxie looked up at him. "But what?"

"I just—well, it's not like Colin was known for his attention span."

"What do you mean?"

He rubbed self-consciously at the back of his neck. "I

mean . . . well, it's a shitty thing to say about your dead brother, but he might have just gotten . . . bored."

Roxie shook her head. "No. There's no way. I saw them together!"

"I did, too. And I don't want to believe it. But relationships end all the time. Especially high school relationships. She was going off to Yale soon. Maybe he just decided that the long distance wouldn't work. I don't know." He shrugged. "Whatever it was, we can't ask him now. Let's just be glad he never had the chance to give Skylar the note. If she'd found out—"

Catching the pained look on Roxie's face, he stopped. Then he sighed again, pressing his fist hard between his eyes. "You gave it to her without reading it first, didn't you."

"In my defense—" Roxie began, holding up a finger to argue on her own behalf. But then she deflated, letting it fall pathetically to her lap. "I was just—I was so sure he'd say something nice. He was always saying nice things to her. I never thought he'd hurt her. Not in a million years."

But as impossible as it all seemed, she supposed Tristan was right. They'd never find out what Colin's reason had been. All that was left to do was deal with the fallout. The fallout *she* had caused.

Roxie hung her head in her hands for a moment, the guilt making her feel sick to her stomach.

Tristan pressed a comforting palm to the back of her neck. "Hey. I know it sucks. But she's going to be okay. She'll come back from this eventually. Maybe this will even make it easier on her."

Roxie lifted her head to give him a doubtful look. "How?"

"Maybe she'll get pissed at him. Might help dull the edge on her grief."

She was pretty sure he only said it to make her feel better. But she agreed, "Maybe."

She stood to go. But before she did, Tristan said, "This might not be the best time, but since you're already here, I might as well give you your other birthday present."

"Another one? The tour bus of my dreams wasn't enough?"

"This one isn't from me. It's from Colin."

"Really? How?"

"Not long before he died, he was cleaning some of the new items Gertie had gotten from an estate sale. He found one he thought would be perfect for you. So he bought it and told me to keep it in the storeroom for you so he could give it to you on your birthday last year. I forgot all about it when he died, but I found it again a few weeks ago."

Roxie narrowed her eyes at him, wary. So far, she wasn't having the best luck with Colin's posthumous gifts.

But then he went into the back room and brought it out for her, and she gasped.

It was an antique mirror. It was massive—taller than Roxie—and almost too heavy for Tristan to lift. He strained to get it leaned against the wall and was breathing hard when he took a step back to examine it with her.

The frame was made from gold-painted wood, carved in an impossibly ornate pattern, a beautiful design of whorls and starbursts and hidden images—a wilting rose, and a moth, and a snake. At the very top, there was a lion's head with a gaping mouth full of sharp teeth and smooth, blank eyes.

And sure enough, there was a Post-it note on the glass, scrawled in Colin's handwriting.

FOR ROXIE. DO NOT TOUCH.

It wasn't nearly enough to make up for the way he'd probably just irreparably shattered her sister's heart. But it made it just a little harder to stay mad at him.

"It's incredible," Roxie said. "But he's never gotten me a birthday gift before."

Tristan shrugged. "I guess he saw it and thought it was too perfect to pass up. Pretty but creepy—just like you."

She gave him a look of mock indignation, slapping him lightly on the arm, and he smiled back, the tension from a few minutes ago with his father almost completely forgotten. Almost.

"Well, Colin was right," she said. "It's perfect. Maybe I can use it on the tour somehow."

"Might as well leave it here until you decide what to do with it. It's way too heavy to take back to the house by yourself. Just let me know where you want it, and I'll hang it for you."

She nodded in agreement. Then she looked at the time on her phone and said, "I better get back to check on Skylar."

She started to leave. But she couldn't shake the uneasy feeling she'd had about Luke Riley. And she was sure she hadn't imagined the look of fear on Tristan's face.

She turned back to him. And when he met her gaze, she asked, "You'd tell me if you needed help. Wouldn't you?"

"Why would I need help?"

"I'm not saying you do. I'm just saying . . . if."

He offered her a slight smile. "I thought you didn't like to worry about *ifs*, Rox."

She leveled a glare at him.

With a quiet laugh, he relented. "Yes. Of course I'd tell you."

She didn't believe him. But she smiled back before she headed home.

12

For a century and a half, Ward Manor—a crumbling Victorian tucked into Whistler Woods—had sat empty. The paint was peeling away, the roof disintegrating, the walls choking with vines. Nature was springing up through the floorboards in its slow but inevitable mission to absorb the house back into the earth. The close-pressing trees blotted out the night sky almost entirely, wrapping the place in a silence and isolation that made it feel as though it were a hundred miles from anywhere else.

That night's tour group huddled behind Roxie as they all stared up at the manor, strangers drawing subconsciously closer together against the cold wind. Or perhaps the ominous sight of the old house gave them the urge to seek safety in numbers. But Roxie knew bad things didn't only happen when you were alone. In fact, the danger came from other people more often than not—which was certainly true when it came to this house's story.

She walked up to the front door and pushed it open slowly, drawing out the high-pitched creak of the hinges, letting the sound thrill down the spines of her patrons before she turned to them, saying with a flourish of her hand, "After you."

The group filed inside, the warped floorboards creaking and whining under their feet. Roxie came last, shutting the door with a firm tug. It banged with a finality that made them all jump as they were cast into the pitch-dark.

Counting off a few seconds, Roxie clicked on her lantern and carried it to the center of the living room.

She had furnished it with some items she'd found at the Resurrection Emporium that felt appropriately worn and regal at the same time—a blue carpet with a faded gold pattern, a stained-glass lamp dripping with clear beads, gauzy lace curtains that danced with the wind sieving through the broken windows, a velvet couch with minimal tears and a dramatically winged back, as well as a cocktail cart she'd stocked with dusty vintage bottles.

And then there was the pièce de résistance—the gold-framed mirror Colin had given her. Roxie hadn't taken long to decide it would be perfect for Ward Manor, and Tristan had come by right away to put it up for her. It looked stunning, tying the whole look together. She whispered a soft *thank you*, hoping Colin could hear it, wherever he was.

She had no idea who owned this old house, if anyone did at all. But she'd been coming here since she'd first learned the place's history and never been chased off before. The discovery hadn't come from her own research this time but rather from a popular story told around the school playground and at slumber parties. A tale usually followed by a dare—*Go to the house in the woods and touch the bloodstain on the bedroom floor.*

"In 1866," Roxie began, "this house was owned by a wealthy man named Nicholas Ward. He had three sons—or at least, he did when the Civil War began. By the end of it, he had only one son left. And one heir to his fortune."

Roxie lofted her lantern toward the wall to illuminate the framed photograph of a tall, lanky man in his military uniform. She'd found a copy of it in the library archives, made one for herself, and salvaged a worn gold frame from the Emporium to display it.

"His last son, Charles, was described by his friends as shy. But I've always thought the look in his eyes told a different story. He was a man hollowed out by what he'd witnessed in battle—men torn apart by musket balls and trampled in the mud. His own brothers lost to the carnage. And then his father died a short time after, leaving him entirely alone in this big, extravagant house. Still so young, but already too broken for falling in love. And certainly too broken for anyone to fall in love with him. Until . . . someone did."

She moved her lantern to the right, revealing another photo, this one of a dark-haired girl in a plain black dress with a white collar.

"Lucy Clark saw the same sadness in him that everyone else saw. But instead of being put off by it, she had the urge to coax out the light that she knew was still in him. Her slow, quiet courtship of Charles Ward was a subtle, delicate thing—a look from under her long lashes, a flutter of her fingers against his, a sympathetic ear when everyone else told him to stop dwelling on his sorrow. Slowly but surely, the color started to return to Charles's cheeks, and there were whispers of an imminent proposal.

"Until Lucy's sister, Eleanor Clark, took notice."

The last portrait on the wall was of a girl with thick, blond curls, a button nose, and a slant to one eyebrow that could only be described as insolent.

"Rumor was that she had no interest in cultivating Charles's happiness. Her eyes were on the fortune he had to offer. And her sister had already lain the groundwork—Lucy had opened his heart, and before she could take a step inside, Eleanor swept in past her and slammed the door.

"Lucy's seduction had been intentional and soft and loving. Eleanor's was a lightning strike—a well-timed meeting at the tavern, a night of drinking and dancing and laughter, coy glances and bold touches. A walk in the woods under the stars.

"In the span between a sunset and a sunrise, Lucy had lost her beloved to her sister. People whispered about how tragic it was for her, how dramatically and suddenly her fortunes had turned, how deep the betrayal must have cut. It was like a ballet or a Shakespearean plot. They waited for her to fade quietly into the shadows or perhaps take her own life in a fit of sorrow for the love she'd lost.

"But Lucy did neither. She attended the wedding of the young lovers in the spring—an extravagant ceremony at the church in the center of town. She sat near the front, all alone, a slight smile on her lips during the entire ceremony. She was praised for her grace and understanding and what people thought must be an infinite well of forgiveness.

"After the ceremony, the happy couple immediately moved into Ward Manor. Charles had been preparing it for months, redecorating and rearranging it to Eleanor's exacting standards. They passed their first evening together at their big, beautiful home in the peaceful quiet of the woods.

"A peace that was disturbed after they fell asleep that night, when their front door opened.

"Lucy stepped calmly inside, wafted up the staircase, and entered the bedroom with the grave silence of ghost. She approached the bed—the bed that should have been hers—and watched Charles, her Charles, sleeping peacefully beside his new wife.

"Then she pulled a gleaming knife from the folds of her dress and slit his throat so quickly that he never opened his eyes to see the face that brought his death.

"To her sister, she didn't offer the same mercy. She woke her by pulling a fistful of her hair, dragging her from the bed and onto the floor.

"Eleanor grabbed Lucy's wrist before the knife drew across her neck.

"The women struggled against each other, and Eleanor shouted for her husband. She was too busy holding off Lucy to see his throat was laid open to the ceiling. He was already beyond this room, beyond this world, beyond stopping his first love from plunging a knife into his pretty wife's chest.

"Afterward, Lucy did not run and hide. She walked into

town that very night with her dress soaked in her sister's blood, the knife still in her hand, her chilling laughter drawing the people of Whistler from their beds to watch through the windows as she paraded like a nightmare come to life down the quiet streets."

Roxie had been told many times by people who had been on her tours that the Ward Manor story was their favorite. She could understand why. The house itself made the story seem so present in a way the other stories couldn't. And many of them had heard the tale before they ever came on the tour—it had spread all over the Midwest. All the drama and betrayal and revenge made for a juicy tale people loved to sink their teeth into.

But Roxie had never been able to understand Lucy and Eleanor Clark like she had her other ancestors. Having a sister of her own, she just couldn't imagine it. She and Skylar had, of course, fought bitterly before. Hurt each other physically and emotionally. Couldn't even call each other friends most of the time.

But killing each other? Especially over some *guy*? Roxie couldn't conceive of it. No matter how angry they made each other, she and Skylar were still sisters at the end of the day. Nothing could change that.

At least, that's what she'd thought. But it had been almost a week since she'd given Skylar the necklace and accidentally handed over Colin's breakup note. And at this point, she wouldn't be the least bit surprised to find Skylar standing in her bedroom doorway in the middle of the night, ready to exact her vengeance.

All Roxie had wanted to do was help. But the more she tried, the bigger mess she made of things. So she'd decided to give Skylar her space. Though that didn't keep Roxie from eavesdropping, stopping by her door on the way to and from her own room and listening for a while.

Mostly, Skylar was silent. The meals Grandma brought her had been almost entirely untouched. But sometimes, Roxie had thought she could hear pacing.

For the old Skylar, this wasn't unusual. Whenever she got stuck on a tricky homework problem or was having trouble finishing a report, her brain seemed to benefit from the steady movement, accompanied by some unintelligible muttering as she worked through possible solutions in her head.

But Roxie hadn't seen her do it since Colin died. Her sister hadn't seemed capable of thinking through much of anything after the funeral, as though her brain had been mired in a thick cloud of fog for the past year.

Roxie had no idea what this development could mean. And she didn't know if she should be relieved her sister had at least gotten out of bed or if she should be even more worried about what she could possibly be thinking.

Grandma was worried. Neither of them had had a single sighting of her all week. *Is this still about Yale?* she'd asked. *Or is she just getting . . . worse?*

Roxie had debated telling her about the breakup note. The words were on the tip of her tongue more than once. But truthfully, she was embarrassed to admit how she'd meddled in an already bad situation. After all, she hadn't told Grandma about her plan in the first place because she'd *known* it was a bad idea. But she'd done it anyway because she had thought things couldn't get worse.

Lesson learned: things could *always* get worse. Especially when Roxie stuck her nose in places where it didn't belong.

After she finished her story, Roxie allowed the tour group to wander the house for a few minutes. Most of them immediately took the stairs to the second floor, wanting to get a glimpse of the bedroom where it had all happened. Rumor had it, there was a smear of blood that had absorbed into the floor, and if you touched it, you would see Lucy Clark over your shoulder the next time you looked in a mirror.

Roxie told Lucy and Eleanor's story in the living room instead of the bedroom for two reasons—one, she doubted the old staircase could hold the weight of more than a couple of people at a time, and two, she was pretty sure the "bloodstain" was just a patch of moldy wood.

But she waited patiently while the group did their exploring. Though Lucy and Eleanor's story wasn't her favorite on the tour, she had fallen in love with Ward Manor at first sight. She'd been a frequent visitor over the years. When she'd been younger, before her grandmother allowed her to wander the neighborhood alone, she'd drag Skylar here all the time so she could explore. Roxie knew the cold and the melancholy of the place should have scared her, but there was something that always relentlessly drew her back. She thought it might be the way the house seemed to breathe, almost alive with its long, dark history.

Every time she made a new discovery—chipped bowls and

glass cups in the kitchen cabinets, a scuffed pair of heeled boots in the closet—it felt like a moment of transcendence. A glimpse of timelines rubbing against each other. Past and present, life and death, occupying the same space. They were reminders that she shared this world with so many others that everyone else had forgotten years ago, and that one day, they would forget her too and she'd be nothing more than an echo in the halls of her own home. It was a thought that might paralyze some people with terror, but it had never frightened her.

Skylar claimed she'd never been afraid of Ward Manor either, though for precisely the opposite reason—she was so thoroughly logical that the place was just like any other house to her. *People die everywhere all the time*, she'd told Roxie once. *If an old story is enough to scare people away, then the whole world should scare them.*

Roxie had responded, *Well if you're too smart to be scared, go touch the bloodstain yourself.*

Skylar had declined, saying, *I don't need to prove myself to you.*

Roxie was still caught up in her thoughts when someone grabbed her shoulder from behind. She was so startled, she jumped and was immediately embarrassed for it. This was her tour—she was supposed to do the scaring.

She turned to glare at whoever it was who had the nerve to sneak up on her. But then, her annoyance turned to shock.

"Skylar?"

She had to lift her lantern to be sure. She had barely seen Skylar out of the house in months. Roxie would have been less surprised to see the blood-spattered ghost of Lucy Clark standing in front of her.

Skylar lifted her hand, squinting against the light. "Yes, it's me. Get that thing out of my face."

Roxie lowered the lantern but kept on staring. Skylar looked too thin, and there were circles under her eyes, like she hadn't gotten enough sleep. But she had brushed her hair and pulled it into a ponytail—something she hadn't bothered to do in a year. She wasn't wearing pajamas but a pair of black jeans and a denim jacket thrown over a green sweater.

She looked so . . . like herself. Roxie was too taken aback for a moment to say anything. When she did finally speak, she asked, "What are you doing here?"

Even before Colin's death, Skylar had never come to one of her tours. She'd made it clear early on that she thought it was nothing more than a morbid phase that shouldn't be encouraged.

"I needed to talk to you," she said. She reached into her pocket and pulled out an envelope.

Roxie recognized it as Colin's breakup letter. After she'd shown it to Tristan, Roxie had taken it home and stashed it in her bedside drawer.

"You snuck into my room?" Roxie asked.

Skylar shook her head. "Not important. All that matters now is that I figured it out."

"Figured what out?"

Whatever cloud had been hanging over Skylar's mind seemed to have lifted entirely. Her eyes were wide and shining. Roxie hadn't seen them look this clear in a long, long time.

"I know who killed Colin."

Roxie gaped at her sister. Then she turned to the rest of the house and shouted, "Listen up! Tour is over! Everybody out!"

They still technically had one more stop at the creek to hear Aurora Clark's story, but Roxie had a feeling Skylar shouldn't be kept waiting.

She hurried a few resistant patrons out the door, some of them mumbling things about rip-offs and refunds, and she said, "All complaints can be directed to the contact form on my website. Have a great night."

And then she shut the door behind them and turned back to Skylar.

"All right," she said. "Now . . . run that by me again."

"The letter," Skylar said, holding the envelope between them. "It explains everything."

Roxie took it, turning it over in her hands. "And what exactly is *everything*?"

Skylar grabbed her by the shoulders, a shaky smile spreading across her face.

"It proves Tristan murdered Colin."

13

Roxie blinked at her sister. "Was that supposed to be a joke?"

Skylar narrowed her eyes. "Why would I joke about my boyfriend's killer?"

"Does Grandma know you're out?" Roxie asked. She grabbed Skylar's wrist and started to lead her to the door. "We should get you home. I think you need to go back to bed."

Skylar wrenched her arm free. "Don't talk to me like I'm crazy. I'm *not* crazy. And I've been in bed long enough." She crossed her arms over her chest, planting her feet in defiance. "Now are you going to listen to me, or do I need to do this on my own?"

"Do what on your own?"

"Prove my theory."

"That Tristan is a murderer. That he committed—patricide?"

"*Patricide* is the word for murdering your father. *Fratricide* is brother murder. And yes, that's exactly what I think Tristan did."

Roxie shook her head, squeezing her eyes shut for a moment. "You're going to have to give me a little more detail than that."

Skylar nodded. "Of course." Then she went to the carpet in the middle of the room and sat cross-legged, pulling a backpack from her shoulders that Roxie hadn't noticed. She started to unload things from it, laying them out neatly on the floor. She took a quick look around as she did so, seeming to notice her surroundings for the first time since she'd arrived. "I like what you've done with the place," she said.

Her gaze paused on the gold-framed mirror. What Roxie loved about it most was the way the glass had fogged with age, so that when it reflected the room back at them, it gave the impression of an alternate dimension, identical in every way except darker and slightly distorted—just a little more sinister.

Skylar tilted her head, and her shadow-self followed suit. Then she shuddered and looked away.

She motioned to Roxie. "Bring that light over here."

Too stunned to do anything else, Roxie obeyed, sitting across from Skylar and setting the lantern between them.

Roxie had a flash of incongruous memory—her and Skylar sitting on this same floor, years ago, playing a game of UNO while the summer sunset slanted through the windows. It must have been one of the last times they were in Ward Manor together. Not long before Skylar outgrew her.

Now the windows were dark, and games were clearly the furthest thing from her sister's mind.

Skylar had spread out two maps, a pile of newspaper articles, and a spiral notebook open to a page filled with her precise handwriting.

The *first* page, Roxie realized when she reached across to flip through it. More than half of the notebook was filled with lines and lines of black ink. "You've been busy," Roxie said.

Skylar slapped her hand lightly away. "We'll get to that in a minute. First—the letter."

Roxie was still holding it. She opened the envelope, slipping out the note to read it over again. She turned the paper this way and that, looking for something she may have missed the first time. A secret SOS message written in invisible ink? A code hidden in the words that Skylar had picked up on?

Skylar watched her, impatiently drumming her fingers against her knee, until Roxie finally said, "I don't get it. It says exactly the same thing as the last time I read it. It's not a cry for help. It's . . . well, it's a breakup note. That's it."

Skylar waved away her words like gnats. "It doesn't matter *what* the note says. What matters is the note itself."

Roxie frowned. "I'm still lost."

"Look at the paper. At the bottom right corner."

Angling toward the light, Roxie could see the word *Riley* printed in an elegant script.

She frowned. Since when did Colin have personalized stationery? The boy could hardly be counted on to wear matching socks.

Skylar caught the look on her face and nodded eagerly. "I thought it was weird, too. Really unlike him. I thought maybe he'd gotten it from his mom or something. But then I realized I had seen this stationery before. Remember Colin's candlelight vigil?"

Roxie nodded, biting her lip. It had taken place at the Whistler High School football field the Saturday after he died. The bleachers had been packed. Unlike his brother, Colin's charm had won him more friends than he could possibly keep track of. Though the size of the crowd also probably had something to do with the swarm of reporters looking for a quote. Not to mention the casual citizen dying for a morsel of gossip about the first murder to occur in Whistler in recent memory (and one where the victim didn't have the last name Clark, no less!).

There'd been a stage erected on the field with a podium, a blown-up picture of Colin in his baseball uniform, and a collection of flowers around the base.

The principal had asked Tristan to make a speech. He'd been reluctant, his feelings still too raw to talk about his brother easily. But he did it anyway, his voice wavering in a jumble of nerves and grief, the paper he was reading from shaking in his hand, and Roxie had been so proud of him while she sat next to Grandma and watched.

Grandma had urged Skylar to come with them. She said it might help with closure. Back then, they'd had hope that Skylar would be able to get back on track in time to start at Yale just a semester late.

"I let Grandma talk me into it because I didn't want her to worry about me," Skylar said now. But I should have known better. People kept coming up to me and telling me how sorry they were, and expecting me to say something about how I was going to be okay and I just . . . couldn't. So I went and cried under the bleachers before it even started. And that's where Tristan found me."

Roxie remembered how Skylar had slipped away before it was dark enough for the vigil to begin, saying she had to go to the bathroom. It had been clear she wasn't all right, and Roxie had asked Grandma if they should go after her, and the woman had shaken her head sadly. *I think she wants a minute to herself.*

Roxie didn't know Skylar and Tristan had spoken that night.

"He was about to go on stage for his speech," Skylar said. "He was taking a minute to gather himself. And he said, *You look like you want to be here even less than I do.* He offered me his car keys and told me I could go sit in his truck while I pulled myself together. I took him up on it.

"I was out there for a while. Even after I calmed down, I waited until the vigil was at least half over because I didn't want to endure any more of it than I needed to. I was panicking just thinking about it. And well—you know I like to organize when I get anxious. Tristan's car was a mess, just like Colin's always was. Granola bar and Reese's Cups wrappers everywhere. So I started picking them all up off the floor. And that's when I found a box wrapped in paper with balloons on it. And I remembered that it was Tristan's birthday."

Roxie nodded sadly. He always said he didn't want her to make a big deal out of his birthday, though she usually went behind his back and planned some kind of celebratory dinner or movie night. Though she'd known that this time, he definitely wouldn't be up for it. Not on the same night the whole town was gathering to mourn his brother. She hadn't wanted him to think everyone had forgotten it completely, so she'd brought him some of his favorite chocolate cupcakes from Smith & Laurel Café that morning.

But she hadn't gotten him a gift. She didn't know who would have, aside from Gertie, but Roxie thought her grandmother would have mentioned that to her. Though she supposed it wasn't out of the question that one of his teachers or coaches had given him something.

"He'd opened the box just enough for me to tell what it was," Skylar said, leaning in closer now, her eyes shining in the lantern light. "It was a personalized stationery set. I could see his name in the corner." She pointed to the word *Riley* on the note. "And it looked *exactly* like this."

She gave Roxie a significant look, like what she'd just said should make the conclusion obvious.

"This stationery belonged to Tristan," Skylar added, as though that should clarify things.

Roxie bit her lip and squinted, trying to make a visible effort at puzzling out exactly what she was supposed to say next. "So . . ."

Skylar sighed. "Tristan didn't receive the stationery until almost a week after Colin died. Which means Colin didn't write me that breakup note. He couldn't have."

"Then who the hell did?"

"Tristan."

Roxie shook her head. "That doesn't make—"

"He's one of the only people who would have known Colin's handwriting well enough to imitate it, right down to the way he crossed his *t*'s. And he's one of the only people who had access to Colin's room. That's where you said you found it, isn't it?"

"Well, yeah. But—why would Tristan want to pretend to be Colin breaking up with you?"

"I wondered that, too. And there was only one reason I could come up with—he thought I might want to investigate Colin's death. He thought that if he could convince me that Colin didn't love me anymore, I would give up on him." She looked down at her hands, her fingers knotted together in her lap. "But I didn't even pay attention to what was happening with the investigation. I was too—"

She paused. A breeze filtered through the woods, and the old house creaked.

When she looked up, she finished, "He was keeping the note just in case he needed it to throw me off the trail, but because I never bothered looking into it in the first place, he never had to use it."

Roxie rubbed at her temples, feeling a headache starting to come on. "Look, I know . . . I know that letter wasn't an easy one to read. I know you don't want to believe Colin wrote it, but a piece of stationery paper just isn't enough to convince me that Tristan wrote it. And it definitely isn't enough to convince me that he killed his own brother."

Skylar nodded. "You're right. It's not enough. But I have more. First, we need to go over everything we know about the events leading up to the murder."

She flipped to a page in her notebook and turned it

horizontally for Roxie to see the long, dark line she'd drawn down the middle, marked and labeled at intervals with the order of events, along with their approximate times.

She pointed to the first marker on the time line. "August 5, a Shell gas station was robbed by an unidentified suspect with a knife. According to article number one, the man working behind the counter that night said the suspect was dressed from head to toe in black, including his shoes, pants, shirt, and ski mask. Approximately six feet tall, a hundred and sixty pounds, and white. This information is corroborated by security footage. He stole $204."

Skylar pointed to a pile of newspaper articles she had printed out, all of which she had helpfully numbered in the top right corner. She'd also highlighted all the information she'd just gone over and waited as Roxie skimmed it to confirm.

Skylar moved on to the next marker. "August 10, the second robbery occurs at the Smith & Laurel Café. There were two women working that night whose description of the robber matched the details the man at the gas station gave. The robber also threatened them with a knife and got away with $2,134."

The article labeled #2 told the same story.

"On to the third robbery," Skylar said as Roxie picked up the next article. "August 18. This one occurred at the Whistler Community Bank."

Roxie didn't need to read the article to know how this one had ended.

"The bank has a policy that two employees should be present during all open hours, but that night, someone had called in sick, and they were unable to find a replacement. So Roger Patterson was working alone when the robber entered the bank a few minutes before closing. This time, instead of a knife, the suspect had brought a gun. He instructed Roger to retrieve all the money on the premises and put it in a green duffel bag. Roger was initially compliant. But instead of handing over the duffel bag, he attempted to attack the suspect. The suspect responded by shooting him in the stomach and fleeing the premises with $34,852. Someone from a neighboring shop called the police when they heard the gunshot, but Roger died from his wound before they arrived."

Both the girls had known Roger since they were little. He'd been handing them Dum Dum lollipops through the teller window for years, even after they'd both started high school. But Skylar spoke with a clinical detachment as she relayed the facts, moving on to the next marker on her time line without betraying any emotion.

"The robberies paused temporarily, up until August 23, at the Resurrection Emporium. Which was also the night of Colin's murder."

There was an article labeled #4, but it was unnecessary. Because the only witness to the attempted robbery that night was Skylar herself.

She took a deep breath, reaching back to tighten her ponytail—a nervous habit Roxie hadn't seen in a long time.

"Here's what I remember," she began. "I was working the register. It had been a slow day, just a few customers. So I spent most of the shift reading behind the counter. Mrs. Ferguson had given me a book as a gift when she heard about my acceptance letter—a six-hundred-page history of Yale."

"Sounds riveting," Roxie said with a raised eyebrow.

Skylar frowned at the sarcasm in her voice. "As a matter of fact, it was. There was so little going on in the shop all day that I let myself lose track of time. I was supposed to close at 9 p.m. but by the time I remembered to look at the clock, it was already 9:43.

"I scrambled to get through the closing checklist and get home. I knew Grandma would be blowing up my phone soon. She'd been worried about me working at all because of the other robberies, but I pointed out that there hadn't been any incidents in weeks. If the guy was smart, he'd probably fled town after he killed Roger. And I wasn't going to wait around for the cops to figure it out.

"I swept and took out the trash. Counted the till and put the money in the safe. I'd just finished turning out the lights and was grabbing my bag when I heard the bell over the door ring.

"I thought I had locked the door, but I must not have yet. I was about to tell whoever it was that we were closed. I could hardly see him in the dark. But then he started to come into focus—black boots. Black Pants. Black shirt. Black ski mask.

"I knew Grandma kept a gun under the counter. She gave me a rundown on how to use it once. *Just in case*, she said, but I told her that I wouldn't touch it, no matter what the situation was. But once it was actually happening—a known violent criminal standing right in front of me—my body just . . . took over. There wasn't any thinking involved. I grabbed the gun, turned off the safety, and fired.

"Of course, I'd never fired a gun in my life. It's not as easy as it looks. I wasn't expecting the recoil. My hand jerked and I missed—by a lot. I hit the wall, and the guy had already turned and run out the door anyway."

Skylar was silent for a long moment after that. Roxie waited for her to go on, watching her downcast face in the lantern light.

"I thought about that moment a lot, after," she said finally. "The cops couldn't confirm the robber and the murderer were the same person, but . . . if they *were*—"

Roxie shook her head. "What happened next isn't your fault," she said.

"If I had been able to shoot him—"

"You can't think about it that way. It's like you said—you'd never fired a gun. It would have been a miracle if you did manage to hit him. No one blames you."

Skylar tightened her ponytail again, taking a moment to clear her thoughts and get back on track with the story.

"When he was gone, I called the police and told them what happened. While I waited for them, I called Grandma. You guys showed up not long after the cops did. I answered all their questions . . . and that was it. Grandma patted me on the back and told me I was never working after dark again. I went home with both of you. And I went right to sleep. But I woke up again around midnight, when we heard the sirens. And then—"

She stopped, and Roxie put a hand over hers, so she knew she didn't have to say it. But Skylar pulled her hand away and finished, "We walked to the cornfield. And we saw Colin's body."

Without dwelling on the statement, she went on to the next thing, flipping her notebook to a new page. There was another time line—this one limited to the night of the murder. She also pulled her map of Whistler closer to the lantern light.

"As far as the police know, on August 23, Colin was working on an essay with his Summer Volunteer Program partner from 8 p.m. to 10:10 p.m." She pointed to a spot on the map, about halfway down Prospect Street.

And Roxie had the uncontrollable urge to roll her eyes—her automatic response whenever the subject of Jackson Mowery came up.

She'd felt so bad for Colin when the pairings were announced. It was a graduation requirement at Whistler High School that everyone complete at least thirty hours of volunteer work with a partner, which would culminate in a final report written together.

Working with Jackson would have been hard for anyone—he demanded no less than excellence and was known for his thin patience and quick temper when people didn't meet his expectations. But Roxie knew it would be even worse for Colin because it was obvious to everyone that Jackson had a thing for Skylar. And it was just as obvious that he hated Colin because of it.

When Roxie had told him to talk their teacher into reassigning him, Colin had smiled and winked and said, *I'm not scared of that little shit.*

"In the time frame that Colin was at Jackson's house, he made one phone call to Tristan at 8:55 p.m. It lasted for one minute and thirty-two seconds. Tristan claims Colin was asking him where to find the spare house key—he had lost his. Then he left Jackson's at 10:10 and started to walk home," Skylar said. "Around the same time—10:02—the attempted robbery at the

Emporium happened, and the suspect ran away." Skylar marked the spot with another finger. "Police suspect they crossed paths around here," Skylar said, drawing both fingers together on Main Street, just a few blocks away from the Emporium. "They found some of his blood on the sidewalk and dripping in a path that leads behind the Morning Glory Diner, between the kitchen door and the dumpster. Judging by the amount of blood there, they believe that's where he died."

Which was why it had become universally agreed by the people in town that the robber and the murderer were the same person. The events happened too close together to be coincidental, even with no definitive proof.

"At 11 p.m., fifty minutes after Colin left Jackson's, someone noticed smoke coming from the Mayers' cornfield at the edge of town," Skylar continued, moving her finger again to show the approximate location on the map. "By the time authorities arrived, there was a full-blown fire that needed to be put out. In the process, firefighters discovered Colin's body. And while he had been thoroughly burned, there was enough of the body left to determine it was not the fire that killed him but multiple stab wounds on the left side of his abdomen."

There was a pause at the end of her story. Skylar watched Roxie's face, like she was waiting for her to digest all the details. "Okay," Roxie said finally. "And what exactly does all this have to do with Tristan?"

There was a slight twitch at the corner of Skylar's mouth— not quite a smile, but there was satisfaction in it, like she was glad Roxie had asked.

She moved her finger back to Jackson Mowery's house on the map. "I didn't pay any attention to Colin's case after he died. I left it up to everyone else to deal with. At that point, I didn't really care *how* it had happened. All I knew was that he was gone, and I had no idea how to move forward without him. I wasn't sure I even wanted to."

Roxie's teeth clenched, and she almost said something, but Skylar hurried on, "It wasn't until I got the breakup letter that I started looking into the investigation. I didn't know the police thought Colin was at Jackson's house working on their volunteer report the night of the murder. If I had, I could have told them I knew for a fact that he *wasn't* there."

"What do you mean? How do you know he wasn't?"

"Because Colin told me Jackson already finished the report. He did it all himself. Apparently, he was pissed that Colin spent the whole summer slacking off during their volunteer time at the Humane Society, showing up late every day and playing with the kittens while Jackson filed paperwork and cleaned up shit. He was going to tell their supervisor not to give him any credit. So there was no reason for him to be at Jackson's house that night."

Roxie paused, trying to keep up. "So then why do the police think he was?"

Skylar handed her article number five. "Because someone lied to them."

Roxie started to read the article and frowned when she saw Tristan's name.

One of his quotes was highlighted and underlined. *Colin was at a classmate's house that night working on a paper. That's all I know concerning his whereabouts.*

"He did exactly one interview about the murder," Skylar said. "He knew everyone in town suspected him. So he wanted to them to know he had a solid alibi."

She wasn't wrong about the suspicion. Rumors had followed him from the day he moved here, and everyone had been certain the scowling boy with a crooked nose had something to do with Colin's death. The police had had their own suspicions and brought him in multiple times for questioning.

But they hadn't been able to get very far—he'd stayed at his cousin's the night of the murder, and there was security footage to prove it.

Roxie read aloud, "Tristan Riley was in Arden, Ohio, reroofing a house for his cousin. Surveillance footage on the property shows him entering the house at 9:05 p.m. that evening, and he does not reemerge until 6:25 the next morning."

Roxie tossed the article in the air, letting it flutter to the corner of the room, as though that were that. Then she pointed at the map Skylar had printed out depicting the border between Indiana and Ohio.

"Arden is two hours from here," she said. "And that's if you're speeding. The fastest route here is the highway. There were two state troopers patrolling that area on August 23 and they definitely would have seen someone going fast enough to shave off more time. The fire in the cornfield started at eleven, and Colin was likely dead before then. The attempted robbery at the Emporium happened at ten—there's no way he could have gotten back here in one hour. He *could* have made it before the body was discovered, but he definitely wouldn't have had time to kill him behind Morning Glory *then* transport him to the cornfield and set it on fire."

She knew Tristan's alibi in and out. Dealing with grueling rounds of interrogation from the police right after losing his brother had been hard on him. She'd been there after every session to grab a hot chocolate and let him vent.

Skylar had waited patiently through Roxie's spiel, her expression never changing. She was clearly well versed in the story already.

"Let's say all that is true. Pretend he's innocent," she said. "Then why would he lie to the police about where his brother was right before the murder?"

Roxie came up short on that one.

After a long stretch of silence, Skylar leaned in and said, "Here's what I think—Tristan murdered Colin earlier in the day. Around 7 p.m. or earlier. But he wanted the police to think Colin died later, during a time frame when he couldn't possibly have done it. So he said Colin was alive at Jackson's house from 8 to 10:10. He got Jackson to lie for him and confirm the story. Then he hid the body in the cornfield, and drove to his cousin's to be seen on camera and secure his alibi. He snuck out right after he arrived, probably through a window so the camera wouldn't catch him leaving, and drove back to Whistler.

"You're right—he wouldn't have had time to kill Colin and transport the body to the field. But if it was already there because he killed him and hid it there earlier in the day . . . it's possible he could have been back just in time to start the fire. It also explains why he needed to burn the body in the first place—because a coroner can give an approximate estimate of someone's time of death based on the stage of rigor mortis the body is in. So he needed to destroy it enough to make an accurate estimate impossible. Which meant the police had to rely strictly upon their time line to make their guess about when the murder took place—between 10:10 p.m. and 11 p.m.''

Skylar had recited her entire theory without pause. She'd clearly been crafting it all week, locked behind her bedroom door while Roxie thought she'd been in bed this whole time.

She'd come prepared. Roxie hadn't. She stumbled around for a hole in her argument. Until, finally, she found one, snapping her fingers. "What about the 8:55 phone call Colin made to Tristan?"

"Easily could have been made by someone else from Colin's phone to try and fool police into thinking he was still alive at that point. Maybe by Jackson himself."

"But why would Jackson do that for Tristan? And you said Jackson also would have had to confirm his story, that Colin was at Jackson's house that night. The police never would have believed it otherwise. But why in the hell would Jackson lie for him? Can't he get in huge trouble if the police find out?"

Skylar nodded. "He could be charged with obstruction of justice. And you're right—I don't think Jackson would stick his neck out like that for anyone, especially not a Riley. So the only explanation is that Tristan must have threatened him somehow."

Roxie was shaking her head. "He wouldn't—"

"I heard about the fight."

Roxie cursed under her breath.

"Actually," Skylar said, "it didn't sound like much of a fight to me, considering Jackson didn't stand a chance."

"That was after the murder by at least a week," Roxie pointed out. "After the police would have talked to Jackson."

Skylar shrugged. "Maybe Jackson started to get antsy. Wanted to talk. So Tristan gave him a taste of what would happen if he ratted—"

"*Stop.* Just stop it. You know Tristan. Quit talking about him like he's a criminal."

"If Jackson's parents had gone through with pressing charges, he could be in jail on assault and battery alone. *You* need to stop letting how you feel about him cloud your judgment."

That left Roxie speechless for a moment, her cheeks flaring red. "You're the one grasping at straws because you want someone to blame for what happened. Everything you've told me is speculation. Even if it could have happened that way doesn't mean it did."

"You're right," Skylar said, packing her notes and maps and articles into her backpack and pushing to her feet. "Which is why we need to prove it. And I think talking to Jackson is the perfect place to start."

She headed for the door, and Roxie scrambled to follow. "Wait. *We?* Shouldn't we just take this information to the police and let them deal with it?"

"Do you want me to give the cops incriminating evidence against Tristan before I've confirmed it?" Skylar asked with a raised brow.

"Well . . . no," Roxie conceded.

"That's what I thought. And besides—the police have had a year to figure this out. They've wasted enough time. It's my turn to take a crack at it." She paused, looking down at the floor before she added, "I never understood why you were so obsessed with ghost stories. Those people are gone, so I didn't see why it made sense to dwell on the way they died. But I think I sort of get it now. I *need* to know what happened to Colin. I won't be able to move forward until I do. I at least have to try."

Roxie nodded. "I can understand that. But why are you asking for *my* help?"

"You're good at research. Thorough. And you know how to piece together a story without much to go on. You deviate from the facts more than I would like. But the reality is, we don't have all the facts."

"I try my best to stick to the truth on my tours. I add my own flair for the sake of a good story. I'm not going to do that just to give you closure about Colin."

"I'm not asking you to," Skylar said. "I'm just saying that it's useful to have someone around who's good at imagining the possibilities. And besides—you're my sister. Which means you can't say no."

Roxie opened her mouth to argue but closed it again. Skylar had her there.

Her sister gave a triumphant smile and headed out the door.

Before Roxie could follow, she felt her phone vibrate in her pocket, and she pulled it out to glance at the screen.

Tristan was calling. She swore under her breath—she'd forgotten about his promise to her grandmother to walk her home from her ghost tours. He must have gone to meet her at the creek and gotten worried when she never showed up.

Guilt gripped her chest. He was trying to get her home safe, and she was going to repay him by investigating him?

She told herself he would understand. He knew how worried Roxie had been about Skylar for the past year. The way she seemed to have completely lost interest in living her life. This was the first time since Colin's death that she'd looked like her old self again. Driven. Determined. *Alive.*

She typed out a quick text message. Ended tour early. Wasn't feeling well. Sorry, forgot to tell you.

Biting her lip, she hit send. Then she followed her sister into the dark.

14

"So the investigation starts . . . like right now?"

Roxie wasn't a stranger to hard work—she wouldn't have been able to get her ghost tour off the ground without it. But she did prefer procrastinating whenever possible. Besides—she still had her skull makeup on from the tour, and it was starting to itch.

"I don't exactly have anything else going on," Skylar said, gripping the edges of her seat as Roxie took the bus around a sharp turn. "You can go home, if you're not up to it. I can take my own car," she added hopefully. She was looking a little green in the rearview mirror.

Roxie sighed and shook her head. She wasn't about to let her sister dive into the seedy underbelly of Whistler, Indiana—whatever the hell that consisted of—by herself.

"How are we supposed to find Jackson, anyway?" she asked. "Just head to his house and hope he's home? I don't have his number."

"I do," Skylar said.

Roxie gave a mock-scandalized gasp at that.

"Don't you dare read into it," Skylar snapped, leaning her head against the window and closing her eyes against what looked like a bout of nausea. "I only have it because we were both in the Quiz Bowl group chat."

"Oooo, the sexiest of all the chats. Did you all seduce each other with dirty Shakespeare quotes?"

"Honestly, it was mostly just Jackson trying to schedule extra practices and everyone else telling him to give it a rest. But I don't need to call him to know where he is. It's Sunday night. He's always working on the paper on Sunday nights."

The *Whistler Network* was Whistler High School's online newspaper that got updated every Monday. Skylar had been its editor in chief for her last two years of high school, despite Jackson running against her both times. He'd done everything in his power to prove he was completely dedicated to the job, which included coming in every Sunday to tweak each issue until it met his stringent standards.

Which had never won him the position for two reasons—one, because Skylar had usually already edited each piece herself, and there was almost never anything for him to fix. And two, because it was an elected position, and no one liked Jackson.

After Skylar graduated, he'd finally nabbed the title for himself. Mostly because he'd been the only one who wanted it. Now that Skylar wasn't there, he was the last line of defense between the student body and the unthinkable—grammatical errors.

He took the job very, very seriously. Which was why, Skylar informed Roxie, anyone who drove past the school on a Sunday could see his car parked all by itself out front and the light switched on in the journalism room. He'd bullied Mr. Hawthorne into giving him a key card.

It was approaching 10 p.m. Jackson had to have gone home by now. There was no way even he could be that pathetic.

But sure enough, when she pulled her bus into the parking lot, Jackson's BMW (a gift from his equally insufferable parents) was sitting by the west entrance, and the first-floor window of the journalism room glowed. Roxie could just make out a figure moving behind the glass.

Before Roxie had even cut the engine, Skylar had hopped out of the bus, taking a moment to steady her stomach as she leaned against the hood. Then she straightened and walked to the window before rapping her knuckles impatiently against the glass.

Roxie suppressed a laugh when she saw Jackson jump, spilling his coffee down the front of his pristine white shirt.

He shot a glare at the window. But then he met Skylar's matter-of-fact gaze, and he spilled even more of his coffee. They watched him hurry out of the room.

A few seconds later, the girls heard the west entrance swing open.

Jackson poked his head out, eyes bright. "Skylar, I—"

But then he saw Roxie standing behind her, and he gave a surprised yelp at the sight of her face paint. If he'd still been holding his coffee, Roxie was pretty sure he would have dropped it altogether.

"You look horrifying," he said.

Roxie curtsied in her black-and-red plaid skirt. "Thank you," she said.

Even after he got over the initial shock, his face still made it clear he'd been hoping Skylar was alone. He hadn't seen her since Colin's death, so maybe he was just too embarrassed to extend his condolences in front of Roxie. But she suspected it was because he was more interested in taking advantage of her sister's grief. Maybe he'd hoped she'd finally come to cry on his shoulder. Or just skip straight to making him her rebound.

Jackson had a reputation for shamelessly capitalizing on any opportunity that presented itself. Roxie had learned that the hard way when they were interviewing for the same part-time job at the local bookshop. She'd been about five minutes late to the interview because she got stuck behind a fender bender, and when she came in, breathless and ready to dazzle the owner, he'd promptly told her not to bother and sent her home.

She'd found out later that Jackson's interview had been right before hers. Someone had overheard him telling the owner, *You know, I hate to say this, but unreliability isn't exactly out of character for her. I'm not one to make accusations without proof, of course, but*—he'd lowered his voice to a very loud whisper—*I heard she's mostly interested in the job because she was told you don't drug test.*

Jackson was as slippery as they came, and if he wanted time alone with Skylar, Roxie would be damned if she let him have any.

The Clarks both brushed past Jackson, into the school, and he followed sullenly behind them.

The journalism room had a row of ancient computers against the back wall, and three of them were on, humming softly, each displaying a different variation of tomorrow's issue of the *Whistler Network*. If he'd moved on to fiddling obsessively with the layout, that had to mean he'd finished tearing apart and rewriting every article his staff turned in to him. Roxie could see a stack of papers on one of the desks, covered in red pen marks that seemed to scream, *Why the hell is everyone an idiot but me?*

If Jackson thought Skylar had come to finally declare her love for him, he must have been sorely disappointed when instead, she took a seat at Mr. Hawthorne's desk, pulled out her black notebook, uncapped a pen, and said, "Tell me why you and Tristan lied to the police about Colin being at your house the night of the murder."

Roxie cringed at her bluntness. Skylar had barely been out of the house in a year—she supposed her grasp of subtlety and social graces might have gotten rusty. Or maybe she just didn't give a damn anymore.

It was clearly the last thing he'd expected to come out of her mouth. He stared at her for a beat too long before answering, "I—we didn't. He was at my house. From 8 p.m. to 10:10 p.m. we were working on—"

"Your summer volunteer report?" Skylar cut him off. "Colin told me you wrote it yourself."

Roxie could see sweat forming at his hairline, reflecting in the harsh fluorescents. "I changed my mind," he said. "I decided—well, I decided I was being unfair to him. He let me do most of the hard work, but he still showed up most days.

Which was more than I expected from him. So I let him come over so we could redo the paper together."

Skylar searched his face for a moment. And Roxie thought maybe her sister knew as well as she did how unsettling silence could be. She let it stretch out uncomfortably while Jackson's hands fidgeted at his sides.

"I'm sorry, Jackson," she said finally, "but that just doesn't sound like you."

Jackson's eyes darted to Roxie for a moment, a plea in them— like he wanted her to save him from her sister's ruthless gaze. But Roxie took more than a little delight in plopping down on top of one of the desks and propping her feet on the chair with all the bad-cop insolence she could muster.

"You've never exactly been forgiving," Skylar pressed on. "And I've never known you to suffer a slacker. Which is exactly what you thought Colin was, isn't it? I've heard you say it myself. When we started dating, I think you told me something along the lines of, *He'll never amount to anything. He's just going to mooch off you for the rest of your life.*"

Roxie saw Jackson's throat bob with a swallow.

"What made you change your mind about him?" Skylar asked.

Jackson noticed Roxie staring at his twitching fingers and shoved them in his pockets before he shrugged. "It was more out of respect for you than anything else," Jackson said. "I knew he couldn't graduate without the volunteer credit. I knew you'd be angry with him. I didn't want to cause tension in your relationship."

"Well, tension is exactly what it caused," Skylar said. "We had a huge fight about it."

Roxie glanced at her sister, surprised. As far as she'd known, Colin and Skylar *never* fought.

Skylar sighed. "You're right—I knew Colin couldn't graduate without that volunteer credit. And if you convinced Mrs. Bell that he didn't do enough work to deserve it, he was going to have to repeat the entire project the next summer. I told him he needed to go and beg you to let him put his name on the report. He refused—he said he wasn't going to grovel. I told him he was being ridiculous and that graduating on time should mean more than his bullshit pride. He said you'd never agree to it anyway, so there was no point in trying."

She'd been staring down at her notebook while she spoke. She sounded far away somehow, like she was talking to herself. But now she looked up at Jackson and said, "I'm not naïve. I know you would have done just about anything to break me and Colin up. This wasn't going to end our relationship, for the record," she added, making brief eye contact with Roxie. "But it still seems like it was your way of driving a wedge between us."

Jackson sat heavily behind one of the desks, rubbing at his temples. "Glad to know you think so highly of me."

Skylar stood, leaned her palms on his desk, and looked down on him as she said again, "Tell me why you lied to the police."

"I didn't," Jackson insisted. "Colin was at my house on the night of August 23. He was there from 8 to 10:10 p.m. That's what I told the police, and that's what I'm going to keep telling you. So there's no point in asking me again."

"Fine," Skylar said. "Then I've got a different question for you—why did Tristan Riley beat the shit out of you a week after the murder?"

Jackson visibly blanched at that, his gaze dropping to Skylar's hands on the desk. After a long pause, he said. "You know I was always a dick to Colin. I've been a dick to a lot of people. I took it too far, and Tristan made me answer for it."

"What do you mean you *took it too far*?" Skylar pressed.

Jackson shrugged. "I must have said something to him. I don't even remember now, it was so long ago. The point is, I'm sure I deserved it."

There was a tremor in his voice when he talked about it.

"But what could you have possibly said to Tristan that was so bad, he almost killed you?" Skylar said, her own voice going suddenly soft. Like she felt bad for him.

Jackson looked up at her. "I don't understand why you're interrogating me now. It happened a long time ago. It's over now. But you've got so much life ahead of you. All you need to do is move on." He reached out then and covered one of Skylar's hands with his own. "I heard you're not planning on going to Yale anymore."

"How did you—"

Skylar bit off the rest of her question. Whistler was prone to the same wildfire gossip as any other small town. Nobody could keep a secret for long.

Unless you were as tight-lipped as Jackson had suddenly become.

After a moment, Skylar said, "I want to move on. I do. But I can't until I find out what happened to Colin. Then I'll be able to get past this and get my life back on track. Which would mean attending Yale."

Bullshit.

Roxie knew Skylar hadn't changed her mind about Yale. No way in hell. She'd seen the cold resolve in her eyes just a few days ago, and even if the investigation had spurred her into action, she'd been so consumed by it that she probably hadn't even thought about college.

But she knew Jackson was on his own Ivy League track. And how could the girl he hoped to marry one day be worthy of him without the same distinction?

She gave Jackson a long, meaningful look. One that Roxie read as, *Help me solve this case, and I can be everything you want me to be.*

A bold-faced lie. But a convincing one. She was certain that Jackson would jump on the opportunity.

But instead, he dropped his gaze to his desk again and said nothing.

"Are you afraid Tristan is going to hurt you if you talk to anyone about it?"

No answer.

"Jackson, nothing bad will happen if you tell me the truth. I won't let it. I promise."

"And *I* promise," he said, "that it will."

Skylar raised her eyebrows. "What does that mean?"

He shook his head. And then he stood and said abruptly, "I don't have permission to let anyone else into the building outside school hours. I need you both to leave. Now."

"But—" Skylar said.

"*Now*," Jackson snapped, so loud that it made both girls jump.

Roxie watched him run unsteady hands through his hair, which, usually immaculately arranged, stood on end. Upon closer examination, she could just see his socks, peeking out from the tops of his shoes. One green, one white. Mismatched. Which would be normal for any other teenager. But Jackson had never been a normal teenager.

And Roxie had never seen him look so afraid.

What was he scared of? Tristan? Something else? Roxie wanted to shake the answers out of him. There was something he wasn't saying.

But whatever it was, it was clear they weren't getting any more out of him tonight. Both girls headed toward the door.

"Wait," he said, grabbing Skylar's arm just before she stepped out of the classroom.

"I wish I could help you," he said. "I really do. But I think the best thing for all of us would be to move on. Okay? I just—I just don't want anyone else getting hurt."

Skylar opened her mouth to speak, but Jackson cut her off with a shake of his head. "Just—be careful."

He held her gaze for a few moments, until Skylar nodded. Then he let her go and shut the door in their faces.

☽

When the girls made it back to the bus, Skylar whirled on Roxie. "See?"

Roxie braced her hands on her hips. "See what?"

"He's too terrified of Tristan to even talk about him."

"He was acting weird," Roxie agreed. "But I don't think it's because of Tristan."

Skylar put her hands up in exasperation. "What else could it be?"

Roxie stepped closer to her sister, glancing at the light still glowing in the classroom window before she whispered, "You said it yourself. Jackson *hated* Colin. And he's in love with you. He would do just about anything to get rid of him so he could—"

Skylar rolled her eyes. "Jackson is not the murderer."

"Why the hell not?" Roxie said, indignant at her sister's dismissive tone. "He has a motive. And if he wasn't at his house with Colin the night of the murder, then where was he? Either he was the last person to see Colin alive, like he claims, or he has no alibi at all. It would explain why Tristan beat him up."

"No, it doesn't," Skylar said. "If Tristan had reason to believe Jackson killed his brother, he would have taken it to the police and made sure he spent the rest of his life in prison. Not just dole out his own punishment and keep the truth to himself."

Roxie crossed her arms over her chest with a sigh. "Okay. Good point. But that doesn't rule him out. I still think it makes more sense than your theory."

Skylar shook her head. "I know Jackson. He wouldn't—"

"I know *Tristan*. That's what I've been telling you this whole time. He's not a murderer. But if that isn't a good enough argument to make you believe he's innocent, then you can't use it to defend Jackson."

They bickered the entire drive back to the house, both of their phones buzzing the whole way with concerned texts from Grandma. Skylar had told her she'd wanted to get some air and was going to catch the end of Roxie's tour, and she'd been thrilled Skylar had wanted to leave the house at all. But it was getting late, and she was anxious. Understandable, Roxie thought, when Whistler may or may not still be harboring Colin's murderer.

When they made it home, Roxie glanced at the Rileys' house as she hurried up the steps. Every window was dark. When she got to her bedroom and tried to call Tristan, there was no answer.

Her certainty about Tristan's innocence hadn't wavered. Still, she needed to talk to him and see if he had any explanations of his own to offer. But it would have to wait until tomorrow.

15

Not long after Roxie got home from school the next afternoon, her phone vibrated with a text from her sister—Meet me at Smith & Laurel.

The command rankled Roxie. No *if you're not busy*. Not even a *please*. But she put her jacket back on, laced up her boots, and headed out the door anyway.

Her sister's bossiness had been a constant for as long as Roxie could remember. One that had always annoyed her. But it had come in handy on more than one occasion. Whenever something went wrong—like a tornado warning when Grandma wasn't home, or the time Roxie lost the dog she'd been pet sitting and had no idea how to even begin finding it—she knew that Skylar would know exactly what they needed to do next. She'd always found safety in her sister's certainty.

Skylar's belief in herself and her capabilities had gone away after Colin died. Roxie had felt its absence, and she'd never admit it out loud, but she was pleased to see signs of it coming back.

The coffee shop was busy when she arrived. It was one of her favorite places in town, with its soft lighting and cozy booths and large ceramic mugs that fit just right in her hands.

Though she'd thought the owners had missed a golden opportunity with the name. She'd come to them right away, after she heard they'd bought the building and before they'd even started the renovation, to tell them the story of the little gray cat that used to live on this street. He had been hit by cars on three separate occasions and still came back every night to beg passersby for treats. As far as Roxie could tell from her research, the story dated back at least fifty years. But according to multiple eyewitness accounts, to this day, a little gray cat was still known to appear from time to time—a cat with a missing ear and a mangled back paw.

And she'd been absolutely unsurprised when she'd learned the cat had originally belonged to a Clark—a great-aunt named Beatrice who called him Smokey.

But apparently, the owners hadn't been as enamored with the story as Roxie had, because her name suggestion, *Zombie Cat Café*, had gone unheeded. Some people simply had no respect for their town's history.

Still, Roxie could be found most afternoons taking up residence in the back corner booth with her earbuds in and her laptop out, making updates to her website or ghost-tour social media accounts, checking reviews, ordering new T-shirts, or handling other administrative tasks.

Today, she found Skylar already occupying that same booth. And she was sitting across from a woman Roxie guessed was in her early thirties, with bright-red hair cut in a sharp bob, a pair of cat-eye glasses perched on the end of her nose, and a tattoo of a crow on her neck.

Roxie slid into the booth next to Skylar as she was saying, "I really appreciate you taking the time to meet with us, Jessica."

Jessica replied enthusiastically, "I'm always happy to talk to any young people interested in entering the death industry! Especially enterprising young women."

Roxie raised an eyebrow at Skylar, who ignored the skeptical look and introduced Jessica. "This is the director of the Strauss Funeral Home and Crematorium."

Jessica nodded as she took a sip of her chai latte.

Roxie had thought she looked familiar, and the memory came back to her now. She'd been there the day of Colin's funeral, wearing the same glasses with a black pantsuit and a pair of kitten heels the same shade of red as her hair. Roxie hadn't known who she was at the time, though she had appreciated her style. She must have been responsible for organizing the funeral.

Which had to be the real reason Skylar invited her here— she doubted her sister had taken a sudden interest in becoming a mortician overnight.

But Skylar put on a show of being intent on just that, pushing her black coffee aside to lean her elbows on the table. "Tell me what exactly a funeral director does. What are your day-to-day duties?"

"Excellent question," Jessica said, tapping the tips of her long, black nails against the wooden tabletop. "You know, there are a lot of misconceptions about what I do. Most people assume

I'm just filling out paperwork and selling people overpriced caskets all day. Which *is* part of the job—don't even get me started on the ridiculous money people spend on caskets."

Though she proceeded to get *herself* started, talking at length about the various materials one could choose, from wood to copper to bronze to stainless steel and even biodegradable options like wicker. Some people opted for a more personalized experience, like team logos or religious imagery on the lid, or themes that paid homage to Disney, hunting, John Deere, or classic cars. Then there was the even deeper rabbit hole of urn options for her customers who went with cremation.

Skylar listened on the edge of her seat, her eyes never leaving Jessica's. Roxie truly found it all fascinating and normally would have hung on every word. But now she was more interested in what angle her sister was trying to work.

It became clearer when Skylar interrupted Jessica's lecture to say, "I found in my research that most funeral directors are also licensed embalmers."

Jessica nodded, impressed. "You're absolutely right. Most people don't know that body preparation is often handled in-house, especially when it comes to small-town funeral homes like ours. I perform all embalming services myself. The process starts with cleaning the body then replacing the blood with embalming fluid. Some of the corpses I work with have been maimed or mutilated in some way, depending on how they died, so I work my magic with clay and plaster of Paris to reconstruct as necessary. Then I need to set the features, which mostly consists of suturing the mouth to keep it closed and using eye caps for the same purpose—might give mourners quite a shock if they popped open during the funeral! Then I use makeup to provide a more . . . natural appearance. As close as I can get, anyhow."

She had detailed this whole process casually, between bites of strawberry tart. "That's the quick rundown," she said. "I'd be happy to go into more detail—"

"I appreciate the overview," Skylar said. She looked mostly unfazed, but it had to be an act—Roxie herself was feeling a little green around the gills, thinking about Colin's body being subject to what they'd just heard. "I have to be honest," she said, looking down at the table. "I became interested in this line of work after attending a friend's funeral that you handled. Colin Riley's."

Jessica's expression changed at the mention of his name. She pressed her lips closed, eyebrows drawing together in sympathy. "Yes, I remember that one well. Not every day you see something so . . . cruel."

Skylar nodded. She let some of what she must have really been feeling show on her face—the grief and exhaustion.

"It was so hard on everyone," she said. "But you did such a good job of making the whole thing more bearable. I saw how you stuck by his mother the whole time. And the way you prepared the body—it was truly great work. Getting to see him whole again after what happened meant a lot to me. To all of us."

Jessica reached across the table and covered Skylar's hand with her own, clearly unafraid of grief after dealing with it in so many clients but not numb to it either. "That is the highest compliment someone in my line of work can hear," she said.

"It's important to me to give people that same peace," Skylar went on. "But . . . well, I'd heard his body was severely mutilated by the knife wounds and the fire."

More than heard—they'd seen it with their own eyes. Though examining the extent of the damage hadn't exactly been a priority at the time.

"The reconstruction process must have been difficult. I was wondering if you could tell me more about that. You said you'd never seen anything so cruel. Could you elaborate on that and the specific challenges it presented?"

And then it all made sense to Roxie. Because while the basic information about how Colin had died had been public, the full autopsy report wouldn't be released to just anyone. Talking to Colin's embalmer was the only way she'd be able to learn more, if there was anything else to know.

But then Jessica gave Skylar a sympathetic smile and said, "I can't discuss specifics about my clients. I'm sorry. I could lose my license."

Skylar had done a decent job of playing the part up until then, but she was less successful at hiding her disappointment at that answer. She tried to salvage the attempt, unwilling to accept that the meeting had been a complete waste of time. "You can't talk about specifics. I understand that. But in a general sense, I'm sure cases of this kind are —"

Jessica leaned closer to look at Skylar's face. "Wait. I remember you. You weren't just a friend. You were his girlfriend, weren't you?"

Skylar's face froze, caught in the headlights. Jessica nodded in understanding. Then she grabbed her purse. "I see what this is now. You're playing detective, aren't you?"

She stood to go, and Skylar bolted to her feet. "That's not what this is," she lied. "I'm sorry, I didn't mean to—"

"Look, I know you're heartbroken," Jessica said, squeezing her arm. "Death always comes too early—this one especially. And I'm not saying you should give up on getting answers for him. But I can't help you. I'm sorry."

Skylar watched her go then fell heavily back into the booth, cursing under her breath. After a moment, she flipped to a new page in her notebook and started outlining the encounter for her records.

Roxie sighed, knowing from experience that there was no point in interrupting her with questions while she was in angry-note-taking mode. So she went to the counter and ordered some refreshments while she waited.

Skylar was finished writing by the time she got back and watched Roxie as she sat down with her latte and pumpkin-flavored cookie with cream cheese frosting—one of the café's fall specials. "Where'd you get the money for that? Grandma?" Skylar asked.

"No. I bought it myself."

Skylar raised an eyebrow. "How?"

Roxie raised one right back. "I don't know if you've heard, but I run a pretty popular ghost tour around here."

"It's actually profitable?"

"Has been for a while now." She wanted to add, *You would have known that, if you'd ever cared enough to ask*, but she bit her tongue.

Though, truthfully, *profitable* was a generous word for it. Most of the money she made on tours went right back into the tour. But she always set aside enough for a steady stream of coffee and desserts.

She saw Skylar's eyes lingering on the cookie. She hadn't worked since last summer, so she was probably tight on cash.

Roxie slid the plate to the middle of the table.

Skylar held Roxie's gaze for a few moments, as though looking for a catch. Until, finally, she took a bite.

"So that was a dead end," she admitted.

"You wanted to know more about the body?"

"Right."

"He got stabbed to death and lit on fire. What else *is* there to know?"

Skylar shrugged. "I'm not sure. I only got a brief glimpse of it the night of the murder. But even in the dark and with the damage from the fire, I could tell the wound was pretty severe. Not just one stab wound but many. Like someone was trying to cut him in half or something. Jesus."

She closed her eyes from a moment, taking a deep breath.

When she came back to herself, she added, "*Cruel* is the word Jessica used. Definitely not an attack from a stranger just trying to flee a crime scene. But personal. Angry. I wondered if maybe my imagination had exaggerated it. I wanted to know if there were any other clues about the body that might point us in the right direction. But also, I knew Jessica had to deal with Tristan and his mother personally. Suzanna was so upset after what happened, I'm sure Tristan did most of the talking when it came to making funeral arrangements. I wanted to know how he behaved, right after his brother's death."

"I can tell you," Roxie said. "He was a mess."

"I want to know from someone *unbiased*. Someone he wouldn't necessarily feel the need to act in front of."

Roxie scowled. "I think I would know if my own best friend—"

But Skylar cut her off with a raised finger before she could finish—her phone had lit up on the table with a text message, Jessica Strauss's name flashing across the screen. Both girls leaned in to read.

Hey, I just wanted to let you know—no hard feelings. If you ever take any real interest in the mortuary business, feel free to give me a call. Also, I have a friend, Georgia, who does some work for the Keller Funeral Home from time to time. She might be able to provide some interesting insight for you. At the end of the message, she'd typed out Georgia's number.

Skylar immediately pulled out her laptop and started googling *Keller Funeral Home*.

It wasn't far, though it was out of the way and on a street they didn't usually take, so Roxie had completely forgotten about it. She hadn't been there in a few years—not since their mother's funeral, and their aunt Violet's before that.

"This funeral home is closer to the Riley's house," Skylar said. "I wonder why they went to Strauss instead?"

Roxie didn't have an answer for that, and even if she had, Skylar wasn't listening. She was clicking through the website, scrolling down the faculty page. She murmured, "It doesn't look like anyone named Georgia works there. Maybe she does some type of contract work for them."

She dialed her phone and put on her jacket at the same time. When Roxie didn't move, Skylar made an impatient gesture until she followed suit.

Skylar cut through the coffee shop and out the door, her focus on the next task too intent to take notice of anything around her. But as Roxie walked behind her, she felt a prickle on the back of her neck—the sensation she was being watched.

She paused and took a look around the coffee shop, until she met a pair of dark eyes staring right at her.

Luke Riley was sitting by himself next to the window, hunched over in his leather jacket, a cup of coffee steaming in front of him. And he made no secret of watching Roxie.

She almost walked over to him. Almost asked him, point-blank, *What did Tristan mean when he said it was your fault the family is just the two of you now? And what are you so desperate for him to find for you?*

He smirked, like that was exactly what he wanted her to do.

But, before she could, Skylar stuck her head back in the door. "You coming? I told Georgia we're headed there now."

Roxie turned back to give Luke one more glance. He raised his coffee to her in a salute before she hurried out the door after her sister.

And, as she did, she added one more suspect to her list.

16

The Merriest Maids was in the middle of a nondescript strip mall on the other side of town, the sign glowing bright red in a wash of gray stone and boarded windows.

Skylar told Roxie on the way over, "The Keller Funeral Home has a contract with the Merriest Maids for cleaning services. Georgia is usually the one they send."

The bell jangled when the girls entered, but the woman sitting behind a large, cluttered desk didn't look up from what she was typing.

The place seemed to function more as an office and supply closet than a store clients were meant to visit. Which Roxie supposed made sense—the maids would be the ones doing the traveling. Against one wall, there was an army of vacuum cleaners in various colors and sizes, all standing at attention until they would be needed again. The other wall was a row of cabinets, some of which had been left open to reveal paper towels, boxes of gloves, and bottles of chemicals. In the back, a row of smocks hung from wooden pegs.

There were no chairs aside from the one the woman was sitting in, so Roxie and Skylar stood around awkwardly, waiting for her to stop typing and acknowledge their presence. The purposeful tapping seemed to echo against the tile, making the space feel cold and claustrophobic at the same time. It went on for so long that Roxie cleared her throat, thinking maybe the woman just hadn't noticed them come in.

Her fingers paused over the keyboard, and she shot the girls a look of irritation so vicious that they both flinched a step backward.

She returned to her typing with even more ferocity than before. And, when it was finally over, she pushed the keyboard aside, leaned her elbows on the desk, and asked, "Can I help you?" in a tone that made it clear she really didn't want to.

"We're looking for Georgia," Skylar said. "She told us we could meet her here."

The woman frowned. "What for?"

"None of your—" Roxie started to say, rankled by the woman's condescending tone, but Skylar cut her off, nodding at the Help Wanted sign in the window.

"She told us about the job, and we wanted to ask her some questions about what it's like to work for Merriest Maids. Would that be okay?"

Apparently, Skylar was willing to learn every trade in town if that's what it took to find answers.

The woman gave them an appraising look—specifically

Roxie, whom she scanned up and down. "You'd have to lose all that makeup to work here," she said. "And the platform boots. And the attitude."

Roxie gave an indignant gasp and started to say, "*My* attitu—" but Skylar cut her short.

"Thank you for the tips," she said. "Could we speak to Georgia now?"

"She's out back taking her lunch break. She's *supposed* to finish up in eight minutes and head out to her next job." The woman started typing again before she finished, "Don't make her late."

The girls hurried out the door and around the building, where they found a young blond woman, her hair tied up in a knot, sitting on top of a warped picnic table and smoking a cigarette while she scrolled through her phone.

"Georgia?" Skylar said, extending her hand.

Georgia stared at it for a moment before she took it and giggled. "Didn't know this meeting would be so formal. Sorry I'm not dressed for the occasion," she said, gesturing to her sneakers, jeans, and hoodie.

Skylar gave a tense, embarrassed smile back. She was used to college admission interviews and model UN conferences, not clandestine meetings behind strip malls dodging used condoms melted to the asphalt.

"We spoke on the phone," Skylar said. "Jessica gave me your number. She said you might be able to offer us some insight about the Keller Funeral Home."

Georgia nodded, the tip of her cigarette glowing hotter as she dragged in smoke and let it out with the breeze.

"They always send me because I'm the only one who doesn't get creeped out by the place. The other girls think I spend my time cleaning blood and guts off the floor, but mostly they just want me to scrub the bathrooms and keep dust out of the viewing area. The owners tip well, so I don't correct the girls when they think I'm, like, vacuuming up smashed brains all day. Some of them are superstitious as hell. Think the place has to be haunted."

At the word *haunted*, Roxie had a few questions of her own come to mind, but Skylar barreled right past the opportunity.

"Would you happen to know if the Keller Funeral Home considered hosting Colin Riley's funeral?"

Much more direct than she'd been with Jessica—Roxie supposed that because Georgia was providing a service to Keller's from a third-party company, she wasn't held to the same standards of confidentiality.

But instead of jumping on the opportunity to provide Skylar with all the answers she needed, Georgia gave a thoughtful nod and said, "I might know something about that."

The Clarks waited for her to go on. After a moment, Georgia sighed and held out her hand expectantly. They both stared at it.

"What?" Roxie said. "You want, like, a bribe?"

"I'm not pissing away the last six minutes of my lunch break for nothing."

The sisters glanced at each other. Skylar turned out her pockets with a shrug and muttered, "You're the one with a *profitable* business."

With a growl, Roxie dug around in her bag until she found

a crumpled five-dollar bill and a gift certificate to the Emerald Theater. "This is all I've got on me," she said.

Georgia bit her lip, assessing for a moment before she took the offering and shoved it into her pocket.

"Yes," she said. "The Rileys did come to Keller's on a day I was cleaning. The mom and the dead kid's brother. I read about the murder in the paper, and I was intrigued." She shrugged. "Call me morbid. Murder cases have always fascinated me. I watch a lot of serial-killer documentaries in my downtime. So, when I got the chance to get a glimpse at people connected to a real, live case, I couldn't help myself. I dusted the same vase right outside the director's office for maybe twenty minutes. The doors were closed, so I couldn't make out much of what they were saying, but I could see through the little glass pane."

"What do you remember?" Skylar pushed. "Did either of them take the lead on the conversation?"

"She never said a word, as far as I could tell," Georgia said. "He kept his answers short and to the point."

"How did he seem to you? Upset?"

She shrugged. "Kind of numb, I guess? Like he just wanted it all over with. And I noticed—well, this wasn't exactly the first time I've eavesdropped on one of these meetings," Georgia admitted, looking a little shamefaced as she rubbed the back of her neck. "Usually, when family members come in together, they're always touching each other. Like holding hands or putting their arms around one another. Almost like they're trying to convince themselves that the people they've got left are still there. But these two didn't touch at all. Not once during the whole meeting. She just stared out the window the whole time while he answered all the director's questions and made the decisions."

Skylar nodded thoughtfully. "Do you know why the Rileys ultimately decided to have the funeral at Strauss's instead? It would make more sense for them to host it at Keller's. It's closer to their house and to the cemetery where Colin was buried."

Georgia stubbed out her cigarette on the bottom of her shoe and shook her head. "That's where it got weird. So it seems like the meeting went okay. The mom and her son shake the director's hand and start walking out. I pretend to be busy on the other side of the room wiping down doorknobs, like I haven't been snooping this whole time.

"The guy grabs his mother's coat from the hook and tries to help her put it on. But she pushes him away. Like, hard. He wasn't expecting it, and he falls back against the wall. I forget to pretend I'm not paying attention, and I walk right up to her and tell her that behavior is uncalled for. She starts screaming in my face and grabbing my clothes, going on about how I don't know what the hell I'm talking about. *This is all his fault*, she kept yelling. *This is all his fucking fault.* Total meltdown, completely out of nowhere. And then she turns on the guy again and spits right in his face, *It should have been you.*"

The Clarks exchanged a look.

"That's when the director and a security guard got to her. They were a lot nicer to her than I would have been, and once they got her calmed down, they escorted her out. But they still told her and her son not to come back. So the Rileys didn't *decide* not to have the funeral at Keller's. They were banned."

"Have you told the police any of this?" Skylar asked.

"No. Just a couple of friends, like Jessica. I thought the whole thing was really weird, and it's been kind of nagging at me. But I don't talk to cops unless I have to, and they never asked me about it." She leaned her elbows on her knees. "You guys don't look like cops. What are you asking all these questions for? You got a true-crime podcast or something?"

Skylar shook her head. "Just trying to get some closure. Colin was . . . a close friend of ours."

"Well, good luck. I hope you find the answers you're looking for. That's all I know."

"Thank you. And we'd appreciate your discretion. We don't want it getting around that we've been asking questions about the Rileys."

Roxie agreed—she absolutely did not want Tristan catching wind of this. He'd been through enough interrogations.

Georgia smirked. "And how exactly are you going to pay me off for my silence?"

"We don't have anything else," Roxie said.

Georgia chewed on her lip for a moment, considering. "Just leave a nasty review for Merriest Maids on Yelp, and we'll call it even. Say Christina from the office was bitchy to you and you took your business elsewhere."

"You got it," Roxie said, already pulling out her phone.

☾

Roxie had hardly settled into the passenger seat of her sister's car and shut the door behind her when Skylar said, "Try and tell me what could possibly make a mother hate her own son so much that she'd say she wishes he were dead. Just try."

"Tristan isn't her biological son," Roxie reminded her. "And she's never treated him like one. He's just a reminder of his father's infidelity. She's always hated him."

"Not liking him and wanting him dead are not the same thing and you know it," Skylar said as she pulled out of the parking lot and turned toward home. "And speaking of Luke Riley—you conveniently forgot to tell me he'd been released from prison."

Roxie glanced at her sister, startled. "I just found out."

"Interesting, considering he was released last summer—over a year ago."

That took Roxie by surprise. According to Tristan, he'd only gotten out recently. Why wouldn't he have told her?

"Are you sure? How did you find that out?"

"I was doing some research on him last night. Colin had mentioned to me once Luke had gone to prison before for burglary—"

"*What?*" Roxie said. Another detail Tristan had neglected to share with her.

"Among many other things," Skylar said. "The way Colin always talked about it, I assumed Luke was serving one long sentence. But it seems that he was in and out of prison many times for different reasons. Right before Colin and Tristan moved to Whistler with Suzanna, he got five years for robbing a home with a knife. But since, he's been picked up for possession of illegal drugs, shoplifting, aggravated assault, and vehicle theft."

"Jesus. He's been . . . busy."

Skylar nodded. "I wanted to make sure he had nothing to

do with the robberies that happened leading up to the murder. And he *was* released in time to commit the bank robbery. His release date was after the ones at the gas station and coffee shop, though, and he has a witness-verified alibi the night of the murder—he was hanging out at a bar in Indianapolis from 6 p.m. until almost midnight."

"He was at a bar for six hours?"

"Hitting on the bartender the entire night, apparently," Skylar said, rolling her eyes. "They kicked him out when he started to get aggressive." She added as she pulled up to a stoplight, "It sounds like Tristan had a shining example growing up."

"What the hell does that mean?" Roxie said.

Skylar sighed. "You know what it means."

"I know you aren't saying *the apple doesn't fall far from the tree* or some bullshit like that. You're a Clark—you know what it's like to have a complicated legacy. You always told me the curse meant nothing. That our lives are determined by our own choices, good or bad. Why should it be any different for Tristan? Having a dad with a criminal record doesn't mean anything."

Skylar had one hand on the wheel while the other toyed with the daisy pendant on her necklace—a new nervous habit. "Fine," she conceded. "You're right. I'm sorry I said it."

They drove the rest of the way home in silence. But the comment still made Roxie uneasy. It was something the old Skylar never would have said. She told Colin all the time that blood had nothing to do with his chances of success. That his own past didn't determine his future.

As much as Roxie wanted to believe Skylar was returning

to normal, she couldn't deny the changes that still clung to her sister like smoke. She'd always been driven by ambition and accolades. But also her desire to use her brain to make the world better.

She'd regained that old energy, but now, she seemed to be fueled by something different. Roxie watched the fidget of her hands on the wheel, the bitter twist of her chapped lips, and the half-moon shadows under her eyes. Her glance seemed to dart nervously as she drove, like every alley or dark corner they passed hid something malicious. Something she needed to root out and destroy.

17

The cafeteria had quickly become the worst part of school for Roxie.

Before Colin had died, she would sit in the back corner with him, Tristan, and Skylar. Her sister had largely ignored the rest of them. She'd considered half an hour to be far too much time to eat lunch and, unwilling to waste the extra twenty-five minutes on socializing, she always had a textbook open on the table and headphones in to tune out whatever the rest of them were doing. Which was usually talking about the movie they'd watched at the Emerald over the weekend, recounting the latest hallway fistfight, or just throwing bits of food at each other while Skylar shot them nasty looks.

Last year, she'd had Tristan. And while he'd always been her favorite person to hang out with, she'd felt the absence of the others like an ache.

And now, Roxie spent every single lunch period sitting by

herself. As confident as she was, even she hadn't figured out how to be alone in a high school cafeteria without feeling a little bit like a loser.

At least today she wouldn't have to face it—because today, she had an assignment.

Skylar had whispered it to her over breakfast that morning while Grandma did the dishes. *Assuming Tristan and Jackson were lying, and Colin wasn't at Jackson's house the night of the murder, then someone else was the last person to see him alive. As far as I can tell, it would have been at school. His last period was study hall.*

Skylar had said he had a friend in study hall named Eric Norton he always sat next to in the back of the room. It was Roxie's job to talk to him and see if he could give her any insight into what Colin planned on doing later that day.

She had managed to talk the librarian, Ms. Sawyer, into giving her a pass to the library during her lunch period to pick out a book for a research paper she hadn't actually been assigned. When the bell rang, she walked against the flow of students as they headed to the cafeteria.

In the midst of her clumsy progress upstream, she managed to run right into Jackson Mowery, making him drop his stack of books and notes, flash cards scattering over the speckled tile.

She saw his expression contort with annoyance as he prepared to lay into her. But then he looked up and saw who she was, and the color drained from his face.

Roxie helped him pick up the flash cards. "Sorry," she said.

"No—no worries," he mumbled back.

His stack reassembled, they both stood staring at each other for a while, ignoring the sea of students parting around them like they were boulders in a river.

"Tell me Skylar is going to drop all this stuff about Colin."

Roxie crossed her arms over her chest. "Tell me why she should."

"Can't you just trust me?"

Roxie couldn't stifle her laugh. "I wouldn't trust you not to slit my throat with one of your flash cards if you thought you'd get extra credit points out of it. Just tell me what the hell you're so worked up about."

He sighed deeply, like he was searching for the words. But he must not have been able to find them, because he scowled and stormed off instead.

Skylar didn't take him seriously as a suspect. Roxie wasn't ready to cross him off the list yet. But interrogating him further would have to wait. Hitching her bag back up on her shoulder, she hurried down the hallway.

When she walked into the library, she found Eric Norton scanning in returned books behind the desk.

You can't just walk up to him and start asking questions without making it obvious we're investigating. You have to start a conversation, Skylar had instructed her. *Make it feel organic.*

Improv. Roxie could handle that.

She made a show of walking around the room for a few minutes, weaving through the shelves and tracing book spines with the pointed tip of her fingernail. She stopped every few feet to pull one down, skim the description, and put it back.

Gradually, she inched closer and closer to the checkout desk.

She and Eric were the only two people in the library, but he seemed to have no idea she was there. She waited for him to take notice of her so she could start with casual questions. *How is your day going? Do you like working in the library?*

But he never glanced up from his work long enough to meet her gaze. So, finally, she had to grab a book at random off the shelf and bring it up to the counter for him to check out.

He looked up, startled, and she realized he'd had headphones in this whole time—he hadn't heard her come in. "Hey, Roxie."

She could see the dark-blue bands of his braces when he spoke. He had a fresh buzz cut, which he kept running his hand over.

They knew each other from classes they'd had together. Or more like knew *of* each other. When Roxie thought about it, she wasn't sure they'd ever had a direct conversation before.

Maybe that's why she panicked and went straight for, "You were friends with Colin Riley, weren't you?"

The question took him off guard. "Uh . . . yeah? Why?"

"I was just—well—" She scrambled for a connection. "I was thinking of him because I saw that book, and he told me once that it was his favorite."

Eric frowned, turning the book over to glimpse at the cover. "*The Life and Legacy of Amelia Earhart?*"

"Oh yeah," Roxie said immediately, going with it. "He thought she was fascinating. A feminist icon—though he probably just said that to impress Skylar. But I think he was really interested in all the theories about her disappearance. There's a lot in there about the history of airplanes, too, which I know he was really into."

She bit down on the urge to keep rambling. She considered herself a good actress, but with the weight of Skylar's expectations on her shoulders, it didn't come as naturally as usual.

"Hmm," he said. "I didn't know that. Didn't know he'd ever even *read* a whole book, to tell you the truth."

"He was full of surprises," Roxie said.

"I guess so."

He handed the book back. And then he started scanning in returns again.

Roxie stood there for a few moments, pretending to be interested in the row of books on display beside the counter. She struggled to think of a way to salvage the conversation. More seconds ticked by, and Eric peeked at her, wondering what she was still doing there.

Roxie turned her back to him.

And then she started to cry.

At least, she tried to. She was so desperate to summon at least a little moisture, she bit the inside of her cheek as hard as she could. When nothing happened, she buried her face in her hands, letting her shoulders shake with what she hoped were convincing sobs. She rubbed hard at her eyes, trying to make them look red. It helped that she was wearing thick, black eyeliner that day, which she smudged as much as she could.

For a few moments, there wasn't a sound from Eric. She assumed he was stunned into silence.

But finally, she heard his chair scrape back and his slow footsteps as he walked around the counter to look at her. "Hey," he said, his voice unsteady and awkward. "Hey, what's the matter? Are you okay?"

Just then, a group of girls walked into the library. Eric grabbed Roxie's elbow and said, "Come on. You can hide out in here a minute."

He took her to the librarian's office, which was currently empty. But Ms. Sawyer had left her purse on the desk chair, and Roxie didn't want to disturb it, so she took a seat on the floor instead, leaning her back against the wall.

Eric returned to the library for a few moments to help the girls find and check out the books they needed. While he was gone, Roxie stuck her finger into a vase on Ms. Sawyer's desk that held fresh-cut flowers, dabbing the water over her eyes and down her cheeks. She made it back to her spot on the floor just seconds before Eric came back in.

He shut the office door behind him, and after a little hesitation, he sat on the carpet next to her.

"I'm so sorry," Roxie said, wiping at her eyes, her makeup coming off in black smears on the backs of her hands. "I don't know what came over me. I just—he was a really good friend, you know? A great guy. I try not to think about him being gone too much, but then something will remind me of him, and I just . . ."

Eric gave her hand an awkward pat. "Hey, you don't need to explain it to me. I get it. Happens to me, too."

Roxie felt a squeeze of guilt in her chest at that. She really *did* miss Colin, she reminded herself. Even if the tears were a lie.

"I remember the last time I saw him," she said. "We had bio together that afternoon. He sat in front of me, and I know we talked about . . . something. It just seemed like any other day, so I didn't take notice of the details. Later, I wished that I had. If I had known—"

She shook her head, biting her lip. Then she looked hopefully at Eric, waiting for him to describe *his* last encounter with Colin.

When he didn't say anything, she prompted, "You had study hall with him, didn't you? Did you see him that day?"

"I did. I don't really remember what we talked about either. We probably just watched YouTube videos about cars or sports or dudes hurting themselves doing skateboard tricks. Normal, stupid shit."

She nodded. He didn't volunteer more.

"Nothing seemed . . . different to you that day?"

"What do you mean?"

Worried she'd pushed it too hard, been too obvious, she said, "You know, sometimes people will get this sense when something bad is about to happen. A premonition. I was just curious if you felt anything . . . off. Just any details that stuck out."

"A premonition," he repeated. "No, I don't think so."

Roxie tried to mask her disappointment at his answer. But then he continued, "He did seem kind of down, though. Stressed about something. He wouldn't tell me what it was, but I invited him to hang out that afternoon to cheer him up."

"Really?"

He nodded. "We were together for a few hours."

Roxie sat up at that, forgetting for a moment to look sad. "Like how long?"

He shrugged. "Maybe until eight? Could have been a little earlier. I hadn't really been paying attention to the clock, but I needed to be home before my dad got back from work."

"Did you tell the police about being with him the afternoon of the murder?"

"Well . . . no."

"Why not?"

He chewed on his lip for a moment before he answered, "Because I was afraid I'd be in deep shit if they found out what we were doing."

18

"Tristan couldn't have murdered Colin at 7 p.m. or earlier because Colin was playing video games at Eric's weed dealer's house until eight," Roxie said unceremoniously when her sister picked up the phone. She had her cell pressed to her ear and tried to keep her voice low as she navigated through the end-of-day chaos in the school hallways.

It had taken a while to get the story out of Eric. He hadn't gone to the police because his dad had been threatening to send him to military school if he got caught smoking weed again. But the guilt of withholding information that might have helped with the investigation had been eating at him, so once the floodgates opened, he'd given her everything he knew.

Skylar was quiet for a long moment before she said, "Does he have proof?"

Roxie had anticipated the question, which was why she had convinced Eric to show her the text messages between him and the dealer, time-stamped August 23 at 4:38 p.m. Coming over with Colin. That work? And the response—Sure I'm home.

She explained this to Skylar then added, "The dealer is some guy named—"

"Caleb," Skylar finished for her.

Roxie frowned. "How did you know?"

"Because Colin had the same weed dealer. But I didn't know that's what he *was* for a long time. Colin told me he went over to his house so frequently because he was his math tutor. I lost it when I found out. Mostly, I was upset that he lied to me. But also because he got fired from his summer job at Hermann Construction after he failed a drug test."

"Oh," Roxie said, suddenly uncomfortable.

There was a long silence before Skylar muttered, "God*damn* it, Colin."

Roxie bit her lip. "Sounds like you guys had been arguing more than usual."

Another pause. "Maybe we were. What's your point?"

"Listen. I know you're certain Colin wouldn't have written you that breakup note—"

"Not just he *wouldn't* have," Skylar interrupted her, a hard edge to her voice. "*Couldn't* have. Only Tristan had access to the stationery it was written on, remember? And he didn't even receive it until after Colin died. But even if that weren't the case—Colin and I talked about a lot of other things you didn't know about. Like getting married. He brought it up constantly. He told me he wanted us to have a big family. At least four kids. Two dogs. He wanted to spend the rest of his life with me. And he would have, if it hadn't been cut short."

She hung up the phone without another word.

Roxie sighed deeply, looking up at the ceiling. Then she shoved her phone in her backpack and stepped out into the parking lot. And that was when she spotted Tristan.

He was leaning over the open hood of her tour bus, the sleeves of his flannel pushed up over his elbows, dark curls hanging in his eyes. When he saw her walking over, he pushed the hood firmly closed and gave her a smile. "Hey, stranger," he said. "Where have you been?"

It had only been a couple of days since they'd last seen each other, but Tristan likely had gotten used to her knocking on his door every afternoon to drag him along on tour research or to a movie. At the very least, she usually texted him funny things she saw on the internet at least three times a day. It was unusual for them to go so long without any contact at all.

She shrugged. "Been busy with school. And what are you doing to my precious?"

He gave the hood of the bus a firm pat. "Just wanted to check on the alternator. How has it been running for you?"

"Like a dream. But once I get it decorated, it'll look more like a nightmare."

"Have you been able to use it on tour yet?"

"Not yet. Grandma wants me to get more practice driving it before I endanger the lives of strangers."

Tristan nodded. "Probably a good move."

An awkward silence ensued—another thing that was unusual for them.

Roxie knew Skylar wouldn't like her talking to Tristan, but that wasn't what made her hesitate—she wasn't even a little bit convinced he was dangerous. It was the guilt of everything she was keeping from him that ate away at her. It was hard to face him when they'd been looking into his brother's murder behind his back.

She debated telling him everything. But she didn't want to dredge up painful memories either. He'd explained and defended himself enough. Roxie would just have to do it for him to Skylar.

She hitched her backpack higher on her shoulder as she started to say she needed to get going, but Tristan said at the same time, "I saw you and your sister walking together in town the other day."

Roxie blinked, taken off guard. "Yeah, we, uh—went to get coffee."

Tristan nodded, a slight smile forming. "I didn't know she'd started leaving the house again. That's great news. I was worried the breakup note was going to set her back even more. How did you get through to her?"

Roxie swallowed. "You know. We're sisters. We just . . . had one of those heart-to-hearts Grandma kept telling me to try."

He raised an eyebrow, like maybe he didn't quite believe it. But then he said, "Smart woman."

He shoved his hands in his pockets, his boot scuffing the pavement.

Finally, he said, "Well, I've got to get back to the Emporium. I was in the area on another job, so I thought I'd check on the bus."

"Thank you," Roxie said.

This was where she normally would have hugged him good-bye. And she wanted him to think everything was normal, so she stepped in close, putting her arms around his neck. He hugged her back.

"Roxie?" She felt his breath hot in her ear.

"Yeah?"

His grip on her hadn't loosened. She couldn't help tucking her cheek against his chest, relishing the warmth there.

He didn't say anything for a long moment. His chest had gone completely still, like he was holding his breath. Until, finally, he eased it out and told her, "I miss you."

Roxie looked up at him. He'd rejected her last year, and she was going to respect his decision. But that didn't mean she could just turn off her feelings like a light switch. The way his fingers were pressing into her spine made her imagination run to dizzying heights, wondering how his hands might feel on other parts of her body.

"Tristan, I—"

But then his phone rang. And he let her go.

He pulled his cell from his pocket. Roxie saw Luke's name flash briefly across the screen, but he hid it quickly, cursing.

Did she imagine the way he seemed to scan the parking lot, like he was looking for someone?

"Don't want to be late," he said. "It was good seeing you, Rox."

And, without another word, he jogged back across the parking lot to his truck and drove off.

19

Roxie came home later that night to Skylar interrogating Grandma Gertie.

It was a more casual interrogation than the others, to be fair. This one involved cookie dough—Skylar was helping Grandma roll it out into little balls on cookie sheets. She was careful to keep the balls spread out in orderly rows and didn't constantly lick her fingers, the way Roxie always did when she was assigned the same job.

As Roxie hung her bag by the door, took off her jacket, and kicked off her boots, she heard Skylar asking Grandma if Tristan had been acting unusual around the time of the murder or if he'd said anything suspicious to her.

Grandma hardly even seemed to be listening, rolling out her haphazard dough balls with abandon, swaying to a song playing on her radio as she said, "He's a very nice boy. Such a hard worker."

"You've employed him at the Emporium for years," Skylar pressed, never taking her eyes from the dough she was rolling into a perfect sphere. "I just want to know what your real opinion of him is."

"He's a nice boy," Grandma said again between licks of a dough-coated spoon. "And a hard worker. That's what I really think of him."

Skylar made a frustrated scowl then turned it on Roxie. "Where have you been?"

"Doing research on a new ghost story," Roxie said, dragging her finger through the dough stuck to the side of the mixing bowl and popping it into her mouth.

"What do you mean by *new*? As in *recent*?"

"I meant new to me. It happened a hundred and thirty-four years ago, but I'm just now learning about it."

"A little late to the party, aren't you?" Skylar said, scrubbing her hands clean in the sink.

Roxie shrugged, leaning back against the counter and crossing her arms over her chest. "Better late than never."

Grandma slid the cookie trays into the oven, switching off the radio and yawning at the same moment. "Can you keep an eye on these for me, girls? They need to bake for ten minutes, and I think I'll be lucky if I last another five."

The girls agreed, hugging her good night. But for Skylar, Grandma had an extra-long squeeze and a kiss on the cheek. "My little soldier," she whispered before she padded off to bed.

Skylar and Roxie exchanged a look.

"All I did was make cookies," Skylar said.

"Yeah. Which is a thousand times more than you've been up for in the past year. We're allowed to be proud of you."

Skylar rolled her eyes, hard. Then she grabbed her notebook and sat on the floor, leaning her back against the island and facing the oven.

It was something they'd always done, whenever Grandma asked them to watch the cookies. An unspoken tradition that had started when they were little and Skylar had taken the request very seriously and very literally, never taking her eyes from the dough as it rose through the little glass window.

"I've been busy while you were gone," she said.

Roxie joined her on the floor with a sigh. "Of course you have."

"First, I tried to contact Suzanna Riley. I called her a few times, but it kept going straight to voice mail. Then I tried looking through all her social media accounts to see if it might give me an idea of what she's been up to, but she never kept them updated much. She hasn't posted anything for years. Has Tristan mentioned hearing from her recently?"

Roxie shrugged. "He said she calls every few weeks to check in. She's still down in Florida with a friend, as far as he knows. She's probably just not interested in picking up calls from a Whistler area code. She wanted to leave this place behind and start over." She paused, thinking for a moment. "Do you think she should be a suspect? It is weird that she would just take off like that."

Skylar shook her head. "Not that weird. She didn't really have any friends here, as far as I know. Colin was the only person she seemed to care about. And she has an alibi—she was working a shift at the ER on the night of the murder. I was more interested in hearing about her side of what happened at the Keller Funeral Home."

Skylar scribbled something in her notebook before she moved on. "The next thing I focused on was reworking the time line. Colin being at Caleb's house with Eric until 8 obviously ruins my initial theory about Tristan murdering him at 7 or earlier. He wouldn't have been able to kill him at 8 and then get to his cousin's house by 9 to be seen on his security camera."

"Exactly," Roxie said with relief. "So now we can drop all this—"

"Unless," Skylar plowed on, "he was somehow able to reduce his travel time. He must have found a shortcut. That's the only explanation."

"Not the *only* explanation," Roxie argued. "There's also the possibility that he's completely innocent."

Skylar seemed not to hear her as she went on, "If he found a quick enough shortcut, there's also the possibility he could have gotten back here in time to be the man I saw at the Emporium. Maybe the police were right, and the robber and the murderer are the same person. Either way, with a shortcut, his alibi goes completely out the window. I just need to find the right route. I've been mapping out all sorts of scenarios, back roads he could have sped on without being noticed or maybe even something that wouldn't show up on a map."

"He would have needed to shave off a whole hour, Skylar. It just sounds like a stretch to me."

"A stretch," she agreed. "But I don't think it's impossible. I just need more time to figure it out. In the meantime—"

She reached up and grabbed her phone from the counter before bringing up a video. It showed a grainy, black-and-white stretch of road, with a corn field on the other side. Roxie would have thought it was a still photo if not for the numbers running at the bottom of the screen.

"It's security footage from Hannah Macon's house," she said. "It shows all the footage she had from the night of the murder, from 8 p.m. onward."

Hannah Macon was a friend of their grandmother's, and she just so happened to live right down the street from where Colin's body had been discovered. She'd been one of the first people to see smoke and dial 911.

Roxie peered closely at the footage, startling a little when a car flashed briefly across the screen, headlights blazing white, then drove on. "How did you get access to this?"

Skylar gave a wince, like she'd been hoping Roxie wouldn't ask. "Well . . . I told her our printer was broken and asked if I could use hers. I figured she'd have the footage from that night saved, so she could share it with the police. And I was right—I found the file on her computer and downloaded it to a flash drive."

"Sneaky," Roxie chided, though not without admiration. Skylar had always been a rule follower to a fault. But she'd adapted to lying faster than Roxie ever would have thought possible.

"I've already watched it through once. I wanted to see if you noticed anything I didn't," she said.

"How long is the footage?"

"It covers a span of three hours."

Roxie groaned loudly. But she took the phone from her sister anyway and trained her eyes on the screen while Skylar peered at it over her shoulder.

After a stretch of silence, Skylar said, "What ghost story were you researching?"

Roxie frowned. Her sister had always made a point not to ask about anything to do with her tour. "You really want to know?"

Skylar nodded.

"Well, you know Gary Fuller, right? The old guy who owns the pizza place on Third Street? He just bought some property that's been sitting empty for a long time. There used to be a church there that burned down, but there's still a little cemetery just outside the woods. And he noticed that one of the headstones was for a nine-year-old girl named Analise Clark, who died in 1885. He'd heard about my tour, so when he found it, he called me.

"The story goes, she was known for being ornery. Her mother was in the church choir, and her father played the organ, so every Sunday, she had to sit in the back of the church all by herself. And, to pass the time, she liked to chew up wads of paper and spit them at the people in the pews in front of her.

"One Sunday, her mother slipped away from the choir and snuck up on her so she could catch her in the act. She watched Analise stick a big wad of paper in her mouth, chew it up, then rear back to launch it.

"But just before she let loose, her mom smacked her on the

back of the head. Analise was so surprised, instead of spitting the paper out, she sucked it in, lodging it right in her windpipe. She jumped up and started dancing around, trying to signal that she needed help, but her mother told everyone she was being dramatic, playing another one of her jokes to get attention and that they should all ignore her. So they went on singing hymns while Analise Clark choked to death on her own spitball."

Skylar raised a skeptical eyebrow as Roxie finished. "Do you have any proof that really happened?"

"That's what I went looking for," Roxie said. "I checked the library's database of old newspaper articles to confirm it, but couldn't find anything. But they have a digital archive of local death certificates dating pretty far back. Analise's official cause of death was recorded as asphyxiation. As far as the rest of it— the church spectacle and the spitball—" She shrugged. "No way to know about that for sure. Gary told me the story, and he'd heard it from his uncle, who'd heard it from God knows who. It's a big game of telephone that's been going on since 1885. Some of the details are bound to get twisted and exaggerated."

"So what do you do? You can't tell it on the tour if you can't determine that it even happened, can you?"

"Says who?" Roxie countered. "It's my tour. They're ghost stories, not history lectures. And when I visited the gravesite . . . well, it *felt* true to me."

Roxie could tell by her sister's silence just how credible she thought her *feelings* were.

"You want to know the best part?" Roxie pressed on, certain she was about to get on her nerves even more. "Old Gary told me that every time he walks out to that little cemetery, he feels something hit him in the back of the head. Something little. Almost like . . ." She leaned in close, and Skylar was already rolling her eyes by the time she whispered, "A *spitball*."

Skylar shoved her away, though Roxie thought she caught the ghost of a smile on her lips. "Like there aren't a million acorns falling off trees around here all the time."

"I prefer supernatural explanations."

There was another stretch of silence, the girls' attention alternating between the monotonous surveillance footage and the cookies turning golden in the oven, the smell thickening the air of the kitchen.

Until finally, Skylar said, "What does the story mean?"

"Mean?" Roxie repeated.

"Yeah. Aren't stories supposed to teach you something? You know, it's kind of like the boy who cried wolf. If you lie all the time, no one will believe you when you're telling the truth. I don't believe in the Clark Curse—I never will. But maybe all the stories are meant to teach us something. Like we shouldn't be too reckless, like mom. Or too careless, like Aunt Violet. Or vain, like Becca when she got the boys to play that game of chicken. Maybe we tell their stories so we can learn from all their flaws."

"I think you're being too hard on them," Roxie said, a sense of protectiveness surging for these women, some of whom she'd never met. "But I guess I never really thought about it. I just find it all interesting. I like connecting to them, even if they don't teach me anything. Maybe they were flawed. But sometimes bad things just happen, and there's nothing to learn from them. You know?"

Skylar nodded but didn't offer any other response.

"Besides," Roxie added, tipping her head back against the island and reaching her black-painted toenails toward the warmth of the oven as the timer counted down the last few seconds on the cookies. "I think all the lessons in the world couldn't keep us out of trouble."

And she was pleasantly surprised when it made her sister laugh.

20

The Emerald Theater was a large, brick building at the center of downtown Whistler. It opened in 1922 but went out of business in the seventies. It sat mostly untouched for a few decades, until around ten years ago, when the Whistler Historical Society bought it and renovated it to its former glory.

After the renovation, the concession stand was in full operation, with massive candy bars and popcorn that made the whole theater smell like buttery heaven. Art Deco patterns had been painted on the walls to match the original design, with help from old black-and-white photographs for reference. The neon sign outside was lit up every night, the green giving it an eerie, radioactive glow. Big, bold letters advertised the movies that played there on the weekends—everything from *Alien* to *Rebel Without a Cause* to *Hocus Pocus*.

From the moment Roxie first stepped inside, a wide-eyed twelve-year-old who'd convinced her grandmother to take her to see *The Thing*, she knew the place had stories to tell—and not just on the screen. The Emerald Theater was a big, beautiful time capsule that, with some digging, Roxie was sure she'd be able to crack wide open.

But to her disappointment, she had yet to squeeze a single morbid morsel out of the place.

She'd scoured every newspaper article she could get her hands on that even mentioned the theater and asked the people involved with the restoration millions of questions, trying to tease out some drama or scandal. But, as far as she could tell, not a single death had taken place within the walls of the Emerald during the entirety of its century-long history. Apparently, it was one of the only places in town where the Clarks had always been safe.

Though, perhaps, she thought darkly, a Clark simply hadn't met their end at the theater *yet*, and she needed to tread more carefully there than anywhere else.

Whether there were any sordid details to be discovered about the Emerald or not, there was no way in hell Roxie wasn't including it on her tour. It was too gorgeously dramatic not to be utilized.

It had been a negotiation process with the Whistler Historical Society. At first, they weren't sure they wanted to encourage a haunted reputation. But they'd eventually worked out a deal once she pledged to donate a portion of all proceeds to the upkeep of the theater.

On Friday night, Roxie's tour group looked doubtful as they approached the Emerald. It appeared the place was shut down for the evening, completely dark. But she marched right up to one of the glass doors, knocked twice, and stepped back. A few seconds later, the marquee blazed to life, and music started to play from the tinny outdoor speakers—the theme from *Pyscho*.

Then the door opened, and a balding man in his sixties wearing a green *Emerald Theater Volunteer* T-shirt poked his head out, a somber expression on his face.

"Enter," he said in a deep voice. *"If you dare!"* And then he topped it off with his best evil laugh.

"Thank you, Charlie," Roxie said, and she filed past him with the rest of the group while he held the door.

The theater was mostly dark, except for a few lights Charlie had switched on to make the walkways visible without compromising the tone of the tour. Roxie led her guests down a few winding hallways and ushered them through a door marked Employees Only.

Because she hadn't found any Clark ghost stories to tell, she'd decided to take advantage of the space by transforming it into an abbreviated haunted house experience instead.

Some of the Whistler Historical Society volunteers—mostly the teenagers—had been generous enough to come in two nights a week from September through Halloween and help her put on the spectacle, dressing up as villains from the classic horror movies the Emerald showed every fall—Freddy Krueger, Jason Voorhees, Michael Myers, Pennywise, and Leatherface. They'd set up black bedsheet labyrinths backstage, along with cheap, animatronic skeletons and clowns with glowing eyes propped up throughout, all for the simple joy of chasing screaming patrons with plastic knives and chainsaws.

There were, of course, some people on her tour who did not

consider this kind of thing their cup of tea. Anyone who wanted to opt out would follow Roxie and Charlie up to the projection room, where they could watch the others' journey through the security monitors.

But tonight, everyone had decided to go through with the haunted house, which left Roxie and Charlie alone in the projection room to laugh themselves hoarse over a bucket of fresh popcorn. The security feed had no audio, but they could still hear the shrieks through the walls.

Roxie had about ten minutes of downtime before she had to meet them at the end of the haunted house. Usually, when they weren't watching the monitors, she and Charlie talked about the latest horror films—which mostly consisted of Roxie gushing about a new favorite and Charlie arguing that the crap Hollywood was churning out these days couldn't beat the classics.

But tonight, there was clearly something else on his mind. He put the popcorn bucket aside, wiping his buttery fingers on his jeans before he said, "I heard Luke Riley is in town."

"Oh?" Roxie said. "Didn't know you attuned to the hot Whistler gossip, Charles."

"You think the shade of paint we should use on the walls is the only thing we talk about at these historical society meetings?"

"Interesting."

"I know you're good pals with Tristan. How is he doing, having his father around?"

"Not great," Roxie admitted. "I don't think they get along."

Charlie nodded, looking unsurprised. "I hear the guy is bad news. I hope he gets bored of this place and moves on soon."

"Me, too," Roxie agreed. "I think Tristan wants the same. He won't let Luke stay at the house with him." She averted her eyes to one of the monitors, hoping her voice sounded casual when she said, "I wonder where he's been living."

"I've heard that sad, little white house. Out by the Garrisons' place. You know the one? With the green roof."

"I think so," she said.

But she knew exactly which one.

As she was leaving the Emerald that evening, her slightly traumatized patrons trailing behind her, teasing each other about who'd screamed the loudest, Roxie sent Tristan a quick text. Not feeling well tonight. I canceled the tour, so no need to walk me home.

He texted back a few minutes later, Hope you feel better. And she tried not to let the lie eat at her.

She couldn't rush the rest of her tour stops or just tell everyone to go home, as much as she wanted to. She'd been forced to cut more than one tour short lately, and she had a reputation to uphold. But the second she was done with the story at the creek in Whistler Woods, she would tell everyone to feel free to search for Aurora Clark's face in the water for as long as they wanted—on their own. She had somewhere to be.

☽

Roxie thought she knew all the scariest places in Whistler. But she was surprised by how unsettled she felt when she approached the white house with the green roof at the edge of town, isolated in the middle of a barren field. The foundation was slanted, and long strips of siding had been ripped away by the wind. The mailbox had been crushed to splinters by a baseball bat or a drunk driver, and the weeds and grass were growing wild.

She had driven past it a hundred times to get to the interstate but had never looked at it closely. It was a house that didn't want to be noticed, ashamed of itself, a body curling in with hunched shoulders and head hung low. Unloved and starved, waiting for someone to wander close enough so it could snatch them up in its jaws.

Roxie still wasn't allowed to use her bus on tours quite yet and hadn't finished decorating it to her standards anyhow, so she had come here straight from Whistler Woods on foot. Which suited her purposes, because she wasn't about to roll up to Luke Riley's house with her headlights blazing and engine rumbling.

There wasn't a single light on inside that Roxie could see. No car in the gravel driveway. It wasn't quite nine o'clock yet, so it was unlikely he was already asleep. Maybe she had gotten lucky and he wasn't home.

She approached the house quietly, tiptoeing through the pockmarked yard. She hoped Luke's rent was cheap—the landlord hadn't even bothered to get rid of trash left behind by the previous tenants, left to decompose in the mud. She found a discarded paint bucket and flipped it upside down below one of the windows, using it as a stool to peer inside. She found a mostly barren room, with an old recliner positioned in front of a television and a few beer bottles toppled like bowling pins around the floor.

She moved on to the next window and the next. No one in

the bedroom or kitchen either, as far as she could see. She listened, but couldn't hear anything either.

She knew it would be a good idea to watch for a few minutes longer, just to make sure the house was really empty. But he could come home at any second and ruin her chance to search the place.

An even better idea would be to not sneak into the house of a known felon at all, a voice said in her head that didn't quite sound like her own. Was it Tristan's? Skylar's? Grandma's? She was sure all of them would give her the same advice.

But as much as she loved all three, she couldn't stop herself from being exactly who she was. And her own voice rose over the other, telling her, *Now's your chance.*

The front door was locked. So were all the windows. But one of them, around the back, had a long crack in it. Would it be so unbelievable that something hit it and broke it a little more? There was a strong breeze tonight.

She took a rock and knocked at the crack. Not enough to shatter the glass completely, but she was able to break out a large enough piece to fit her arm through and unlatch the lock.

She cursed her platform boots as she scrabbled to find purchase on the siding and pull herself through. She made a much clumsier job of it than they did in the movies, crawling in head-first and falling heavily on the floor—she winced at the *thud*. If there was anyone home, they would have heard it and come running. But she waited and listened for a few moments, and no footsteps came.

She stood, brushing off her skull-printed skirt and orienting herself in the dark. She didn't want to flip the switch because the barren land surrounding the house was completely flat. You could probably see the glow of a single window from miles away. She used her phone flashlight instead, casting it around the bedroom.

It was bare of any defining details—just a bed covered by a musty quilt and a dresser with missing handles. It could have belonged to anyone.

She didn't even know what she was looking for exactly. Luke had an alibi for the night of the murder, but Skylar said he was out of prison before the bank robbery. And while it was likely all three (almost four) robberies would be committed by the same person, the one at the bank had been different. The robber had used a knife to threaten workers at the other locations, and no harm had come to them. But at the bank, Mr. Patterson had been shot.

Maybe Luke committed the robbery himself. Maybe he knew who did and was working with them. Or maybe he had nothing whatsoever to do with any of this—but he still had something on Tristan. Something he was using as leverage to force his son to find something for him.

She was going to figure out what had brought Luke Riley to Whistler. And, more importantly, what she could do to make him leave.

She started in the closet, sorting through a handful of worn shirts and frayed jeans. A pair of boots were strewn on the floor. A rosary hung from a hook on the door.

She spotted his wallet on a table in the entryway, which made her freeze, her whole body tensing. Why would he have left without it?

She held her breath, listening again, counting off the seconds. Still, she didn't hear a sound—but she knew better than anyone how unsettling silence could be.

After a minute had passed, she ventured forward, the floorboards creaking under her boots. She picked up the wallet and examined it by the light of her phone.

There wasn't much in it—his ID, a five-dollar bill, and an old bus ticket. A credit card with someone else's name on it. And behind that, a photograph.

It was a picture of Luke, Suzanna, and the boys when they were young. Tristan and Suzanna sat in chairs side by side, her smile mostly convincing while his was noticeably forced—whether because he was uncomfortable taking pictures or something else, Roxie couldn't tell. Luke stood behind them with his other son in his arms, and there was nothing artificial about Colin's smile. He clung to his father's neck, curls spilling over his face while he laughed.

The edges of the photo had gone soft, like it had been handled frequently—taken out and looked at all the time. Roxie was careful when she slid it back into the wallet.

There wasn't much to look through in the living room, aside from a stack of magazines and empty cigarette cartons. The kitchen was just as nondescript. It held the dregs of a transient life, of someone ready to take off at a moment's notice, with no food in the refrigerator to be forgotten or bread in the cabinet to mold. Just beer bottles and cans of beans and stew to heat in the pot on the stove.

She was starting to think that breaking into the house had been a pointless risk. She was looking quickly through the kitchen drawers, just to cover all her bases before she made her escape. They scraped and whined with years of disuse. She found silverware and dish towels and spices and even a few packets of tea, no doubt left behind by previous renters.

And then, when she pulled open one of the last drawers, a gun clattered to the bottom.

She flinched backward as though a snake had jumped out at her. Then she made herself move closer, studying the weapon.

She didn't know what kind of gun had been used in the bank robbery. She supposed it wasn't all that abnormal for someone to own one. But she was fairly sure it wasn't legal for a recently released felon.

She was about to take a picture when she heard a floorboard creak behind her.

She didn't have time to scream before someone clamped a hand over her mouth.

21

Roxie didn't go without a fight. She kicked and threw her elbows, getting at least one firm hit on Luke Riley's face, but it didn't slow him down. He had her around the waist and carried her to one of the rooms, forcing her in so hard, she fell on the floor.

He slammed the door shut after her, and when she'd oriented herself enough to get back on her feet, she tried to let herself out. But he'd blocked the door with something, and it wouldn't budge.

The room was dark with no windows. She felt around the walls frantically for a while before she found the switch and flipped it on to reveal a dingy bathroom with cracked floor tiles, rust stains in the tub, and a ripped shower curtain on the floor.

She heard Luke's muffled voice from the other side of the door, but she couldn't make out what he was saying, and whoever he was talking to, she heard no answer. He must've been on the phone.

Phone. Roxie patted her pockets, looking for hers, and

realized that she must have dropped it during her struggle with Luke.

She wished desperately that she'd told Skylar where she was going. Or anyone, for that matter. She'd considered sending her sister a text on the way over, but truthfully, she'd been afraid of what she might find at the house. She didn't think Tristan killed his brother—of course she didn't—but he and Luke were clearly mixed up in something he wasn't telling her about. She remembered their tense conversation at the Resurrection Emporium and the way he'd reacted when his father called him in the school parking lot. Whatever was going on, if it had even a little bit to do with Colin's death—

Roxie didn't know what she'd do. And she definitely hadn't wanted Skylar there to make the decision for her.

Though she sure as hell wished she had a Yale-worthy genius on her side now, because she had no idea what to do next.

A few minutes later, the bathroom door opened again, and when Luke appeared, he wasn't holding his gun or any other weapon. Still, he didn't step aside to let her out either.

"You can't just lock me up," Roxie said. "That's kidnapping. I'll tell the cops."

"You broke into my house," Luke countered. "I'd be within my rights to kill you. I still could." He shrugged, like he hadn't decided yet.

Roxie felt her heart kick with panic, but scowled rather than show her fear.

It struck her now, how much he looked like Tristan. Colin had taken after their mother, with narrow features and pale eyes.

But Luke's wide jaw, black hair, and intense gaze were all unsettlingly familiar.

"Let's talk," he said, making a vague gesture toward the toilet like he was inviting her to sit down.

Roxie wrinkled her nose, opting to perch on the lip of the tub instead.

"Okay."

"You're friends with my son."

It didn't sound like a question, but she nodded anyway.

"Why did you break into my house?"

She chewed on that for a moment, pretty sure that this was where she was supposed to lie. But what *good* reason could she have for being here?

"I heard you and Tristan fighting the other day. He's been tense since you got to town. I've been worried about him. I know you wanted him to find something for you, but he won't tell me what." She shrugged. "I came here to get answers and figure out how to get rid of you."

He didn't quite laugh, but the corner of his mouth quirked, and it almost felt like the same thing. She'd seen that identical expression on Tristan's face a thousand times.

"The boy likes his secrets," he said.

Before he could say more, they both heard a car skidding to a stop outside the house.

Luke gave a deep, tired sigh before he stepped out of the bathroom again, shutting and barricading the door behind him before she could follow him out.

"Roxie!"

She pressed her ear to the door when she heard Tristan yelling for her—Luke must have called him.

"Relax, kid. She's fine," she heard Luke answer.

"Where the hell is she?"

"In the bathroom."

"How did she get here? If you touched her—"

"*Me* touch *her*? She broke into my house! Pretty sure I'm going to have a black eye tomorrow from that elbow she threw."

"I don't believe you. Why would she come here?"

"She's looking for answers to some tough questions."

There was a long, heavy silence after that.

Finally, Luke said, "Did you find the money?"

Tristan didn't answer.

"That's what I thought," Luke said. "I'm not going to let you keep putting me off. There are going to be consequences. Maybe Roxie—"

Tristan growled back, "Don't bring her into this. Your son is dead, and all you care about is the fucking money. If you ever loved him—"

"Loved him?" Luke gave an incredulous laugh, devoid of all humor. "That's why I've done everything I've done. Why I've made the sacrifices I've made. For you boys. I did what I had to do to take care of you—*that's* what love is."

"Maybe you should have loved us a little less, then. Let some stepdad give us a life that wasn't always on stolen time. Maybe Colin would still be—"

Roxie heard a *thump*, and a tremble went through the house, like something had hit the wall. She held her breath, waiting, listening.

Finally, she heard Luke say, "I did the best I could for my family. And sometimes that meant I had to do the wrong thing. I *had* to, son. And I think you understand that better than you like to pretend."

After a tense pause, Tristan said, quieter now, so Roxie could hardly make it out, "I'll find it. But you have to stay away from Roxie and keep your goddamn mouth shut, or you'll never see the money again."

Roxie didn't hear them speak more after that. But they must have come to an agreement, because a few moments later, she heard the scraping noise of whatever blocked her in being pushed away, and she stepped back just in time for Tristan to throw the door open. He grabbed her hand with hardly a glance at her face. "Let's go," he said. She followed behind him without argument. She looked around for Luke as they left, but they were gone too fast, Tristan pulling her out into the cold night.

Once they were in his truck, he pressed the pedal to the floor. The tires spun beneath them, spitting gravel, until they caught and shot down the driveway and onto the empty road.

Roxie gripped the edges of her seat. "What the hell is going on?"

He ignored the question. Didn't even seem to hear her, his hands white-knuckled on the wheel, engine roaring as he took the turns too fast. He didn't speak until he skidded to a stop in the parking lot behind the Resurrection Emporium. And when he did, he turned on her with a question of his own: "What the hell were you doing at my dad's house?"

Roxie didn't shy away from him, even though he looked angrier than she'd ever seen him before. She was angry, too. "I knew you were keeping secrets from me, and I needed to figure out why."

"They've got nothing to do with you."

"If they're about Colin, then yes, they do. I heard you talking about him to your dad. *And* you said that you're trying to find money for him. Want to explain that to me? Would it happen to have anything to do with all the money taken during the robberies that summer?"

He stared at her. Opened his mouth. But then he shook his head and pounded his fist on the steering wheel. "Shit," he said. "Shit, shit, shit."

He looked helpless in that moment, so desperately unsure of what to do next, that watching him made the anger ease slowly out of her chest. "Tristan, you can tell me the truth. I'm your best friend. If you did something . . . wrong, maybe there's still time to fix it. I want to help you." She put her hand on his back, willing him to look at her.

He wouldn't. And he didn't respond for a long time.

It was a cold night, the wind making the truck rock. Roxie's teeth had started to chatter. "Why don't we go inside?" she said, getting out of the car.

After a moment, Tristan followed her, unlocking the Resurrection Emporium's door, then switching on the lights. He must have come from here when his dad called. He'd been working on repairing a table for someone, a Folgers can of screws knocked over and scattered across the floor, like he'd left in a rush to get to her.

She cleared a space on his worktable and jumped to sit on it, legs dangling.

"You dropped this at Dad's house," he said without looking at her, pulling her cell phone from his pocket and handing it to her.

"Thanks," she said quietly, setting it aside. She'd completely forgotten about it.

He leaned against the worktable beside her, arms crossed over his chest, eyes trained on the dusty concrete floor. She waited patiently for him to find the words. Until, finally, he turned to her and said, "I never wanted to lie to you."

"Why did you feel like you needed to?"

"Because . . . because I knew I was doing something wrong. I didn't want you to be implicated if it all went south."

She waited for him to go on, but at the same time, wished he wouldn't. She was afraid—terrified—that he might be about to confess to something that would change everything.

With a deep, steadying breath, he said, "My dad committed the robberies. All of them. The gas station, the grocery store, and . . . the bank. He shot Mr. Patterson."

Roxie swallowed, holding back any kind of snap reaction, waiting for him to get the rest out.

"And at the Emporium, the night of the murder," Tristan said. "When your sister was there. That was him, too. He got his buddies at the bar to lie about him being there so he'd have an alibi. What he wasn't counting on was for Skylar to still be there, and when he saw her pull the gun, he got spooked and ran off."

"I thought your dad just got out of prison," Roxie said.

Tristan chewed on his lip. "I lied about that, too. He was out at the end of last June."

"Why didn't you tell me?"

"I didn't even know, at first. And I definitely didn't know he was here in Whistler. He was lying low. I didn't find out until after he hit the bank, and by then—" He raked his hands through his hair. "God, everything's gotten so complicated."

"But there's no way he was out last June" she said. "He—"

She stopped before she blew the cover on the investigation. She considered for a moment, trying to decide if this would be a good time to tell him about it. He was finally opening up to her, after all. But she knew Skylar would be livid, and he'd probably be hurt about her going behind his back, too. She decided it was best to talk about that later.

Instead, she tiptoed around the topic, saying, "I did a little research on him before I went to his house. I wanted to figure out what he might be holding over your head. And it looked like he wasn't released until mid-August, after the first two robberies."

Tristan shook his head. "I don't know what the official record says. I haven't looked. But it wouldn't surprise me if he managed to get it modified somehow, to make the cops not look too closely at him. He knows a lot of people and always seems able to call in a favor. All I know is that he got out in June and came here looking for some easy targets."

"So, if he committed the robberies himself, why doesn't he know where the money is? Why would he expect you to find it?"

Tristan released a tired breath, rubbing his temples like he had a headache coming on. "He didn't want to keep all that cash on him. So he showed up on our doorstep out of nowhere with the duffel bag stuffed full, saying he'd been sleeping in his car and didn't want someone breaking in and taking everything. He wanted me to help him find a place to hide it and wanted to stay at the house with me and Colin. I told him to go to hell.

"But then Dad went behind my back and talked Colin into taking it and stashing it somewhere for him. I didn't know about it, or I would have talked him out of it. I only found out after he was dead. Dad took off for a while, waiting for the investigation to die down, but he started hounding me with phone calls just a few months later, threatening to come back if I didn't send him the money. I told him I had no clue where it was, but he didn't believe me. Now he's come back to hassle me about it in person. Says he won't leave until he has it."

Roxie swallowed before she asked her next question. "Did Luke kill Colin?"

Tristan paused. She held her breath.

"No," he said finally. "At least I don't think he did." He ran his hands through his hair. "My dad has always been good at getting into trouble. But, at the end of the day, I think he truly believes he did it all to take care of us. And I think he really did love Colin and wouldn't do anything to hurt him. Not on purpose, anyway. Besides, if he did kill him, he wouldn't have done it without finding out where he hid the money first. But I've started to wonder if maybe someone caught wind that Colin had all his cash. One of Dad's old enemies or associates. He owed a lot of people money—there were always guys stopping by the house when we were younger. Scary guys, looking to collect debts. One of them might have cornered Colin, trying to get him to fess up about his hiding place. Maybe Colin wouldn't tell them. So they killed him."

Roxie gripped the edge of the workbench hard, blinking to keep her whirring thoughts straight. She felt a fresh wave of grief for Colin. He'd been trying to please a father he'd hardly had time to know, and he might have gotten killed for it. But mixed in with that feeling was some relief, too. She hadn't thought for a second that Tristan was a killer. Though she had sensed he wasn't being honest with her, and it was good to finally have an explanation from him—one that didn't make her a liar when she told her sister he was the same boy she had always known.

"Do you have any idea which one of your dad's enemies might have come after him?" she asked around a thickness in her throat.

Tristan shook his head. "I wish I did. But Dad has dealt with so many shady people, he probably doesn't even remember them all. And even if he did, most of them use fake names and are good at covering up their tracks. Digging into it would be pointless, and it would probably end with more people getting hurt. So I've just been trying to make peace with the fact I'm probably never going to know exactly what happened to my brother, or who's responsible."

Roxie noticed that, at some point during the conversation, Tristan's hands had hardened into fists, his knuckles white.

"Do you blame your dad?" Roxie asked quietly.

"I do," he said, without hesitation. "He shouldn't have gotten Colin involved in his mess in the first place."

That left just one more question. "Then why haven't you turned him in to the police?"

Tristan took longer to respond to this question than he had any of the others. Almost like he didn't quite know how to answer.

Finally, he said, "He swears up and down that he never meant to kill Mr. Patterson. Says that the guy was trying to wrestle the gun away from him and was going to shoot him with it. He claims the gun went off by accident during the struggle. There's no way for me to know for sure. But it's possible that, in court, he might be able to get off with a lighter sentence if he can convince them the killing was accidental.

"But, if he goes down for the robberies, I know for a fact they're going to try and pin Colin's murder on him, too. And no way in hell could anyone argue *that* was an accident. Not with the state the body was found in. If they convict him of that murder, he'll be put away for the rest of his life.

"And, hell, maybe that's what he deserves. It's just—well, he's the only family I have left, Roxie. Whether it's right or wrong, I don't want to leave him to rot in a cell. So I thought maybe I would find him the money, and then he could take off and build a new life somewhere else."

He dropped his head back, gazing at the ceiling. He looked so exhausted. "And now I've put you in a tough spot. Which is why I didn't want to tell you any of this in the first place."

He was right. Now that she knew Luke had killed Mr. Patterson, she couldn't just ignore it. And if Tristan wasn't going to turn him in, now the burden was on her.

"I'm not going to make you responsible for him" he said, heading her off before she could say anything. "I'm going to be the one to tell the police myself."

"When?"

"Soon. Really soon."

She knew she should press him harder for specifics. But all this was clearly taking a toll on him, and she didn't want to add to the weight on his shoulders. She realized it had probably been there for a long time, pushing him down further and further since the day Colin died.

She grabbed his hand gently and told him, "Okay. I trust you."

He surprised her by bringing her hand up to his face. He pressed it to his cheek, and without thinking, Roxie opened her fingers and rested her palm against his warm skin. He leaned into it, closing his eyes. And, for the first time in a long time, he seemed to relax.

He kept his eyes closed when he said, "That's why I walked out after you kissed me at prom."

Her breath caught. They hadn't spoken about it since the day he tried to apologize to her. She'd thought the idea of them ever being anything other than friends was already dead and buried.

"What do you mean?" she said back, her voice catching. She ventured a step closer, tilting her head back to look up at him.

"I didn't feel right kissing you when I was lying to you about so much. Dad had started calling me almost every day at that point. I had a lot on my mind. I wanted to wait until things got less complicated before I started anything with you." He opened his eyes. "But I'm beginning to realize my life is going to stay complicated for a while. And I can't keep letting that stop me from living it."

Roxie's heart was pounding so hard, she didn't think she'd be able to get the next question out. "Does that mean you wanted to kiss me back?"

There were so many other things to worry about right now. Questions and responsibilities and consequences that were so much bigger than them. But in that moment, all Roxie could think about was her hand on his cheek and the narrowing gap between them.

"Roxie," he breathed, touching her waist, pulling her in even closer. He brought his hand up to the back of her neck, threading his fingers into her hair, dipping his face toward hers.

And then, someone opened the door.

Roxie cursed, turning toward the sound, ready to tell off whoever had just ruined her moment. But she froze when she saw her sister standing in the doorway, arms crossed over her chest, eyes narrowed.

She was angry. She didn't make any secret of that.

"Where the hell have you been?" she snapped.

"I—" Roxie glanced back at Tristan. "Tristan was walking me home from my tour and mentioned some new inventory Grandma got in. I wanted to come here and see it. We lost track of time."

Skylar raised an eyebrow at that. She'd clearly seen what had almost happened. But she didn't press it.

"Time to go," she said.

Roxie's cheeks blazed with mortification—not only over being caught almost kissing Tristan but also him witnessing her getting ordered around by her sister. But Skylar was already walking, and she hurried to follow.

"Wait," Tristan called after them. "It's late. Let me drive you guys home."

"That won't be necessary," Skylar said without turning back or breaking stride. "I can take care of my own sister."

22

"Bullshit."

Skylar whispered the word across the kitchen table, though Roxie could tell she would have preferred to yell it. But their grandmother had been asleep upstairs by the time they got home, and they didn't want to wake her.

She'd just finished telling her sister Tristan's story—about his dad committing the robberies, Colin stashing the money, and Tristan's suspicions that he'd been killed by one of Luke's many enemies.

She knew Tristan wouldn't want her to say anything to Skylar, especially before he'd had time to go to the police. But he didn't know Skylar suspected him of murdering Colin. Roxie had hoped she could convince her sister of his innocence on his behalf. Maybe Skylar wouldn't give up on the investigation altogether, but Roxie hoped she'd at least lay off him.

Yet she'd barely gotten the whole story out of her mouth before Skylar dashed those hopes.

"He told you someone fudged the records of his dad's release date? There's no way you believe that. Who do you think he is, Al Capone, for Christ's sake? Low-profile criminals like Luke Riley don't have that kind of sway."

Roxie shrugged. "Tristan said that he does. I think he knows more than we do about what his own father is capable of."

"Roxie, he's lying to you. We've already established he's a liar. His story doesn't explain why he'd tell the police that Colin was at Jackson's house the night of the murder when we know for a fact that he wasn't."

"Maybe it was to protect his dad somehow."

Skylar shook her head. "That wouldn't make sense. Let's say Luke is the robber—telling the police that Colin was walking home from Jackson's house at the same time as Luke was fleeing the Emporium only makes him look guiltier."

Roxie slumped back in her chair, rubbing at the fresh blisters on her feet. Not for the first time that night, she cursed her choice of footwear.

"Maybe Colin was the one lying. Did you think of that? Maybe he told Tristan he was going to be at Jackson's and he was actually stashing the money for his dad or moving it or—"

"There's no way Jackson would lie to the police to cover for Colin. Not in a million years. Besides, I know Colin didn't hide any money for his dad in the first place—he wouldn't keep something that big from me."

"Clearly you didn't know him as well as you thought you did," Roxie snapped back.

Skylar visibly flinched at that, going quiet for a moment.

Roxie sighed, rubbing at her temples. She felt the dull, persistent pain of a headache coming on. "I'm sorry. I didn't mean that. It's been a long day. I don't know why Tristan told the police Colin was at Jackson's house that night, but he must have had his reasons. We didn't get into all the intricacies of it. He's been dealing with so much over the past year, and now he's got to turn his own dad in for murder. We need to drop all this instead of making things even harder on him."

But Skylar clearly wasn't about to let up. She stood from her chair and started pacing around the kitchen, her footfalls muffled by her socks. "It's impossible to be logical with you when your judgment is so clouded by your feelings for him. God, I just—I knew you were reckless, but making out with a suspected murderer? Really?"

"I don't suspect him. And I didn't even get to make out with him, thanks to you," Roxie added, crossing her arms sullenly over her chest.

"You could have at least waited until the investigation was over, if you're so sure he's innocent."

"It wasn't exactly planned. And besides—I don't think this investigation is ever going to be over for you. You've gotten it in your head that he's the killer, and you're not going to stop until you prove it. And you're never going to prove it because he didn't do it."

"What makes you so sure?"

"I trust him."

Skylar gave a short, bitter laugh at that. "That's all you've got? Now I'm really worried."

"You don't need to worry about me. I can take care of myself."

"Roxie, you were two hours late getting home. What was I supposed to do, just *trust* you were okay? Grandma was getting upset, so I covered for you and told her to go to bed. And *then* I had to go searching all over town for you. I called you a million times, and you never answered."

"I'm sorry. I should have texted you. I didn't mean to upset anyone. But that doesn't mean—"

"I don't want you seeing Tristan anymore. Especially not alone. Not until we can prove he isn't dangerous."

Roxie felt indignation surge hot up her throat. "Since when do you get to tell me what to do?"

"If you're going to make self-destructive choices, you can't expect me to sit by and watch."

Roxie threw up her hands. "I'm not going to put up with—"

"I don't care if you want to put up with it or not. I don't care if I hurt your feelings. I don't know how to put it more plainly—it's not wise to hang out with someone who committed"—she held up a finger before Roxie could argue—"who *may* have committed murder."

Roxie shook her head. "So all you've done for the past decade is call me a freak or ignore me completely, and I'm just supposed to take orders from you now?"

"I've never called you a freak."

"My tenth birthday party."

Skylar blinked. "What?"

"The one with the Halloween theme."

"Grandma always took us to the pumpkin patch for your birthday."

"Except for the year I turned ten. You really don't remember? I planned the whole thing out—made Grandma buy tons of candy, decorated the whole house, made cupcakes with those little plastic spider rings. There was going to be a costume contest and pin-the-fangs-on-Dracula. The works. Which still sounds like a pretty damn good time to me. But, of course, not a single person from school showed up. I was trying not to cry because I didn't want Grandma to feel bad for me, so I made a joke about it being the Clark Curse's fault—like it was all just bad luck, not something wrong with me. I knew better. But then you had to jump in and shove the truth in my face—*Nobody came because you always act like such a freak.*"

It had happened years before Roxie started her tour. Before Tristan moved to Whistler. Plenty of people had called her a freak before that moment and plenty more since. All those times, she'd just told herself they were wrong. They didn't really know her.

But if her own sister said it—someone who was supposed to know her better than anyone—then it had to be true.

"I absolutely *did not* say that," Skylar insisted.

Roxie scoffed. "What, you think I just enjoy making up traumatic childhood memories?"

"You're just remembering it wrong. I would never say that. Maybe I wasn't as supportive as I should have been, but that was years ago. It's time to move on and focus on more important things. In case you've forgotten, my boyfriend got *murdered.* And since when do you care about parties anyway?"

"That's the day I made myself quit caring, oddly enough," Roxie said. "About parties and about what you thought of me."

"You're being dramatic."

"I'm over it," Roxie said. "I was just bringing it up to illustrate a point."

"Which is?"

Roxie stood from her chair and stepped close to Skylar, coming almost nose to nose with her. They were exactly the same height. They used to measure themselves obsessively while they were still growing, down to the eighth of an inch.

"You've never been a good sister to me, so you don't get to waltz into my life and pretend like you have any kind of claim over it. I won't be taking any orders from you. I'm going to hang out with Tristan whenever I feel like it. Because unlike you, he has always had my back."

Skylar looked stricken for a moment. Or perhaps it was just a trick of the dim kitchen lights, because her face hardened again as she said, "If that's how you feel, then I'll finish this investigation on my own."

"Fine by me," Roxie said before she stormed up the stairs to her room.

23

Roxie had wanted to help Skylar. And she'd done that. Her sister had a purpose again—even if obsessively trying to solve a murder wasn't exactly the *healthiest* purpose. At least it got her out of the house.

Over the past few days, Skylar had been disappearing for hours at a time to talk to God knows who about God knows what. She'd stopped sharing anything about the investigation with Roxie.

Which was fine by her. Skylar would tire herself out eventually. All her leads would turn into dead ends, she'd realize Tristan was innocent, and she would move on. Roxie could go back to sleeping easy—she'd done her part.

But she couldn't quite let it go just yet. One reason being that nearly a week had gone by since Tristan had told her his father committed the robberies and killed Mr. Patterson, and he still hadn't turned him in to the police.

She'd thought he'd do it the day after he confessed to her. When she'd texted him that morning, there was no answer, and he hadn't come to the door when she went by his house. Understandable, she'd thought, that it would keep him busy. The police would probably want to have some long conversations with him.

But, after hearing nothing from him for three days, she'd started to worry. So she'd driven by Luke's house.

She'd taken her grandma's car so she wouldn't be noticed and didn't even lift her foot off the gas as she passed the sad, little white house. Luke's car had been in the driveway, and Luke himself was sitting on the front steps smoking a cigarette.

Very much *not* in jail.

She'd asked Grandma if she had seen Tristan at the Emporium, and she said he'd been calling off from work—which meant he was alive. Just avoiding her.

And *that* could only mean he still hadn't worked up to turning his father in. She understood—it couldn't be easy to send the last scrap of family you had left to prison. But it still needed to be done. Eventually, if she didn't hear from him, she'd have to go back on her word and tip off the cops herself. Though even that wouldn't be so straightforward, considering she had zero proof.

Then there was that moment at the Resurrection Emporium, before Skylar had interrupted them. She'd been certain he was about to kiss her. And what if he had? Would he still be ignoring her calls? There was no way they would be able to move forward with the unresolved issue of his dad—and she couldn't be sure he even *wanted* that kind of relationship with her.

Either way, her whole body burned thinking of how close they had been. She'd spent more than her fair share of time daydreaming about what it would be like to feel his mouth pressing against hers, his hands exploring her skin, his teeth grazing her ear.

The other thing bugging her about the investigation was that Jackson Mowery was still acting suspicious as hell.

He was sitting in front of her in biology and couldn't seem to stop himself from fidgeting. He tapped his pencil against the desk and kept looking out the window, and a few times during the lecture, she caught him glancing back at her.

She believed Tristan's story about what had happened with his father and thought his explanation of one of his dad's enemies being Colin's killer was likely enough. But what did that have to do with Jackson? Why would he and Tristan lie to the police about Colin being at his house that night? And another question still unanswered—why did Tristan beat the shit out of him the week after the murder?

But her train of thought was completely interrupted when she overheard someone say behind her, "Lydia can't have her Halloween party now."

Halloween? There's no way it's already—

But when she looked up at the calendar tacked to the whiteboard, she realized it was tomorrow.

Roxie had always thought of Halloween the way some people did the Super Bowl or Christmas—all the other days of the year were just a buildup to the main event. She'd deck out their house with decorations (without the input of any of the other residents), stock up on the best candy, watch carefully curated horror movie marathons, bake themed treats like ghost cupcakes and bat-shaped cookies, and inhale pumpkin-flavored everything. Not to mention, it was the busiest time of year for her ghost tour.

But this year, she hadn't even had time to think about it with everything that had been going on.

"Lydia's parents found out she was going to have us all over while they were away," the voice went on, whispering under the drone of a video about cell division Mr. Shaffer was playing on the projector, "so they canceled their trip and now she's on lockdown. Jake's a pussy and won't let us bring alcohol to his place after what happened freshman year. You know, when you puked in his pool. My grandparents are in town all week, so my place is out. I don't know where the hell we're supposed to go."

She knew without looking that it was Tim Miller talking to his friend Brian Thompson. They were both on the football team, tall and broad under their letterman jackets, and probably at least 450 pounds combined.

And yet, they both jumped in their seats when Roxie turned suddenly to face them, like she'd popped out of a jack-in-the-box.

"I'm having a party," she said.

At least, that was the plan as of about three seconds ago. After dredging up memories with her sister about her tenth birthday, she saw this as a stroke of fate—the perfect time for a do-over.

It wasn't that she needed validation from anyone. Truthfully, she didn't really care if anyone showed. After the stress of last couple of weeks, she was just determined to have some fun, and going overboard for Halloween was the way she wanted to do it.

When all the boys did was stare at her, she said, "You know about Ward Manor, don't you?"

"The house in the woods where that chick got murdered?" Brian asked. "With the bloodstain on the floor and everything?"

Roxie nodded. "It's the perfect spot. No one lives close enough to hear the music. No adults for miles to bust you for alcohol."

"Is that place even, like, structurally sound?" Tim said, looking dubious.

Roxie waved a dismissive hand. "Of course it is. I go there all the time. You bring the booze and the people. I'll take care of the rest."

Tim and Brian exchanged a look. Roxie said with a devilish smile, "You're not scared, are you?"

"Hell no," they answered in unison.

"That's what I thought. I'll see you on Halloween."

When the bell rang, she gathered her books and got up to leave. But before she did, she squeezed Jackson Mowery on the shoulder. She knew him well enough to know he'd definitely eavesdropped on the whole conversation. So all she had to say was, "You're invited. Skylar will be there."

Without waiting for his answer, she walked out.

There was no way Skylar was actually going to be there. But

Roxie knew the chance of seeing her was the only reason he would come. And while she'd been kicked off the investigation, she still had a few things she needed him to clear up for her. She hoped that maybe cornering him somewhere outside school might make him more inclined to talk.

24

"I'm worried about Skylar," Grandma said.

She had the receiver of the landline pressed to her ear when Roxie came home from school. She dialed a number, waited, then sighed and hung up again.

Roxie was only half listening. She grabbed a cookie from the jar on the counter then crammed the whole thing in her mouth before she sat at the kitchen table, pulling out her phone and starting a list of supplies she'd need to get together before the party tomorrow.

Grandma sat down heavily across from her. "Have you heard from her?"

Roxie shook her head—and didn't add that they hadn't spoken a word to each other in days. "She can look out for herself," she said. "She's a smart girl."

"I know it," Grandma said, rubbing at her temples. "But I didn't like the look on her face when she left the house this morning. She was . . . determined. Hell-bent on something. That's the only way I know how to explain it."

Roxie shrugged. "Maybe she was researching something. Like that time she got really into eel reproduction. We hardly saw her for a week."

"She did say she was going to the library," Grandma said. But then she gave Roxie a sidelong look, clearly trying to read her face for something she wasn't telling her.

Roxie got up and grabbed another cookie to escape the scrutiny.

"I've been calling her all afternoon, and she won't pick up her phone," Grandma said. "I need to get to the Emporium—Tristan called in sick again, poor thing. Would you be able to go check on her?"

Roxie closed her eyes for a moment, tamping down the annoyed grumbling that almost escaped her. Skylar had kicked her off the investigation, and Roxie was still losing valuable party planning time because of it.

But she couldn't exactly tell her grandmother that she was busy getting ready for a secret night of underage drinking in an abandoned house. So she told her, "Don't worry. I'll find her."

She tried the library first, though she was almost certain her sister wouldn't actually be there. It had been their go-to lie to grandma during their entire investigation because it was one of the only places they were both known to frequent. And she was right—she didn't find Skylar in the aisles or at any of the study tables.

She tried Smith & Laurel next, scanning all the booths and

asking the baristas if they'd seen her. When they told her they hadn't, Roxie was all out of ideas.

Before Colin's death, the only places her sister ever went were the library, coffee shop, school, and the Rileys' house. It was impossible to tell exactly where the investigation would have led her this week. She could've been two towns over trying shake down the manager of an Applebee's for an alibi, for all Roxie knew.

She tried her cell again, and when there was no answer, she texted, Grandma is worried. Call her. She almost added, *I've spent an hour looking for you—I'm not your babysitter.* But, mustering all her maturity, she refrained.

She'd done all she could do for the moment. She wasn't going to let her sister ruin another one of her parties. She would start on the decorations then try to get ahold of her again later.

The good news was she already had most of what she needed. Ward Manor was huge, so she'd been using it as storage space for ghost-tour props for years, and no one had ever stopped her or tampered with her things. Most people who visited the house were only brave enough to stay the length of time it took to run up the stairs, touch the bloodstain, and run back out, squealing and sprinting away with whoever had dared them to do it in the first place.

Over the years, Roxie had amassed a collection of strange and horrendously gorgeous items, most of which she'd found at the Resurrection Emporium. Things like her rocking chair made from a plastic replica skeleton, a handful of copper spiders, rock skulls with iridescent purple crystals glued into the hollow eye sockets, copper bats made from balls of wire, and a set of pottery someone had painted with a variety of fanged mouths. Now seemed like the perfect time to pull out all the stops.

When she stepped into the woods, the sun had started to set, light slanting through the trees and lining the branches in gold. The ground was a blanket of leaves, damp and soft from recent rain, muffling her steps. A peaceful backdrop for her whirring thoughts as she tried to plan the placement of everything in her head. She was sure she had some fake cobwebs in a tub somewhere. Maybe even a bottle or two of fake blood she could squirt on the windows. She was definitely going to cover the couch in the living room with something—she'd spent a pretty penny on it, and she'd be damned if some drunk high schooler was going to throw up all over—

Her thoughts were shattered by a loud *crack* that echoed through the woods. It sounded a lot like a gunshot.

She knew her first instinct should have been to run away. But whatever was hardwired into other people's brains that made them avoid danger seemed to have glitched in Roxie's. Because she took off toward Ward Manor instead, where she thought the sound had come from.

She was panting by the time made it there, stopping where the tree line ended, keeping to the lengthening shadows and peering out at the cold grandeur of the house.

She'd finally found Skylar—and she was holding a gun. She gripped it tightly in both hands, her eyes narrowed over the barrel, which was pointed at a row of glass bottles she'd lined up along the trunk of a fallen tree, about fifty feet away.

When she fired, the bullet whizzed past the bottles and into the underbrush. And Roxie counted herself lucky that she wasn't hiding on that side of the woods.

She took a step into the clearing, and a branch snapped under her boot. Skylar whipped around, gun raised.

Roxie held up her hands in surrender.

"Shit," Skylar said, pointing the pistol at the ground and switching on the safety. "What the hell, Roxie? You don't sneak up on somebody with a gun."

Roxie let her hands fall slowly back to her sides. "Since when are you somebody with a gun?"

Skylar shrugged, upper lip stiffening. Already defensive. "Since today."

"And how the hell did you get it?"

"I found someone online a few days ago who listed it. We met up this afternoon, and I bought it from him."

"Just like that?"

"Just like that. I'm nineteen. You don't even need a background check for a private sale." She shrugged. "So I bought a gun."

Roxie blinked in stunned silence for a few moments. Then she asked, "Why?"

Skylar rolled her eyes and turned back to her bottles. She planted her feet, squared her aim. "For protection against the killer that's roaming free around town. Obviously."

"You mean Tristan," Roxie amended, her voice tight.

The corner of Skylar's mouth lifted. "You said it, not me."

Roxie flinched when she pulled the trigger again. Skylar swore under her breath—another miss.

"You're still grieving," Roxie said. "You're angry. You're not yourself."

"Oh, calm down. I won't shoot your friend until he gives me a reason to."

Another shot. Another miss.

"But—"

"Look," Skylar said, dropping the gun back to her side. "If it turns out the robber who came to the Emporium that night was Colin's killer, that means I had a chance to kill the bastard myself. If I ever get that chance again, I'm going to be ready. Next time, I won't miss."

The Clark sisters stared each other down for a few breaths. When Roxie didn't respond, Skylar turned back to the bottles again.

She steadied her grip. Took a deep breath. Let it out slowly. Fired.

This time, she clipped the bottle on the far right—not enough to break it or even knock it over. Just enough to make it rock on its base for a moment.

But that was enough for Skylar. She pumped a victorious fist in the air, laughing with a manic kind of joy.

25

Roxie waited inside Ward Manor while her sister finished up target practice. She didn't want to watch. Instead, she tried to distract herself with party preparations.

She didn't spend too much time cleaning. Part of the manor's charm, in her opinion, was in its dust and rot. She focused more on tacking up a collection of creepy black-and-white photos she'd amassed—shadows with glowing eyes, uncomfortable close-ups of insects, people wearing the masks of animals or demons.

With each *bang* of the gun, her whole body flinched, and her heart rate spiked. She kept dropping plastic bones as she strung them together like garlands to hang from the ceiling.

Ward Manor had no electricity, but she would work around that with some battery-powered speakers she was sure she could talk Charlie into letting her borrow from the back room in the Emerald Theater. She considered lighting the place with candles but decided against it—she didn't need anyone stumbling into them and setting the whole place on fire.

Another gunshot, followed by the sound of shattering glass, and a whoop of triumph from outside.

Roxie shook her head, refocusing.

She had a few sets of red string lights at the house. They looked like little burning coals in the night, and she was pretty sure she'd also seen a small generator tucked away at the Emerald. If Charlie would lend her that, she could also bring the fog machine she typically used at the theater's haunted house and make the room feel more like a cozy, intimate little graveyard on a misty night.

She was most definitely overthinking it. From what she'd heard of Whistler's past parties, she could have gotten away with a boom box, a stale bowl of candy, and some orange streamers hung from the ceiling. But it wasn't in her blood to do anything halfway.

And the same went for her sister, who was apparently taking the task of honing her aim very, very seriously. The light was almost completely gone, and she still hadn't come inside.

Roxie felt her phone ring in her pocket—Grandma calling.

"Did you find Skylar? Is everything all right?"

Roxie debated telling Grandma about Skylar's new toy. But she decided it wasn't worth giving the old woman a heart attack.

"I found her," she said. "We'll be home soon."

She hung up in a hurry, before Grandma could overhear another gunshot.

She switched on one of the spare battery-powered lanterns

she kept in the closet, putting it in the middle of the living room floor. Then she stood in front of the tall, ornate mirror hanging on the wall—Colin's odd gift to her—and hung fake cobwebs around the frame. She stood there for a while after she finished, watching the shadows the lantern light cast over her face.

When Skylar finally came inside, tucking her pistol into the backpack she'd left on the floor, she said without preamble, "I logged into Suzanna Riley's bank account."

"Excuse me?"

Skylar waved her hand, like the details were negligible. "She kept all their passwords written down in a notebook in their kitchen drawer. I saw her take it out a hundred times. I used the house key Colin gave me to sneak over there while Tristan wasn't home and copied down her login info."

Skylar went on before Roxie could even begin to process that information, "I was trying to see if I could look at her transaction history to determine where exactly she went to start this *new life* in Florida. But that's the interesting part—there *weren't* any transactions. She left last September, a month after Colin died, and she hasn't used that account a single time since. She has almost five thousand dollars just sitting there untouched, and—what are you giving me that look for?"

"Hacking into someone's bank account has *got* to be illegal."

Skylar responded with a derisive laugh. "No one is going to give a shit about that once we prove Tristan killed his brother and maybe his mom, too."

Roxie put her hands on her hips, shaking her head. "I don't like this."

"Like what?"

Roxie pointed straight at her. "You. The way you're acting. You bought a damn *gun*, Skylar. You're not yourself."

Skylar snorted. "Don't start with this *you've changed* bullshit again. I told you, the person I was before is gone, all right? She's buried six feet under with—"

She stopped. Turned her gaze to the wall for a moment and pressed her fist to her mouth, composing herself. Roxie wavered, started reaching for her sister, but Skylar stepped away.

After a steadying breath, she went on, "The sooner you get used to that fact, the sooner we can get the justice Colin deserves."

"Okay," Roxie said. "Fine. You're different now. But that's what worries me. I don't know what you're capable of anymore. How can I be sure you won't use your gun to take justice into your own hands before we have any definitive proof that Tristan is the murderer?"

Skylar growled in frustration. "Come *on*, Roxie. It's pretty obvious at this point that he's a liar."

Roxie bit her lip, thinking back to her own doubts— particularly where his complicated ties with Jackson Mowery were concerned.

"Yes, he's still hiding something. I get it. But I can't force myself to believe it's murder. He has an alibi. He couldn't have made it back here in time to break into the Emporium or kill Colin."

"Well, if you'd stuck out the investigation with me, I would have been able to tell you I found a way around that."

Roxie's stomach dropped. "What are you talking about?"

Skylar grabbed her phone from her bag, pulling up a video. The girls bent their heads together to watch.

It was the security footage from outside Hannah Macon's house the night of the murder, down the street from where Colin's body was found. Roxie had watched the entire thing herself—all three tedious hours of it. "Not this again," she grumbled.

"I watched it all the way through four times," Skylar said. "That's how long it took me to spot this."

She pointed at the bottom of the screen. Roxie squinted. It was mostly cut off, but when she stared at it, she could see part of the top of someone's head, and they were pushing something.

"Is that a bike?" she asked.

"That's what I thought, too," Skylar said. "It seemed weird to me that someone would be pushing a bike down the street at 10 p.m. But then I looked closer."

She pointed to one of the wheels. Roxie squinted—it was hard to make anything out for sure on the grainy video. "See how thick these tires are? And right here—I think that's a battery. This isn't just a bike. It's a dirt bike."

Skylar paused, waiting for this revelation to sink in.

"Okay?" Roxie said.

"It got me thinking," Skylar went on. "It reminded me about these stories Colin used to tell me about him and Tristan growing up. He said they used to ride their dirt bikes in the woods behind their father's house all the time. The same house that belongs to his cousin now."

She pulled up a map on her phone. She zoomed in on the

area between Indiana and Ohio. "I've been looking for short-cuts Tristan could have taken, any roads that might have gotten him here in time to be the one who came to the Emporium that night and then committed the murder. Nothing I mapped out was working. But then I wondered—what if he didn't take a road at all?"

She pointed to a spot in southern Ohio on the map.

"Tristan's cousin's house is right about here. See how it backs up to this green area? They own a lot of wooded acreage. And beyond that, those woods stretch on for miles. The Riley property juts right up against Cardinal Valley State Park—which is full of tons of trails. Not wide enough for a car. But I think a dirt bike would make the trip."

Roxie squinted while Skylar pointed at the map again. "See how the highway curves around the woods here? If Tristan cut through Cardinal Valley from here"—she drew a line down the middle of the green part of the map, from the Riley property to the state line—"to here, then he could have saved himself a lot of mileage. Not to mention avoiding any traffic, stoplights, or police."

Roxie felt herself wincing before she asked, "I'm assuming you checked the trail map?"

She waited for Skylar to say that, of course, she had—and there was one that precisely fit the bill, and Tristan's alibi had just been shot to hell.

But instead of looking smug, Skylar pursed her lips. "I've checked," she said. "And it looks like there isn't a trail long enough to realistically save him so much time."

Roxie released a sigh of relief.

"But," Skylar went on, "I did some more research. I was looking into Tristan's family history. As it turns out, his grandfather—who owned the property before Luke Riley—was a part-time park ranger. He was *also* sent to prison for selling crystal meth in Indiana."

"Interesting hobbies," Roxie said. "But I'm not seeing the connection."

"If he was dealing in Indiana, it would have been extremely valuable for him to have a way of transporting his stash all the way to the state line without the risk of getting pulled over and busted. Because of his day job, he knew Cardinal Valley very well. Maybe well enough to clear his own trail."

Roxie's brow furrowed. "A whole trail no one else knew about?"

"He likely had connections with the other park rangers. Or maybe worked out a deal with them. Something to get them to look the other way."

"But his grandpa has been dead for over a decade. A trail like that would have grown over by now, wouldn't it?"

Skylar was prepared for the argument. "Tristan's cousin also has a record for dealing—it looks like there's criminal activity all over the Riley family tree. Keeping the trail cleared would be beneficial for him, too."

Roxie shook her head. "This is still just speculation. Conjecture."

"Until we find the path," Skylar said.

"We?" Roxie said. "You kicked me off the investigation, remember?"

"Only because you were so convinced of Tristan's innocence—"

"I still am convinced of his innocence." She said it through a tightness in her throat. A holdout of doubt that grew just a little more with each unanswered text and phone call. Every day Luke Riley continued to walk free, and every time Jackson glanced at her over his shoulder like he was waiting for her to pounce.

Skylar looked at the ceiling and pressed her palms hard into her eyes, like she was so exasperated with Roxie now that she was trying not to explode. "You've been so hung up on his alibi, and I finally found a potential way around it. I'm not saying that I'm sure about it, it's just a theory. But you won't even test it out with me? Maybe the reality is that you're afraid I'm right. You don't want me to prove that he's guilty because of your feelings for him."

"That's not—"

"God, Roxie, your crush on him has been obvious for *years*. And I know you're desperate to believe he stayed in Whistler after graduation because he's waiting for just the right moment to profess his undying love for you. But he's had plenty of chances, and he hasn't even kissed you yet. He's probably just hanging around here long enough to make sure his tracks are covered. He doesn't give a shit about you, so stop protecting him."

Roxie was speechless for a few moments, until the heat of embarrassment in her cheeks turned to anger. She took a step closer to Skylar, refusing to let her make her feel small.

"You're the one who can't see past your feelings," she said. "You've been consumed by grief for a year, Skylar. And you have every right to be. But you've hardly been able to function. Do you really think you're capable of thinking clearly now? Objectively? I think you're just desperate for a real monster to blame after battling the ones in your head for so long."

Skylar huffed in disbelief. "Jesus. Just because I'm the only person in this town who gives a shit about Colin doesn't mean I'm crazy."

"I only went along with this investigation in the first place because I was so worried about you. I was desperate to bring you back to reality, and looking into the murder seemed to be the only way to—"

"Stop. Don't act like you care about me. You probably couldn't wait to ship me off to Yale so you could add Colin to your stupid little ghost tour without me finding out."

Roxie's anger became a scorching thing in her throat. She could hardly breathe, hardly get out the words, "You honestly believe I would do that?"

"Why wouldn't you? You like turning our family's tragedies into jokes. Fueling the rumors about the Clark Curse."

"If you'd ever taken an interest in the tour, or me, you'd *know* they're not jokes to me. I want to feel connected to our family instead of being ashamed of them, the way you are." Roxie jabbed a finger in Skylar's chest. "And you don't get to resent me for doing things I enjoy while you spend all your time trying to tear other people down with bullshit accusations—"

That's when Skylar pushed her.

Roxie and Skylar had gotten into plenty of fights before, but that usually just meant shouting at each other, and when they were younger, maybe some pinching while Grandma's back was turned, or a well-placed bite.

But now, Skylar shoved her hard against the wall.

The shock was so intense that Roxie froze for a moment, gaping at her sister.

Skylar glared back, breathing hard, her eyes narrowed. Not sorry.

"Do something about it," she said through her teeth. "I *dare* you."

So Roxie did.

They were on the floor, a tangle of limbs, kicking and scratching and hitting and rolling, letting loose everything that had built up in them over the past year—frustration, betrayal, isolation, hopelessness, loss, and grief. They didn't hold back. Roxie left a deep gouge on Skylar's face with her fingernails and buried her knee in Skylar's stomach. Skylar busted Roxie's lip with her elbow and pulled at her hair.

Both had tears glimmering on their faces in the lantern light.

Some of Roxie's came from physical pain, but most were an overflowing of heartache that had been building in her chest for she didn't even know how long. Missing Colin. Loving Tristan. Feeling helpless as the gap between her and her sister only seemed to grow wider every day.

She wanted to ask Skylar about what *she* was feeling. Wanted to know what this past year had really been like for her, locked away in her room and in her head, nobody else allowed in. But she'd never had any idea how to even begin those kinds of conversations with her sister. They'd shared clothes and hand-me-down shoes, cartons of fries at the mall and tubs of popcorn at the movie theater, and even a bed when they were little and Skylar cuddled up with her, saying she was going to protect her from the thunderstorms when Roxie suspected her sister was actually the one frightened of them.

But they couldn't talk about what was burning up inside them, so they lashed out at each other instead, inflicting more and more damage, and they probably never would have stopped if they hadn't rolled into something hard. And then there was the shattering sound of glass all around them.

It snapped them out of it, like someone had dumped a bucket of cold water over them. They got up slowly, having to brace against each other because they couldn't put their hands against the floor without cutting their palms.

"The mirror," Roxie said, her voice cracking. Her gift from Colin, destroyed.

It wasn't just the glass that had broken but the ornate wooden frame as well, cracked and splintered all the way down one side.

Roxie was brushing glass off her clothes, cursing under her breath as tiny shards stuck to her fingers like burrs, more frustrated tears springing to her eyes at this fresh loss, when Skylar whispered, "What is that?"

Following her sister's gaze, Roxie looked closer at the broken mirror. Behind fractured bits of glass, there was a layer of wood, which she thought was the back of the mirror. But then she saw what Skylar was looking at—a patch of wood they'd knocked out toward the bottom. Through it, she should have been able to see the damask wallpaper on the other side. But she didn't.

Skylar reached her hand through the hole. "It's a false back," she said. "There's a compartment down here. And—"

When she drew her hand back out, she was clutching a crumpled wad of cash in her fist.

There was a beat of silence. And then, the Clarks snapped into motion, glass crunching under their shoes. Roxie hardly noticed now when the sharp grains scraped her fingers as she helped Skylar lift the heavy mirror from the wall and lower it to the floor. They felt around the edges of the back, undoing the clasps that held it in place. Then, together, they pulled it open.

At first, Roxie wasn't sure she was seeing what she was seeing. But then, Skylar brought the lamp closer, and it was unmistakable.

The back of the mirror was jammed full of money.

Skylar said something. At first, Roxie was too stunned to register it. "What?" she asked, blinking.

"I said, *count* it."

Skylar tore off her jacket, swiping it over the floor to clear away enough glass for them to kneel. They both grabbed handfuls of crumpled bills, every denomination from ones to hundreds, smoothing them out over their knees and counting them into haphazard piles.

Skylar finished long before Roxie did, and she ran to get her backpack, pulling out her notebook and flipping frantically through the pages.

The second Roxie put down her last bill, Skylar demanded, "What did you get?"

Roxie took a shuddering breath. "$14,763."

"I got $20,089." It only took a few seconds for her to calculate in her head. "That's $34,852 together." She held her notebook out to Roxie with a shaking hand. "Look how much was taken from the bank."

Roxie knew what it would say, but she checked anyway—$34,852.

There was another beat of silence, while they considered what that meant.

"Tristan gave you this mirror," Skylar said. "He committed the robberies, and stashed the money in here, then passed it off on you so he wouldn't be caught with it, but he'd know how to access it when he needed to. This just confirms everything I've been telling you!"

"Tristan gave me the mirror *from Colin*," Roxie reminded her. "Which lines up with *his* story—that Colin was hiding the money from his dad. Tristan must not have known what was in here when he gave it to me."

Skylar threw up her hands in frustration. "You're going to insist I have every single piece of this damn puzzle before you believe it, aren't you? You'd rather protect Tristan than believe in your own sister."

Roxie sighed. "Skylar, that's not how it is."

Skylar waved her hand, dismissing whatever Roxie was about to say. "If that's what you need me to do, then that's what I'm going to do." And then, without another word, she grabbed her backpack and walked out the door.

Leaving Roxie alone, kneeling in the middle of enough cash to buy her a whole fleet of old tour buses.

She let herself live in that fantasy for just a moment before she swept all the bills into an empty decoration box and went to hide it in one of the long-forgotten rooms upstairs. She'd ask Skylar what they were supposed to do with it later.

26

Grandma had a Halloween date.

Gertie had been resistant to the idea at first. It was with Marvin, who owned the accounting firm across the street from Smith & Laurel Café, and he was known for being competent, responsible, and boring.

But he'd begged and begged for her to give him a chance to sweep her off her feet at a special Halloween performance of *Phantom of the Opera* in Indianapolis. Finally, with some encouragement from Roxie, she'd relented.

"I still don't know about this," Grandma said while she waited by the door. "Two whole hours with him in the car and at least an hour of dinner, and the show has an *intermission* . . . Just because we're the only two single folks over seventy in this town who can still touch our toes doesn't mean we're a good match."

"I don't think *I* can touch my toes," Roxie responded, which led to both of them giving it a try—Grandma's fingers trailed the floor, and Roxie's barely brushed her shins. Skylar rolled her eyes at them, refusing to participate, but after relentless chiding, she gave it a shot. She made it farther than Roxie, down to her ankles, but only at the price of pulling a muscle in her shoulder.

Without discussing it, the girls had agreed not to let Grandma find out about their fight. Roxie had managed to cover her wounds with makeup, and Skylar explained away the scratch on her cheek by saying she'd run into a tree branch.

When it came time to go, Grandma was still wishy-washy, asking the girls if they were certain they'd be okay on their own, assuring them she would keep her phone on vibrate through dinner and the show if they needed her to leave early for anything.

They told her over and over again that they would be fine— Roxie had a tour, and Skylar was planning a low-key night watching movies on the couch, passing out candy to trick-or-treaters who rang the doorbell.

Grandma fished out some cash for them in case they wanted to order a pizza and gave each of them a lingering kiss on the cheek. Then she was out of stall tactics, and there was nothing left to do but paste on a smile and walk out to the curb to meet Marvin, who had already opened the passenger door of his station wagon for her.

The girls waved goodbye from the porch. Once the car was out of sight, they both went back into the house and shut themselves in their rooms without a word to each other.

Roxie didn't have time for any more arguing. It was only five o'clock, and her tour wouldn't start until eight, but she was heading to the party straight after, and she still needed to pull together the most important element of the whole night—her costume.

☽

"Nice shoes," Skylar said.

Roxie was sitting in front of her vanity mirror and spied her sister's reflection above her shoulder, leaning against the doorframe.

Roxie's black, spike-heeled boots laced all the way up to her knees, little red pom-poms hot glued all over them. But that was the least of the costume she'd crafted.

She'd gone full-on creepy clown. Taking her makeup inspiration from Pennywise, she'd painted her face ghostly white, with red stripes slashing vertically through her eyes and curving around her cheeks like she was crying blood. She'd put in yellow contacts to give her irises an unearthly glow and gathered her hair into pigtails, dipping the ends in red dye. She wore a fitted white dress she'd found at an antique store, faded almost to yellow, with a flared skirt she'd spent the previous night sewing her own red stripes onto. Then came her crowning achievement—it had taken every spare second, but she'd managed to paint a row of massive, fanged teeth that covered the entire bottom half of her face.

"A little elaborate for a tour," Skylar said.

Roxie turned back to her mirror, using a fine-tipped brush to smooth out a few finishing touches. "I'm hosting some guests at Ward Manor. Didn't you see the decorations I put up yesterday?"

Skylar crossed her arms over her chest. "No. I was a little distracted."

Roxie eyed her sister in the mirror, almost apologizing for the scratch. But she stopped herself—Skylar hadn't apologized for her swollen lip either.

Instead, she told her, "You're invited. If you want to come."

"No, thanks. I'm busy tonight, too."

Refusing to rise to the bait, Roxie didn't ask what she meant by that.

"I hope this party goes better than the last one," Skylar said. Maybe sarcastically, maybe sincerely. Roxie couldn't tell.

When she turned to go, Roxie spoke up before she could think better of it.

"Wherever you're going, just be careful."

Skylar met her gaze in the mirror and smirked. "I'll start being careful when you do." Then she was gone.

And Roxie thought that perhaps they were cut from the same cloth after all.

☽

As exhausted as Roxie was from throwing together her impromptu party over the last twenty-four hours—not to mention thinking about her fight with Skylar and the implications of what they'd found in the mirror—she wasn't about to slack off when it came to her tour that night. Halloween was the finale of her season, with no more tours until next September, so she always poured her heart into making it special. She was fully booked, and all her patrons had come prepared, wearing costumes and glow sticks, eager to be entertained.

And Roxie was ready to give them an experience unlike anything she'd done before. Because tonight was the night she'd decided to debut her tour bus.

Tristan had done an excellent job with the black paint on the exterior and the stenciling of the tour's name down the sides and above the windshield, but he'd left the interior mostly untouched, knowing she'd want to make it her own. And even with everything going on over the past month, she'd made the time to do just that. If she had to sum up her vision, she would say she'd been going for the design aesthetic of a cozy, vintage train carriage—*after* it had been ransacked by a pack of werewolves.

She had hung tattered red curtains over the windows and made claw marks all over the upholstered seats. She'd found a gold-patterned carpet at the Resurrection Emporium and cut it into strips to lay down the center aisle then squirted countless bottles of fake blood all over it. She'd found a few stained-glass shades that she mounted over the lights, diffusing a soft, eerie glow. The ceiling was a tapestry of fake cobwebs and plastic spiders. And the spot behind the driver's seat was permanently reserved for Roxie's lovely assistant—a plastic skeleton wearing a flapper dress, feather headband, and pearls, whom she had affectionately named Frannie Phantom.

The addition of the bus also meant she could treat tonight's guests to one more surprise—a new stop.

She'd never included the old stone bridge on her tour before because it was too far from the other locations to walk to, even though it was one of Whistler's most popular haunted attractions.

When Roxie had googled *cry baby bridge* for the first time, she'd learned there were towns all over the United States with similar stories. Some of them involved a woman throwing a baby born out of wedlock off the bridge then jumping off in a fit of guilt. Others chronicled an unfortunate car accident with children in the back seat. And others told of young lovers running away with their little girl bundled in their arms, only to slip on a layer of ice and fall together to their deaths.

As the legend went, if you stopped your car on the bridge in the middle of the night and put it in neutral, the ghost of a child would slowly push you across.

Skylar, of course, had been more than happy to put a damper on Roxie's excitement when she'd first heard the story. *The bridge isn't level*, she'd told her. *There's an incline—slight enough that you can't tell just by looking at it but enough to move a car forward.*

Roxie couldn't deny the logic. But it didn't explain why the sound of a young girl crying could often be heard on a cold, clear night.

She'd been determined to find out more about the bridge's history. She'd convinced Skylar once to sneak out of the house with her after dark, and they stood right in the middle of the bridge until they heard it for themselves—thin and faint and sorrowful.

It's the creek water running under the bridge, Skylar insisted. *The stone makes it echo. That's all.*

It doesn't sound like water to me, Roxie had argued.

That's your brain tricking you, matching itself to the story, making you hear what you expect to hear. Brains do that stuff all the time.

But, even in the dark, Roxie had seen the unsettled look on her sister's face. Perhaps her brain was playing the same tricks on her. Both of them had run the entire way home.

Roxie wondered if maybe there was something to what her sister had said—maybe there were so many similar stories about bridges all over the country because it had been told so many times, spread to so many towns, that people started seeing and hearing spirits where there weren't any.

But it turned out she should have been looking for the origin of Whistler's crying-baby bridge story in her own home. Because the girl that had been haunting it for seventy years wasn't dead yet.

Grandma Gertie had lived in a house right next to the bridge. And when she was a girl, her mother had been dying of cancer. Gertie had put on a brave face every day to help take care of her mother—bringing her meals she wouldn't eat, singing her songs she didn't seem to hear, or reading her books she couldn't focus on through the haze of pain medicine. But then, every night, Gertie would hide under the bridge and bawl her eyes out, wailing as loudly as she wanted to, hoping the sound of the creek would keep her father from hearing up at the house.

What she hadn't realized was that one of the neighborhood boys had walked across the bridge once while she was crying in the dead of night. He hadn't seen her in the dark. So he'd gathered up his friends, telling them he was sure he'd found a ghost and made them come and listen to her for themselves. They spotted flashes of her pale dress. She'd only learned she was being watched when one of the boys ran away screaming.

Grandma Gertie had laughed when she'd told that part of the story. *He was the biggest, meanest boy in my class at school, and I'm pretty sure just the sight of me reduced him to tears.*

Even though she'd stopped going to the bridge to cry after that night, the legend had already taken on a life of its own, and to this day, brave kids still ventured there to listen for her voice and look for her in the dark.

Roxie had been given Grandma's permission to tell the true story on the tour if she wanted to. But in the end, she'd decided against it. Because while all ghost stories are tinged with sadness, this one was just too heavy for her to share.

The idea of falling victim to the Clark Curse was a horrible thing to contemplate. But what she thought must be even worse was to see someone you loved perish while you got left behind— which was the same lesson her sister had learned the hard way, after Colin died. It had been happening to Gertie her whole life. First she'd lost her mother and sister. Then her first daughter, Violet. Then the girls' mother, Katherine.

Maybe the sound that still lingered at the bridge was just the echo of the creek running underneath it, like Skylar said. But Roxie thought that maybe even without a death, pain might linger the same way a soul did. And Gertie Clark had experienced more than her fair share, pieces of her broken heart scattered all over this haunted town.

Still, after all that, Gertie always hummed when she did the dishes and danced while she baked cookies and hugged the girls hard each night before bed.

Because Roxie had decided to keep this particular story to herself, she parked the bus on the bridge and just let the group wander for a bit, exchanging stories of the times they had been there before, and what they'd seen or heard, and what they imagined it all meant.

But that night, the creek crawled along quietly, no crying to be heard. And Roxie hoped that was a sign Grandma was having a better time on her date than she had expected to, the pain of the past left behind for an evening.

Once everyone was back on the bus, Roxie put it in neutral and let the phantom of the sad little girl her grandmother had been push them onward, into the night.

27

Roxie arrived late to her own party. When she finally pulled her tour bus into the woods and steered it toward Ward Manor, she found the usually clear path was clogged with so many cars, she had to park in the trees and walk. She could hear the thrum of music before the house came into view—and when it did, she couldn't help the satisfied smile that quirked her lips.

She hadn't really needed the affirmation, and sure, most of them were only here because it was a secluded place to drink and party undisturbed, but the ten-year-old in her still felt validated nonetheless.

There were people everywhere—milling around a bonfire someone had built in the clearing, sitting on the steps, or dancing inside the house, shadows pulsing behind the broken windows. All of them were holding red cups, laughing, touching, swaying, talking loudly over the music.

She could hardly fit into the house. All at once, the girl who was too creepy to have friends had too many, packed from wall to wall, the floors shaking with their feet and the bass from the speakers. She felt it through her boots, vibrating up her legs. Someone had figured out the fog machine she'd dropped off before her tour, and the mist curled around the room, making the whole scene feel more like a dream.

She was caught in a wave of people, drowning at the center of an ocean of limbs. So she went with it, matching the rhythm of the waves. As much as she prided herself on being an entertainer, she had zero experience dancing, but there was too much going on for anyone to notice how bad she was. The more she moved, the easier and more fluid it became.

People talked to her who had never spoken to her before, their slurred voices rising over the noise. *YOUR COSTUME IS SO FREAKY,* and, *HEY, AREN'T YOU THAT GIRL WITH THE GHOST TOUR,* and, *I NEVER BELIEVED IN THAT DUMB CURSE ANYWAY.* They were bolder with the cold night air filtering in and the booze blazing warm down their throats. They touched her makeup and poked at her dress, marveling at the details. Roxie didn't even mind when she started to sweat so much that her fangs began to smear.

She didn't know how long she danced, swirling around the floor in a delirium of fog and dizzying heat. At some point, her grandmother texted her and Skylar to let them know not to wait up—apparently, Marvin had turned out to be less boring than she'd thought.

She was feeling good, listening contentedly to two girls shouting about how cool her collection of crystal-eyed skulls was, when she spotted the couch at the center of the throng.

One end was being put to good use by a couple making out,

pushing aggressively against each other, like they couldn't get close enough—which made her grateful she'd remembered to cover the couch with a sheet. On the other side, there was a boy sitting by himself, slouching and looking miserable.

"Jackson?" Roxie yelled over the music.

He had a beer in one hand, his other pressed over his eyes. She had hoped he would come so she could ask him some questions about his odd behavior lately, but now, he looked so miserable that Roxie felt bad for lying just to get him here.

She squeezed onto the couch beside him, wedging between him and the couple that seemed to be trying their damnedest to swallow each other, and she yelled in his ear, "I'm glad you made it!"

Jackson took his hand from his face, but instead of looking at her, he stared straight ahead, into the mirror hanging on the wall.

It had taken hours last night after her fight with Skylar, but she'd painstakingly managed to salvage some of the larger slivers of glass that were still intact and reconfigure them in the mirror's frame like a puzzle, gluing them into place. The final effect was even more stunning than before, she thought, the red twinkle lights dancing off the cracks. With a sudden stroke of inspiration, she had found an old tube of red lipstick at the bottom of her bag and used it to write on the glass, *She's right behind you!* in homage to the legend of Lucy Clark.

Jackson stared at the words painted over his fractured face and still didn't speak.

"Are you okay?" Roxie yelled over the music.

He looked over at her finally and started to say something, but he stopped to grimace when he saw her makeup. "Holy shit."

"Thanks," she said. "Skylar isn't here. I'm sorry you came for nothing."

Jackson shook his head. "It's probably best I don't see her anyway."

"Okay, then," Roxie said. "Do you want me to give you a ride home?"

"I don't want to go yet."

Roxie frowned. "I distinctly remember you saying once that parties are for *people who wanted to drink away the sorrows of their wasted lives.* Or something like that."

Jackson tipped his almost-empty beer bottle at Roxie, like a salute. "And that is precisely why I'm here." He took another drink. His nose wrinkled at the taste, but he forced it down anyway.

Roxie watched him. Then she noticed four other bottles on the floor beside his feet. "Have you ever had alcohol before?" she asked.

"I drank champagne with my parents when I scored a thirty-five on the ACT," he said.

Roxie gently extricated the bottle from his stiff fingers and set it on a beer pong table someone had set up behind the couch. "Someone with a thirty-five on the ACT doesn't have a wasted life."

He scoffed. "What the hell do you know?"

Roxie pursed her lips and nodded. "All right, then," she said, standing, ready to rejoin the party. She'd invited him here to get information out of him, but this wasn't shaping up to be a productive conversation.

Jackson sighed, grabbing her hand and pulling her back down beside him. "I'm sorry. I don't mean to be that way. I've never known how to *not* be that way." He shook his head, leaning forward with his elbows on his knees. "No, that's not entirely true. I'm an asshole on purpose sometimes. I've learned it makes it a lot easier to beat someone when you act like you're so much better than them from the start."

His speech was slurred, eyelids heavy, cheeks blazing red, and his forehead sheened with sweat. He looked like he was about to throw up or pass out, but he rallied himself again and went on, "Except that tactic never worked on your sister. It was impossible to rattle Skylar. No matter how cocky or condescending I was, no matter how many nights I stayed in the library later than her to prove I worked harder, trying to get inside her head. It never made a difference. Not even a little bit." He shrugged. "I couldn't beat her. So I fell in love with her. She was—"

"Why are you talking about her in the past tense?"

He ignored her, not looking at her, like she wasn't even there. Making his confession to a room too loud for anyone else to listen.

"She was brilliant and beautiful, and we were perfect for each other. That's what I thought. That's why I had to do something. I *had* to. She was going to throw away her whole life on that loser."

He made a choking sound then and covered his face with his hands.

Roxie's fists clenched on her knees. The *loser* he was referring to had to be Colin.

"What do you mean you *had to do something?*" she asked. When he didn't answer, she made an effort to soften her voice, putting a soothing hand on his shoulder, even though she wanted to grab him and shake the answer out of him. "Jackson, what did you do?"

He sat up, dazed and blinking, opening his mouth to say something. But he stopped himself abruptly, like he'd hit a brick wall. He was staring over Roxie's shoulder.

Roxie turned and saw Tristan making his way through the crowd. It looked like he hadn't spotted them yet—he was headed in the direction of the kitchen, probably looking for a drink.

Then Jackson jumped off the couch before pushing his way through the crowd and toward the door.

"Wait!" Roxie shouted after him, trying to follow.

But then Tristan was there, stepping in front of her, offering a crooked smile and a beer. "You're not heading out, are you?"

Roxie stared over his shoulder for a moment, trying to find Jackson again, but he'd been swallowed by the sea of dancing bodies. She refused the drink, shaking her head. "I just—Jackson is acting weird. I need to—"

"Let him go," he said, his expression darkening at the mention of Jackson's name.

Roxie pushed past him anyway. Jackson had gone in the direction of door, so she ran to the front porch, his words making her head spin. *I had to do something.*

She peered all around the yard, lit by the dying embers of

the bonfire, but he was nowhere to be seen. Tristan came up behind her. "What's the matter? What did he say to you?"

With a frustrated sigh, Roxie said, "Nothing. He was pretty drunk, and I'm just worried about him getting home okay." She paused before she added, "I think you scared him off."

"Me?"

Roxie shrugged. "He must still be afraid of you, after the fight."

She paused, waiting for him to jump in with more of an explanation, but he only replied with, "Maybe."

"So what are you doing here? And more importantly, where the hell have you been? I've been calling you for days."

"I'm sorry about that," he said. "I've just been . . . trying to figure stuff out." He looked down at his boots when he added, "I haven't talked to the police yet."

"Why not?"

"Because . . . well, I called Suzanna to let her know what's going on, and she freaked out on me when I said I was going to turn him in. She got really upset, started begging me to reconsider. I didn't let her change my mind, but still, I know the police are going to want proof of the accusations I'm making against him. I thought I'd try to find some first. I don't even have the money from the robberies to show them, and—"

"I do," Roxie said.

He stopped short. "What are you talking about?"

She grabbed his hand and towed him back into the house, pushing through the mob of dancing bodies to the mirror hanging on the wall. "It broke already?" he asked.

Roxie watched his face as he looked at the mirror. According to Skylar's theory, he gave it to her knowing the money was hidden in the back—trying to push it off on her so he wouldn't be caught with it.

But his surprise seemed genuine when she pulled it away from the wall and showed him the compartment behind it. She guided his hand to it so he could feel the opening for himself. "It was stashed back here. All $34,852."

She was thankful he didn't ask how the mirror had been broken, not wanting to explain her fight with Skylar.

But he grabbed her by the wrist and said, "Where is the money now?"

The intensity of his gaze stopped the words in her throat for a moment. And his grip on her was just a little too hard.

"Why?" she asked. "What do you want with it?"

He must have caught the sudden uneasiness on her face, because he let her go, putting his hands in his pockets. "I was just thinking—I can take it to the police," he said. "Maybe this is the proof I need to get Dad put away. They won't believe he committed the robberies if he doesn't even know where the money is, but now that we have it, it will all make a little more sense."

She tilted her head at him, looking straight into his eyes. For some reason, he seemed to be having trouble meeting her gaze when he asked again, "So where is the money now?"

Just then, Roxie's phone buzzed in the pocket of her dress, sparing her from giving him an answer right away. She glanced at the screen. "My sister," she said. "I'll be right back."

She hurried outside, dodging another couple making out on the stairs as she went into the yard, trying to get farther away from the music. "Hello?"

She heard Skylar's voice but couldn't make out her answer. A large group had started a heated cornhole tournament on the lawn, taunting and cheering and making it impossible to hear. "Hold on," she said into the phone and hurried out to her bus before shutting herself inside. "Okay. What did you say?"

"I think I found it." Skylar sounded out of breath.

"Found what?"

She answered with a curse, and then there was a muffled clatter, like she'd dropped her phone. "Skylar?" she said a few times before her sister responded. "What happened?"

"I fell," Skylar said. "It rained here last night. Mud everywhere."

"Mud? Where the hell are you?"

"In the woods."

"What woods?" Roxie said, peering through the trees like Skylar would turn up at any moment.

"In Ohio. Behind Tristan's cousin's house," Skylar said matter-of-factly.

"*What?*"

With a deep sigh, Skylar said, "The one thing you kept getting hung up on was Tristan's alibi. Right? That he couldn't have possibly made it back to Whistler in time to be at the Emporium that night or commit the murder. So I came here to find the shortcut through the woods that would make that possible. And I think I've done it. I'm walking on it right now."

Roxie started up her bus while Skylar spoke, feeling it rumble to life around her. After inching out from between two other cars and trying not to hit any trees, she started down the path toward town. "Send me your location," she said. "You shouldn't be out in the woods alone at night. It's too dangerous."

"I found the paths Tristan and Colin must have ridden their dirt bikes on as kids," Skylar pressed on, as though she hadn't heard her. "They were mostly overgrown and not very long, and they all looped right back to the house. But this one is different. I've been walking on it for thirty minutes now, and it's still heading southwest, toward Whistler. It's wider than the others, and someone has definitely been keeping it clear. It's mostly straight, too, so he could have been driving his dirt bike at top speed the whole way."

By the time Roxie pulled out of the woods, the streets were completely quiet and deserted, all the trick-or-treaters safely at home, probably counting their candy and negotiating trades with their siblings, the way Skylar and Roxie used to do. "You're not going to find any tracks or hard evidence now," she said. "It's been months."

"You're right," Skylar said. "But I don't need to. All I need is to figure out if there's a path that leads from his cousin's house to the highway and calculate a rough estimate of how much time it could have saved him. I just need to prove that Tristan getting there in time to kill Colin is *possible*. That way, his alibi will fall through, and the police will have to make him a suspect again."

"Walking a path that long could take hours on foot," Roxie

said. "And it's pitch-black out. Not to mention freezing. It's not safe."

"I don't care," Skylar said.

"Just come back to Whistler, and I'll go with you another day."

"I'm not waiting around any longer for you to see the truth," she said.

"Skylar, come on, I—"

But her sister had already hung up.

With a frustrated growl, Roxie pressed harder on the gas, speeding through the empty streets. Talking to Tristan and figuring out what the hell was going on with Jackson would have to wait. She needed to go find Skylar.

She didn't see another soul as she navigated out of town— anyone in Whistler who was still awake was at Ward Manor right now. She shook her head, which had started throbbing while she was on the phone. After hours of dancing and yelling over the music—not to mention processing everything Jackson and Tristan had said, and now Skylar—she was running on fumes.

Leaving the town limits, she shot down a dark stretch of road between two cornfields. A stop sign flashed red in the dark ahead of her, so Roxie pressed on her brakes.

And nothing happened.

The bus kept rushing forward, ignoring her command. Roxie lifted her boot and pressed down again, harder. Not really expecting a different result but hoping wildly for one anyway.

Nothing. Her brakes weren't working.

That fact took a few precious seconds to process. The bus

wasn't going to stop unless something made it stop. Something like the massive tree at the end of the street.

The bus shot through the intersection.

With just a few yards to spare, Roxie snapped into motion, yanking on the door handle. It sprang open and she tumbled out, hitting the asphalt hard. She rolled, knocking her head on the ground, her skin ripping open along her left hip and shoulder and temple, hot blood mixing with the grit of the road.

She was too dizzy to see, but she heard her beloved new tour bus crash into the tree. She covered her ears as the glass shattered and the engine gave a final dying roar, before it went silent in a plume of smoke.

Roxie held very still for a few moments, squeezing her eyes shut as the world stilled around her. She turned her gaze inward, assessing the sensations from her toes to the tips of her fingers. Her scoured skin hurt like hell. But everything still seemed to work. No damage that wouldn't heal, as far as she could tell.

She got up slowly and brushed off her dress, which was torn almost completely up one side. She saw the blood gushing there, staring at it like it belonged to someone else.

She scanned the street to see if anyone had witnessed what had happened, but it was still empty. The crash had been loud enough to rattle her brain, but she must have already been too far away from town for anyone else to hear it—or maybe the residents of Whistler just knew better than to investigate strange noises on Halloween night. Either way, no one came.

Roxie patted her pockets, but they were empty. Cursing, she

realized her phone must have gotten lost in the crash. Though she wasn't sure who she could call anyway. Skylar wasn't close enough to help, and Grandma would fly into an absolute panic. Maybe Tristan could drive her to the hospital—

A wave of blackness overtook her for a moment, and she pressed her palms hard to her eyes, trying to keep steady. Maybe jumping out of the bus had caused more damage than she'd thought.

She went around to the front and peered inside. A low tree branch had busted through the windshield and skewered the headrest—the exact spot where her head had been a few moments ago.

Just a few more seconds, and Roxie would have been dead. Her stomach lurched at the realization.

A phone. She needed a phone. Her house wasn't too far, and Grandma had stubbornly held on to her landline, even after all the times the girls had teased her for it.

She turned toward home, limping under the light of the Halloween moon, leaving bloody footprints in her wake.

28

Grandma wasn't home from her date yet when Roxie got there, though she decided that was probably for the best—she would have had a heart attack if she'd seen her granddaughter covered in blood, staggering through the door.

At least someone is having a fun Halloween, she thought as she glanced at the clock above the oven and saw it was just past midnight.

Before she called anyone, Roxie went to the bathroom first, using the mirror to assess the damage, dabbing gingerly at the wound on her ribs with a wet rag. It looked even worse than it felt, and she grabbed handfuls of paper towels to staunch the flow of blood, holding them in place with one hand as she rummaged in the cabinet under the sink for the first aid kit. She found a roll of gauze, and with plenty of wincing and cursing, she managed to lift her dress and wrap her chest a few times, slowing the flow of blood. For now.

And, while she was patching herself up, a thought occurred to her that she didn't like: What if someone had cut her brakes on purpose?

If Skylar were here, Roxie knew exactly who she'd be pointing her finger at first.

Tristan had been at the party. He would have seen her bus parked in the woods and easily could have tampered with it without anyone noticing. And he was the one to give it to her in the first place—if he knew how to fix it, that meant he'd know how to break it, too. What if her best friend, the one she'd been so staunchly defending against her sister's accusations all this time, had just tried to kill her?

But Jackson had been at the party, too. And he'd been acting so strange, guilt for something he'd done wrong clearly weighing on his mind. Roxie didn't think he knew anything about cars, but he knew about pretty much everything else, so why not?

She'd been pushing them both for answers. One of them could have decided she'd started pushing too hard.

Or maybe the investigation had made her start seeing monsters where there weren't any. It was an old vehicle, and old vehicles broke all the time—she was just grateful it hadn't happened during the tour and no one else had gotten hurt.

She shook her head, trying to clear the fog of exhaustion and pain, and went to work on cleaning a gash in her leg. She'd just ripped another bandage with her teeth and tucked in the loose end when she heard the front door open.

She poked her head out of the bathroom and peered into the

kitchen, expecting to see Grandma. But the one who rushed through the door—cheeks flushed, hair disheveled, eyes wild— was Tristan.

His gaze locked on her. "You're alive," he said.

"Against all odds," Roxie said back.

"You left in such a hurry. I got worried, so I tried to follow you, but I didn't see you parked at home, so I went driving around and I saw—I saw the bus crashed into the tree, and I thought— Jesus, Rox, I thought—"

He couldn't finish. Instead, he closed the gap between them with just a few strides and pulled her tightly to him.

She tipped her head back to look at him, to say something, but whatever it was left her mind completely when he bent and pressed his mouth to hers.

She was finally kissing Tristan Riley.

He hadn't shaved in a few days, and she felt the stubble, rough against her lips. His mouth was so warm and urgent, his hands against her back pressing her even closer, his arms enveloping her completely.

There was a tinge of relief in the kiss, too, the kind that only follows fear—a reassurance that the worst had almost happened, but it hadn't, and thank God it wasn't too late.

She'd been fantasizing about this very moment for so many years, staring out classroom windows and imagining what it would be like, but the reality of it was so dizzyingly beyond what she'd thought it could be, and for a moment, her whole body sang with it.

But then the pain of his tight grip around her waist cut

through the euphoria, and she yelped against his mouth, and he let go, stepping back. "I'm sorry," he said, his breath ragged, his hands tense at his sides. "I'm sorry. I shouldn't have done that."

"No," Roxie said too quickly. "I mean—*yes*, but—I got makeup all over you."

The paint from her fangs had come off in a grayish smear around his mouth. But he didn't seem to care. He was too busy staring at her dress—torn and caked with blood. The bandages wrapped around her side had also started to turn red.

Panic flashed in his eyes, and Roxie felt guilt squeeze her heart. All the pain he went through when he lost his brother, and she was still making him worry about her all the time.

She stepped forward to touch his arm, to reassure him that she was fine. But she stumbled, the room spinning. He had to catch her.

"We need to get you to a hospital," he said, and before she could respond, he'd swept her up in his arms. He carried her back out into the cold night, buckled her into the passenger seat of his truck, and then sped away from the house.

Roxie leaned her head against the window and closed her eyes, her stomach lurching with the car's movement. But she opened them again when Tristan said, "I almost killed you."

She turned to took look at him. His hands were white-knuckled on the steering wheel. His eyes burned red.

"*I* fixed the bus up for you. But I clearly didn't do a good job. This is all my fault. I almost *killed* you, Roxie."

"But you didn't," Roxie said, reaching across the console to wipe away some of the paint she'd smeared on his cheek.

She felt awful for suspecting him of cutting the brakes on purpose earlier, even for a second. This was the Tristan she knew—always there for her, ready to do whatever it took so he wouldn't have to lose anybody else. He'd never hurt her. Just like he never would have hurt Colin.

"I'm getting back at you anyway, because I'm bleeding all over your seat."

The corner of his mouth ticked upward, just slightly. But the hint of a smile vanished when she winced in pain as they hit a pothole.

There was a long stretch of silence. Roxie looked out the window as he sped down the road, where she knew there were more cornfields, but it had gotten so dark, it was just an endless sea of black.

Then she looked back at Tristan and asked, "How long have you wanted to kiss me?"

In an instant, his face and neck flushed a deep shade of red. He coughed. "You want to talk about that now?"

"Might as well," she said. Then she leaned closer to him and added, "Before the Clark Curse *really* comes to get me."

He smirked. "Fine. I've wanted to since . . . maybe a week after I met you?"

She gasped, mock scandalized. "We were *children*."

"I was *twelve*."

"You're right. Practically a man."

He thought it over for a moment before he finally said, "I think it was that time I saw you ride the Banshee fourteen times in a row."

For a moment, Roxie didn't know what he was talking about.

Then the memory came back to her—the field trip to Kings Island. It had been for fifth and sixth graders only, so Skylar couldn't go. But that hadn't dampened Roxie's excitement, even if it meant an hour-and-a-half bus ride sitting alone.

"Colin was sick that morning, and I wanted to stay home," Tristan said. "I didn't think it would be any fun without him. But Suzanna made me go because she'd already paid the fee. When we got there, everybody split off into their own friend groups, and I was by myself. I was self-conscious about it. I thought I'd look really pathetic and sad if I went on rides by myself. So I got a slushy and found a bench in the shade to sit on, and I was just going to wait it out until it was time to go home.

"But then I saw you, getting in line to ride the Banshee, all alone. And it didn't make you seem pathetic at all." He gave a little laugh. "I wish you could see the way your face looked, every time you ran to get back in line. I swear, nobody else in that goddamn park was having a better time than you were that day.

"You were enjoying yourself so much, I thought you hadn't noticed me sitting there staring at you like a creep. But then you walked over, and you held out your hand to me, and you said, *Are you just going to keep watching me having fun, or are you ready to come have fun with me?*"

"And you finally got on the ride with me," Roxie said. "So tell me—were you thinking about kissing me *before* or *after* you threw up?"

"Definitely both."

Roxie laughed, even though it made her ribs throb with pain.

And that's when they both heard the muffled *ping* of an incoming text message. Tristan frowned, twisting in his seat to dig in his back pocket. "I forgot—I found this on the ground at the crash site before I came to find you."

He handed Roxie her cell phone. The screen was shattered, but when she pushed the home button, it lit up. Still working. And she had dozens of notifications—all from the same person. Roxie sighed.

"What is it?" Tristan asked.

"Skylar," she said.

"What does she want?"

Roxie typed in her pass code. "Who knows. She's probably just . . ."

Her voice trailed off into silence.

The first text said, Where are you?

The next said, Please tell me you're not with Tristan. If you're with Tristan, you need to get out RIGHT NOW.

Tell me you're safe.

Call me.

Then there was a voice mail. With a suddenly unsteady hand, Roxie hit Play and pressed her phone to her ear.

I found Suzanna Riley's body, was the first thing her sister said.

Roxie kept her face carefully blank, her eyes on the road ahead.

She was off the main path, Skylar went on. Her voice, usually so sure and steady, sounded like it might quiver to pieces. *I saw a shoe, stuck in the mud, almost completely covered. I thought it was weird that someone would just leave it there. They would have had to walk all the way home barefoot. So I yanked it out myself to get a good look at it. And I recognized it—a blue, Nike tennis shoe.*

Roxie listened to Skylar take a deep, shaky breath.

Colin got them for his mom for her last birthday. I helped him pick them out. They were Suzanna's, I was sure of it. And she was wearing those shoes the day she packed up her car and left Whistler. I remember. I watched her leave from my bedroom window.

It was an effort for Roxie to keep breathing, the weight of panic settling on her chest.

I searched the area, trying to see if I could find the other shoe. I went into the woods, in the direction it looked like she must have been going. And it—it didn't take me long to find her. And . . . she wasn't in good shape. I think she's been here a while.

"Roxie?" Tristan said beside her. "Everything okay?"

Roxie forced a smile and a slow, calm nod while she listened to Skylar say, *Tristan killed her, Roxie. I know you don't want to believe it, but he took this path to Whistler to kill his brother, and then Suzanna must have found out somehow, and he murdered her too and hid her here. This trail isn't on any maps—Tristan is one of the few people who even knew it existed. It's the only thing that makes sense. I'm with the police now, and they're out looking for him. If you're with him, I need you to get away now. He's dangerous. And there's no telling what he'll do when he realizes we're closing in on him.*

Roxie hung up the phone.

"She wanted to talk my ear off about some book she just finished," she told Tristan. "Something about peapods? She's into the weirdest shit. I'm sure I won't hear the end of it for months."

Her voice sounded too thin to her own ears. She was sure the lie was written all over her face.

But Tristan smiled and said, "Sounds like the old Skylar to

me. I didn't think it was possible, but I'm glad she's acting like herself again. You were right not to give up on her."

"I'm happy, too," Roxie said quietly. She had her hands in her lap now, and he reached over and took one, giving it a squeeze. She squeezed back, trying to pretend absolutely nothing had changed in the past couple minutes.

She did her best to muster a casual tone when she asked, "You said earlier that you talked to your mom. You know, about turning in your dad. Right?

Tristan nodded.

"When was that?"

He shrugged. "I don't know. A couple of days ago, I think. Why?"

"I just hadn't heard you mention her in a while. How is she? Is she still in Florida?"

"Yep. I think she's all right. She told me she's been enjoying all the sun."

"Hmm," Roxie said.

They lapsed into silence again.

The way Skylar had described the body, there was no way that anyone had spoken to Suzanna in the past few days. He was lying right to her face.

Skylar's accusations against Tristan had seemed so impossible from the beginning. Not just because she didn't think he was capable of murder but because his alibi had been solidly in place from the beginning. But now that Skylar had found the path in the woods, that certainty had crumbled.

Roxie guessed they were another ten minutes from the

hospital now. But ten minutes has a funny way of stretching out when you might be sitting a breath away from a murderer.

She glanced at him again and again, her heart thumping in her throat, her hands gripping her knees. He didn't look cold or bloodthirsty. He didn't look like someone who would stab his own brother to death. Or someone who would kill his stepmom and stash her body in the woods.

He looked the same way he always had.

Her head was spinning. How could she have been so wrong about him? She had such a good feeling for people, could draw out their stories with nothing more than an old photograph or a few lines in a newspaper. And she *knew* Tristan.

Or she'd thought she did. And her certainty—her arrogance—had led her here.

"I'm going to call Skylar back and tell her to meet us at the hospital," she told Tristan.

Skylar picked up on the first ring. "Roxie. Are you okay?"

"So, don't freak out," Roxie said, "but I had a bit of an accident." Skylar started to speak, but Roxie cut her off. "I'm fine. Or I will be. I just need you to meet us at the hospital."

Skylar paused for a moment. "Us?"

"Tristan is taking me," Roxie said, keeping her voice neutral.

"Tristan?" Skylar snapped. "Didn't you get my message? He—"

"We'll be there in five."

And then Roxie hung up.

Skylar was smart. She would understand Roxie had to pretend nothing was wrong while Tristan was listening in. She would tell the police, and they'd be at the hospital to meet them. And then this would all be over.

She leaned her head back against the seat and closed her eyes to hide all the emotions warring inside her—fear, anger, betrayal. But most of all, a deep, deep sadness that burned her eyes, tears threatening to give her away.

"Hanging in there?" Tristan asked.

Roxie didn't trust her voice, so she just nodded.

He held her hand the rest of the way there, until they pulled up to the emergency room doors, and he got out of the car and ran around to her side. He eased her out, wrapping her good arm around his neck. Gentler than she ever knew he could be, his grip never faltering, never squeezing too tight.

She limped with him toward the door. She could hear sirens now, getting louder, but that wasn't unusual at a hospital.

"You're going to be okay," Tristan said, his lips pressed to her ear. And then her tears finally did spill over. "I know it hurts," he said. "But I'm going to get you taken care of."

They were about to walk in the door when the first cop car screeched to a stop behind them.

There was yelling. Someone screaming at Tristan to get away from her and put his hands up.

Roxie turned and saw the guns pointed at them. At him.

More cop cars pulling up. More guns.

He looked at Roxie. She couldn't even feign surprise.

"I'm sorry," she said. And she was, even though she knew

she shouldn't be. He'd murdered his family. He didn't deserve anyone's sympathy.

So then why did she still feel it? Why did she want to tell the police to leave him alone? Why did she want to whisper in his ear that if he ran, she would run with him?

He was looking around, bewildered, blinking against the brightness of the hospital lights and the ones flashing on the police cruisers. But Roxie grabbed him hard by the shoulders, forcing him to look at her.

"Tristan Riley," she said. "If you have ever been my friend, you'll tell me the truth right now. Did you murder Colin and Suzanna?"

He stared at her.

"Tristan," she said again, ignoring shouts from the police officers to step away from him. "Just tell me the truth."

She knew how bad things looked for him. But if he told her now that he was innocent, against all evidence to the contrary, she would believe him. She held his gaze, just short of begging. *Please, please, just tell me you're innocent.*

Tristan opened his mouth. But then he closed it again. With each second of silence that ticked by, she felt her heart break a little more.

Please, please, please.

But he didn't deny the accusation. Instead, his face hardened. Turned cold. And in that moment, for the first time, he finally looked like a killer.

Tristan slid his hands around her waist, his grip tight. Roxie's heart felt like it was kicking in her chest. Maybe he was going to take her hostage so he could get away. Or maybe kill her like Suzanna and Colin—one final act of violence to feed some well-hidden, sick need in him, before they locked him away forever.

But Tristan didn't do either of those things. Instead, he let her go. And then he raised his hands to the sky.

29

It was morning. Finally morning. The girls hadn't slept all night.

After Roxie had gotten her wounds stitched up, she'd gone to the police station and met Skylar, who'd greeted her with a change of clothes and open arms. They'd held each other on the steps for a long time, Roxie starting in on a million apologizes, practically begging her big sister to say *I told you so*, but Skylar cut her off every time. *It doesn't matter. It's all okay now.*

They'd gone through round after round of questions, while all of theirs went unanswered. They told the police about the awful things Tristan's mother had said to him at the funeral home, the way he'd been lying about her whereabouts, the security footage of the dirt bike near the spot where Colin's body was found, the secret path behind the Riley property, and the money they'd found in the mirror. But the girls had no idea what was happening to him, where he was, or what he was saying.

The sky had flushed pink with dawn by the time Grandma

took them home to get some rest (though she had some pointed questions of her own concerning their whereabouts last night and made a few vague threats about punishments for lying to her). Roxie had gone straight to her bedroom when they got back, closed the blinds, curled up under the covers, and shut her eyes to the world. But after two hours of fidgeting and relentless thoughts flitting behind her eyelids, she'd wrapped a blanket around her shoulders and decided to get some air.

She was going to sit out on the front steps but found them already occupied. Skylar had showered and changed but apparently hadn't been able to sleep either. When she heard Roxie open the door, she looked up from the book she had open in her lap.

Which, despite everything, made Roxie smile. Most of their lives, it had been rare to catch her sister without a book. It was one of the few things the girls had in common, though Skylar didn't have the time or patience for the kinds of stories Roxie gravitated toward—which usually involved monsters, romance, or both. Skylar only wanted to read things that were true, like dense biographies, essay collections, case studies, and long-form journalism. And she always had a highlighter and pen to take notes in the margins.

The tome she had in her lap now looked thick and heavy enough to anchor a ship. Roxie sat beside her and turned it over to look at the cover, only to realize she recognized it—it was the same history of Yale she'd been reading when Colin died.

"I restarted it," she said.

Roxie nodded and refrained from commenting. Of course,

she was dying to know if she'd picked the book up again because she'd changed her mind about going back to Yale, but she knew that now wasn't the time to be pressing her sister with questions about the future when they'd barely had time to process the events of the past twenty-four hours.

The morning was cold and gray, and Roxie noticed Skylar shiver with the breeze, hugging the book close to her chest. She lifted the edge of her blanket before wrapping it around both their shoulders. Skylar leaned into her gratefully.

"Grandma talked to her friend who works at the police station," she said. "Tristan hasn't confessed to anything yet. But I think he'll fess up eventually. He'll realize he doesn't have a choice. There's no point in fighting now. The least he could do is make this whole process quick and easy. For everyone's sakes."

Roxie nodded, offering a tentative smile to mask the tangled knot of feelings wedged under her ribs. She'd felt sick since last night, ever since she had asked Tristan if he'd killed his brother and Suzanna. In all the years she had known him, she had never seen a look on his face like the one he'd given her. It had chilled her to her core.

"She also said the cops got the money from where you hid it at Ward Manor," Skylar said. "And they drove by Luke Riley's place to question him, but it looked like he was already long gone."

Roxie huffed, completely unsurprised. "Now that the money is the with cops, he's run out of reasons to stick around," she said. "So much for family."

Why he felt Tristan owed him that money in the first place

was another unanswered question. Had Tristan been honest when he'd said Luke was the one who'd committed the robberies? Or maybe he helped Tristan with them somehow? With Luke gone, they wouldn't know until Tristan gave them a new story. And there was no telling if it would finally be the truth.

"I'm sorry," she said to Skylar, though she'd already said it dozens of times. "If I had believed you from the start, we would have caught him a lot sooner."

Skylar laughed. "Are you going to keep apologizing for that forever?"

"Maybe."

"I'm sorry, too," Skylar added, taking Roxie by surprise. "I know I've been a little . . . obsessive these past couple of weeks. I know I wasn't always making sense. I know all I had to go on was a gut feeling most of the time. Just because it all turned out to be true doesn't mean you didn't have a right to question me. And—" She took another deep breath. Eased it out. "It doesn't mean I had any right to say the things I said to you. About your tour. I know you've never done it to be mean. I know you've never made fun of the people in your stories. I know you care. And I know you've worked really, really hard on it."

Roxie felt tears prick at her eyes. Again. She'd cried so many times since last night. She managed to keep them in check as she said, "It's okay."

Skylar went back to reading. Roxie stared out at the mostly empty street. It was Saturday, and most people were still in bed, tired from a night of trick-or-treating or partying in the woods. Roxie groaned inwardly, thinking about the shape Ward Manor must be in now. The best she could hope for was that everyone had done their puking in the woods instead of the house.

She stole a few glances at her sister's face. Roxie knew the events of last night had been traumatic. Just hearing her sister's description of Suzanna's body, which had been in a state of advanced decomposition, made her shiver. And before Skylar had come to the police station to endure interrogation, she'd been hiking miles through the muddy woods. There were hints of exhaustion in the dark circles around her eyes and the drawn look of her mouth.

But still, all things considered, she looked okay. Or like she was finally on the path to being okay.

Which was why Roxie didn't want to bring up what was still bothering her. Because while Skylar might finally be ready to let the past rest and step into the future, there was still one loose end that hadn't been resolved.

"Jackson said something weird to me at the party."

Skylar's finger paused on the page as she looked up.

"He told me he did something. Something he needed to do to stop you from throwing your life away on Colin. But he left before he told me exactly what it was."

Skylar shrugged. "It wasn't murder. We know now that. He probably just said something shitty to him and feels bad that he never got the chance to apologize. Whatever it was . . . well, honestly, does it really matter at this point?"

Roxie bit her lip. "I guess not."

Still, the words wouldn't stop swirling in her head.

Skylar hadn't seen the look on his face—the weight of the guilt pressing down on him.

But she was right. Whatever it was he felt so bad about, Colin was beyond forgiving him now.

⟆

Roxie managed a few hours of sleep that night, but she was woken before dawn by a strange, unsettling dream.

In it, she had walked into the kitchen to find a woman with long, wet hair sitting at the dining table. Her dress, which stretched to her ankles, was completely drenched, dripping brown water, a huge puddle spreading on the floor beneath her. And when the woman turned to look at her, Roxie knew the moment she saw her face—gray and bloated with creek water—that it was Aurora Clark.

And then, her head had started to slowly spin.

Every time the face came back around, it belonged to another Clark woman. Eleanor, with the slit throat. Becca, eyes wide with the glow of headlights and the bottom half of her face smashed nearly flat. Analise, turning purple as she choked. Aunt Violet, the side of her head leaking blood. Roxie's mother with shards of windshield glass stuck in her eyes.

There were other women, too. Hundreds of them that she didn't recognize as the heads spun faster and faster, like a top, until they were just a formless blur.

And then abruptly, the spinning stopped. And Skylar stared back at her.

Roxie rushed forward, relieved her sister didn't look like the others. She was whole. Unhurt. Alive.

You're safe, Roxie told her. *Nothing bad is going to happen to you. I won't let it.*

But then the floor started to shake. And pieces of the roof

began to fall in clouds of dust and plaster. Water burst from the sink and between the tiles and through the cracks in the cabinet doors.

Roxie put her arms around Skylar, both of them crying because she'd been *wrong, wrong, wrong, wrong*—no matter what she did, no matter how hard she tried to stop this, no matter how much she loved her sister, she couldn't keep the world from ending.

30

"Grandma, do you think our family is really cursed?"

Roxie was at the kitchen table with her cold hands wrapped around a warm mug of coffee. She sat in the exact same spot where Skylar had been in her dream last night. But the roof, thankfully, was still intact, and her sister was sleeping soundly upstairs.

Grandma was busy making breakfast, the window over the sink just starting to glow with morning light. She didn't say anything for a moment, taking her time as she slid the eggs from the skillet onto two plates and brought them to the table. Then she sat across from Roxie, and Grandma said, "Why do you ask?"

Roxie shrugged, popping a yolk with the tip of her fork. "I was just thinking. I took my tour to the bridge on Halloween."

"Oh," Grandma said with a little smile. "Could you hear me?"

Roxie shook her head. "Not this time. But whenever I'm there, it always makes me remember how much you've been through. So I can't help thinking . . ."

"That we *must* be cursed."

Roxie nodded, taking a bite as she waited for Grandma's answer.

Finally, the old woman said, "A lot of bad things have happened to me, true. But a lot of bad things happen to everyone. And the ones who haven't experienced much hardship or sadness in their lives . . . well, the unfortunate truth is that it simply hasn't happened to them *yet*."

"You've seen the family tree, though," Roxie said. "Clark women seem to have worse luck than most."

Roxie had drawn it out numerous times, and it never painted an optimistic picture. There were exceptions, of course—Grandma Gertie being one herself—but many of her female ancestors hadn't lived to see forty, their years cut short by accidents and illnesses. And the occasional murder.

Grandma gave a sigh. "Death does love a Clark," she said. "But there are other tragedies one can endure, and they don't always make the headlines. Every family in the world knows suffering, I can tell you that. Ours is just easier to pinpoint, I suppose. You know, whenever something bad happens, people like to believe it happened for a reason. That's why men have been making witches out of women for centuries—crops die, lightning strikes, babies don't last the winter. So they find someone to blame, and they burn her to ashes, because they can't face the fact that sometimes, horrible things happen, and there is no explanation for them and no stopping them from happening again. Just like people in this town don't want to believe death will come for them or the ones they love. They say we're cursed, and they're not, and they think that will keep them safe."

Roxie rested her chin in her hand. "I guess that makes sense. It's just—well, it's easy to *feel* cursed lately."

She tried to hide the tears that sprang suddenly to her eyes, turning her head away. Grandma reached across the table and covered Roxie's hand with hers.

"You miss Tristan, don't you?" Grandma said.

Roxie nodded, pressing her lips together. "I'm not supposed to miss a murderer. But I do." She said it in a whisper, not taking any chances that her sister might overhear upstairs.

She shouldn't be this miserable. The mystery had been solved. And the most important thing to come out of all this was that she finally had her sister back, even if she wasn't the same as she had been before.

Roxie wasn't the same anymore either. How could she be, with Tristan gone?

"You don't miss him, sweetheart," Grandma said. "You miss the person you thought he was."

"I just don't understand how I could have been so stupid. I was so *wrong* about him, Grandma. Right up until the very end. I thought—"

She thought she was in love with him. But she couldn't admit that out loud, so she just shook her head.

"We were all wrong about him, darling. Myself included," Grandma said. "He never gave me any reason not to trust him.

He always showed up on time. Never complained. He wasn't exactly friendly with customers, but that was fine so long as I kept him in the back. He was a hard worker. I sent him to the bank with deposits all the time, and there was never a penny missing. I wonder if maybe he wasn't always what he is now. If something changed him. Either way, I feel awful for encouraging him to pursue you."

Roxie frowned. "You did?"

"Well, it was evident he had feelings for you. So I told him to be honest with you about them. But I was afraid he was too shy to ever say anything to you directly, so I bought him some nice stationery for his birthday, just to give him a little push. I know sometimes it's easier to express your feelings in a letter than—"

"Wait," Roxie said.

She paused. Blinking against tiredness as she processed what her grandmother had just said so casually. Like a set of stationery wasn't exactly what had spawned the whole investigation in the first place. But Grandma had no way of knowing that— the only people who knew the breakup note existed were her, Skylar, and Tristan.

"*You* were the one who bought him the stationery?" Roxie asked.

"I was. Did he show it to you? I never would have pushed him to admit his feelings for you if I'd had even an inkling that something wasn't right."

She remembered the thick paper the breakup note had been written on, with *Riley* printed in cursive at the bottom. Skylar had known it was a birthday present, but up until now, they had no idea who it had come from.

Finding that out had never been a priority in Skylar's investigation, because a forged breakup note wouldn't be strong enough evidence to take to the police. That explained why she hadn't wasted the energy on it as she pursued more solid leads.

Or maybe she hadn't *wanted* to look too closely into the note. Because she'd decided it wasn't from Colin, that it couldn't possibly be real. The idea he would ever break her heart wasn't something she could face—so she hadn't.

Roxie told herself it didn't matter now whether Colin had really broken up with Skylar or not. She had no reason to dig deeper. The only thing it could bring was more pain for her sister.

She shouldn't ask. She shouldn't dig. She shouldn't. The murderer had been arrested, and the letter was in the past. It was time to move on.

But she found the question rising to her lips anyway.

"Grandma. Is there any way Colin could have gotten his hands on a piece of that stationery before he died?"

"No," Grandma said, and Roxie sagged with relief for a moment.

But then Grandma went on, "He didn't need to take any of Tristan's. Because I gave him some of his own."

Roxie felt as though she'd just walked over a grave. Like the ground was rumbling beneath her feet, fists pounding the underside of a closed coffin lid.

Like the ghosts they thought they'd laid to rest still had something to say.

"He was so proud of Skylar when he found out she got into Yale," Grandma went on. "But I could tell it made him nervous, too, even though he never told me he was. Long-distance relationships aren't easy. Of course, he'd be worried about staying in touch. So I gave him the stationery and told him he should write to her." She shrugged. "I know Skylar has never been much of a romantic, but I thought it would help him keep things interesting."

She wasn't wrong—it had certainly made things interesting all right.

This didn't mean beyond a shadow of a doubt that Colin had written the breakup note. But Skylar had been so certain it was completely impossible. It was that certainty that had spurred her to launch an entire investigation. The same certainty Grandma had just shattered.

And if Colin *had* broken up with Skylar—why?

Did it have something to do with what Jackson said at the party? Could Jackson have been the cause of the breakup somehow? And if he was, could that have been the reason Tristan beat him up? But why would Tristan defend his brother when he'd just killed him?

The questions whirling in her mind were making her feel dizzy suddenly. She pressed her forehead against the table and squeezed her eyes shut.

Grandma leaned down and pressed a reassuring kiss to her temple. "You've been through so much, my dear. But you will survive it. And you will be happy again."

"Clark women aren't exactly known for being good at surviving," Roxie pointed out, which made Grandma laugh.

"Well, there are three Clark women left, aren't there? It doesn't matter what the others have done before—*we* get to decide what it means to be a Clark now. Isn't that exciting?"

Roxie groaned.

31

Jackson's house was on the opposite end of Whistler from Roxie's. It was the side reserved for the doctors and dentists and lawyers, with immaculate lawns and picket fences. The kind of people who would never dream of running to Target in pajama bottoms and a messy bun, even if all they needed to get was butter.

Roxie was sure Jackson usually fit in just fine. But the boy who answered the Mowerys' front door that evening looked like he'd wandered into the wrong house.

He looked sick. His cheeks had a feverish flush to them, the skin under his eyes puffy, like he hadn't been sleeping. His hair was wild as an untended garden.

The boy who usually seemed to operate at a higher frequency than anyone else moved like he had syrup in his veins. He had opened the door slowly and blinked at Roxie, taking a few seconds to process who she was. And once he did, he dropped his gaze—not with the arrogance of someone who thought he was too good to give her the time of day but with something that looked more like shame.

No one knew Roxie was here. She didn't tell Skylar about the stationery belonging to Colin—she didn't want to break her sister's heart over nothing. She'd get to the bottom of Jackson's strange comments and tie the loose ends, just to be sure. Then she'd move on, and Skylar would never have to know.

Her plan had been to get right down to it—no more vagueness or evasions. She would grill Jackson for an explanation, put the pressure on until he caved and explained what he was hiding from her.

But instead, she just watched him for a few moments.

She'd always been confident in her ability to read people—though that skill had failed her spectacularly when it came to Tristan. But, looking at Jackson now, something told her that putting pressure on him wasn't the right move. So, instead, she asked, in a soft voice, "Are you okay, Jackson?"

At first, it seemed like he hadn't heard her. She almost asked again. But then, all at once, his face crumpled. His shoulders started to shake, and his chest hiccuped with quiet sobs. "No," he got out between them. "No, I'm not."

He stepped outside with a quick glance behind him, probably to make sure his parents didn't notice. Then he shut the door and sat on the porch swing. Roxie joined him, her toes grazing the ground as they rocked slightly forward and back.

"Tell me what's bothering you," she said, her voice just barely above a whisper, like he was a rabbit in the woods she was trying not to frighten off.

He *wanted* to tell her. She could see it in the way his

shoulders slumped, like his secrets had become too heavy a burden to bear, and he was ready to pass them to someone else to carry.

His eyes were wet, red-rimmed, when he finally met her gaze.

"I can't," he said.

"Why not?"

"Because I love Skylar," he said.

"You think the truth is going to hurt her somehow?"

"I know it will. She won't be able to take it, Roxie."

She felt a little light-headed as something like fear pulsed through her.

"Maybe she doesn't need to know," Roxie said.

"That's what I thought. That's why I went to all this trouble to keep it a secret. But now—now Tristan is in jail." He buried his face in his hands. "I don't know what to do."

"Are you saying Tristan *shouldn't* be in jail?"

He didn't respond.

"Jackson," Roxie whispered, putting a hand on his back. "I can tell this has been hard for you. But you don't have to do it alone anymore. Let me help you. Tell me what you know, and we can decide what to do about it together. Okay?"

Slowly, he lowered his hands from his face and looked at her.

"If you have a reason to believe Tristan is innocent, we can't just let him rot in prison. No matter what secrets you're keeping, or how you think this is going to protect Skylar, it isn't worth ruining his life over something he didn't do."

After another agonizing stretch of silence, Jackson finally said, "Tristan didn't kill Colin."

Her heart pounded. She gripped the edge of the bench, hard, so her hands wouldn't shake. But she wouldn't get her hopes up just yet.

"How do you know?" she asked.

He took another long pause.

And then, he started his story.

"I got paired with Colin on the summer volunteer project at the Humane Society. I knew before we even started that he wasn't going to be very helpful—I'd seen him slack off in every class we shared. But I'm used to taking over group projects and doing everything on my own. I prefer it that way, actually, because I don't trust anyone with my grade but me.

"It wasn't a surprise when he showed up a half hour late most days. And I wasn't shocked he skipped out on almost all the actual work, usually chatting and laughing with the lady at the front desk while I scooped shit and cleaned cages and handled all the feedings. But I was filing some adoption paperwork in the back one day when I overheard a conversation he was having with one of our supervisors.

"He was going on and on about how him and Skylar were going to get married someday. How they were going to have four kids. How she was going to be *doing something with her genius brain* while he opened a construction company. And . . . it made my blood boil.

"I couldn't bite my tongue. I *had* to shatter his grand delusions. So, when we walked out to the parking lot at the end of the day, I stopped him by his car and told him he'd never have the money to start his own business, and even if Skylar gave it to him with what she made with her *genius brain* job, he'd just

297

waste it all anyway, because he wasn't smart enough to run a business. And who the hell was going to take care of all those kids while he was squandering her money? Skylar?

"He just shrugged at me, barely listening. But I still couldn't leave it alone. I thought I couldn't let Skylar throw her life away on someone who wasn't an equal to her. Someone who would never push her to fulfill her greatest potential. I was convinced *I* was the only person capable of doing that. And that Colin Riley sure as hell wasn't. I convinced myself I had to do something. For her sake."

Roxie tried not to let any judgment show on her face. She just nodded and waited for him to go on.

"I told him he wasn't right for Skylar. That he was only going to drag her down into the dirt with him if he didn't let her go. That she would never be able to do all the things she was meant to do. I told him he didn't realize how brilliant she was, how important she was going to be.

"He didn't say a word at first, just listened while I berated him, probably waiting for me to tire myself out so he could go home. But I wanted to get a rise out of him. I kept going, getting into his face and telling him he was destined for minimum wage or unemployment checks."

Roxie felt any sympathy she might have had for Jackson shrivel in her chest. But she kept her mouth shut and waited for him to give her more.

"Finally, he started to fight back. He told me I didn't know anything. That he'd never drag Skylar down, and he'd do whatever it took to be a man who was good enough for her.

"And I laughed. I laughed right in his face, and I told him, *Well, you'd better get something figured out soon before she goes off the Yale and realizes the world has a lot more to offer her than you do. Maybe go get some tips from your dad—because the only way you're ever going to have anything is by stealing it from somebody else.*"

"You knew about his dad?"

"I might have done a little nosing around, when Colin and Skylar started dating." He shrugged. "I was looking for reasons to talk Skylar out of it. I told her his dad was an ex-con, thinking that might scare her off. But she didn't care—she already knew anyway."

He glanced at her from under his lashes, waiting for her to tell him what a piece of shit that made him. Roxie just pressed her lips together, nodding for him to go on.

"That last part really got to him," Jackson went on. "He pushed me. Told me to mind my own goddamn business. Then he got in his car and drove away.

"He didn't show up for his next shift at the Humane Society. I wasn't surprised. But I was a little shocked when I asked our supervisor what excuse he gave her. She told me he was going to visit his father at the prison.

"I didn't really think much of it, at the time. I thought it was a lie to cover up the fact that he couldn't face me, because he knew that I was right.

"But then . . . then the first robbery happened a few nights later. At the gas station."

Roxie had been nervously digging the tips of her fingernails into the wood of the bench, but when he said that, she froze.

"And then the second robbery, at the coffee shop," he said. "I didn't—I didn't really think there was any way Colin had actually taken my joke seriously. But I ran into Skylar at the library not long after. She was with one of her friends, showing off this new pair of shoes she said Colin had surprised her with."

Roxie remembered Skylar's daisy necklace. She'd wondered vaguely at the time where he'd gotten the money for it. And he'd bought it around that same time.

She said quietly, "You think Colin committed the robberies?"

"I started to suspect it. But not seriously. And once I heard about the one at the bank and how the robber killed Mr. Patterson, I decided there was no way it could be him. Even though I didn't think much of him, I knew he wasn't a killer.

"But, by then, he'd stopped showing up for volunteer work almost entirely. He missed five shifts in a row but managed to come to our very last one. And that's when I told him I was going to inform Mrs. Bell that he hadn't participated enough to receive credit. I'd already completed the essay component of the project on my own, and I said there was no way in hell I was putting his name on it.

"I knew Skylar would be angry with him. I waited for him to beg me to change my mind. But he didn't. He just said, *I guess you were right about me.* Then he got back in his car and drove off.

"I finished my shift and went home. But—well, I couldn't stop thinking about it, for some reason. Colin hadn't looked good when I saw him. Tired. Stressed out. I don't know, I just got the feeling that he had a lot going on, and I was just making it worse. I felt bad."

It's called having a conscience, Roxie thought. *And you should have felt bad a hell of a lot sooner than that.* But she kept the thought to herself.

"So I decided to stop by his house and tell him I'd changed my mind. I'd let him put his name on my report.

"But when I pulled onto his street, I saw Colin's car heading the other way. Toward town. I figured he was probably picking Skylar up from work at the Resurrection Emporium. And to be honest, I saw it as an opportunity. I'd follow him there, and I'd get to save the day right in front of her. She'd know it was because of my generosity that he'd get credit and graduate on time. But I was going to make it clear I wasn't doing it for him. It was out of respect for her."

Roxie closed her eyes for a moment to hide how hard she was sure they were rolling.

"So I followed him. But he didn't drive to the Emporium. He turned before he got there, pulling off into an alleyway and cutting his engine.

"I could tell he was up to something. But I had to drive past without stopping so he wouldn't notice I was following him. I found a parking lot a little farther down, and then I went back on foot.

"He was still sitting in his car. I crouched behind some bushes across the street and watched him. I thought maybe he was waiting for someone. How perfect would it be if I caught him cheating? I'd film the whole thing, and then I'd have the proof to show to Skylar. I'd be her shoulder to cry on. So I got out my phone, and I started recording."

He pulled his phone out of his pocket now, his hand shaking.

"And I still have the video."

As he pulled it up, she had the sudden urge to tell him not to show it to her. Because once she knew the truth, there would be no unknowing it.

But she didn't stop him. And he pressed play.

The screen showed the back of Colin's car parked in the alleyway, taillights off. No movement for a minute. Until finally, the driver's side door opened. Colin stepped out, his reddish-brown curls flashing on-screen for a moment. Until he covered them with a black ski mask that he pulled down over his face.

Black boots. Black pants. Black shirt. Black gloves.

Roxie took in a sharp breath, covering her mouth. Then she stole a glance at Jackson. He wasn't watching the video—he'd probably seen it hundreds of times by now. He was watching her reaction to it. And there was a sadness in his gaze that told her it was only going to get worse.

The street was mostly dark. All the businesses had closed for the night, including the Resurrection Emporium. From Jackson's point of view, it looked like Skylar had already locked up and left. Most of the lights were off, and Skylar was supposed to have gone home almost an hour before. But Roxie knew she was in there, tucked in the back of the building and reading her book about the history of Yale by the glow of the lamp behind the desk.

But there was no way Colin could have known that. Skylar said they hadn't spoken all afternoon—she'd been too angry with him for slacking off on his volunteer work.

Roxie watched Colin dig in his pocket for a moment, and he pulled out his key. Gertie had let him have one because he helped out often enough at the shop. Skylar had told her she *thought* she had locked the door but assumed she must have forgotten because the robber pushed it right open.

She hadn't forgotten. Colin hadn't needed to break in.

He disappeared from view as he stepped inside.

Roxie couldn't see what happened next. But she knew from Skylar's story.

She'd seen the robber come in. In a panic, she'd pulled the gun from under the desk and fired while he ran away.

Even though Roxie was expecting it, she still flinched when she heard the gunshot.

She watched Colin run back outside. He turned the corner around the building right beside the Emporium, the Morning Glory Diner, and disappeared.

"I waited for a few seconds to see if Skylar would come out," Jackson said.

But she didn't. She was ducking behind the desk, calling the police.

Then Jackson got up to follow Colin, running behind Morning Glory.

"I wanted to see if I could catch up to him. I wanted a clear shot of his face, so I could show all this to Skylar later. So she'd know beyond a shadow of a doubt it was him."

Because even with everything that had just happened, breaking them up was still at the top of his mind. At least he had the decency to look ashamed about it now.

The camera shook erratically as he ran. Roxie could hear his heavy breathing. The picture went light and dark, light and dark as he passed under the streetlights.

The screen went completely black as he ran around the side of Morning Glory. Roxie couldn't see anything until a single light came into view, mounted over the kitchen door, illuminating a dumpster.

And stretched out on the ground beside it was Colin.

His mask was torn off. He was heaving breaths in and out. His eyes were rolling with panic. And a bright pool of blood was spreading underneath him, coming from a hole that had been ripped through his shirt.

No. That didn't make sense. Skylar had said the bullet had missed him.

Roxie saw him only for a second. Then there was a blur of motion and darkness again.

"That's when I dropped my phone," Jackson said.

But it was still recording.

"Oh my god, oh my god, oh my god," Jackson was saying. "Holy shit, holy—uh, I—okay, I'm gonna call an ambulance, it's gonna be—"

"*No*," Colin said, his voice sounding thick. Like he was choking on something. "No, don't tell anyone. Skylar can't find out. It'll kill her if—"

He started coughing, the sound wet and shuddering and full of pain.

"If you love her like you say you do, you won't let her find out."

"But, Colin, I—"

More coughing.

"Tristan is on his way to the house—" Colin could barely get the words out. "Get Tristan—"

And then a succession of horrible sounds—choking. Gasping. A faint whimper.

Silence.

After a few moments, she could hear Jackson muttering, "Shit, shit, shit, shit, shit, shit, *shit*!" Then he picked up the phone, and she saw his face for a moment—pale with panic and shock—and the video ended.

Roxie didn't know at what point she'd started crying. The tears were coursing down her face and neck, blurring her vision, making her voice hoarse as she said, "I don't understand."

"Tristan didn't kill Colin," Jackson said again, his voice faint, still holding the secret tight in this little bit of space, just between them. So Roxie was the only one who could hear when he spoke the terrible truth: "Skylar did."

32

"No," Roxie said, shaking her head, even though there was no denying it. She'd seen it all unfold right in the video. "Skylar said she missed. She hit the wall."

Jackson nodded. "She did. But the walls of the Emporium are made of concrete. The bullet ricocheted and hit Colin as he was turning to run out the door. It was a freak accident."

"But he was killed by a knife, not a bullet. I saw the body myself."

Jackson rubbed at the back of his neck. "We were afraid that if the cops knew it was a bullet that killed him, they'd be able to trace it back to Skylar too easily."

"We?"

Jackson nodded. "After Colin was dead, I—I had no clue what I was supposed to do next. Couldn't think. But I could hear sirens coming. Skylar had called the police right after Colin ran off. I didn't have time to process or weigh my choices. But I knew

Colin was right—It would kill Skylar if she found out what she'd done to him. So I made a snap decision. I found his keys in his pocket. His car was closer than mine, and I could carry him behind the Emporium to get him there instead of crossing the street to my car and risking being seen. So I shoved him in his own trunk and took his advice—I went to find Tristan so he could help me figure out what the hell we were supposed to do.

"It was about 10:25 when I got back to the Riley house. Tristan pulled up on a dirt bike at 10:30. He found me standing in his driveway, covered in blood, and I had to tell him his brother was dead."

Roxie couldn't imagine what a shock that must have been for Tristan. How painful. Her stomach twisted at the thought.

"If he showed up on a dirt bike, that means he did take the shortcut back to Whistler from his cousin's house," Roxie said. "Why was he in such a rush to get back? Did he know something had happened?"

"He said Colin called him earlier that night. He sounded off. Kept saying he was sorry and calling himself a fuckup. Tristan asked him what the hell he was talking about, but he wouldn't say. He could tell something was wrong. Really wrong. So he told Colin he was coming home, and he got back here as fast as he could."

"He didn't know Colin was committing the robberies?"

Jackson shook his head. "It was all news to him."

"And he helped you cover up what really happened? He went along with all this?"

Jackson shrugged. "It was his brother's dying wish. And he

didn't have much time to think about it. We had to work quickly. We drove him out to the cornfield and laid out the body. Then we dug out the bullet and used a knife to make it look like he'd been stabbed. We probably overdid that part a little—we were worried about the bullet fragmenting inside of him, shards of it dispersed around the wound. So Tristan basically cut out an entire side of his stomach. He looked like he wanted to vomit, but he got through it. I don't know how.

"We were worried about DNA evidence on the body and in the surrounding parts of the cornfield we'd been in. Not to mention our footprints. Which is why we brought matches and a can of gasoline. The fire didn't burn long enough to destroy his body completely, but it got the job done.

"And then . . . there was nothing left to do but go back to the house. Tristan left on the dirt bike right away to get back to his cousin's before he was missed—he knew he'd be one of the first suspects, and he needed to secure his alibi. But we got our story straight before he left. We were going to tell the police Colin had been at my house from 8 to 10:10. The break-in at the Emporium happened at 10, and we didn't want the cops to consider that it could have been Colin. It also made for an easy explanation—the break-in happened around the same time as Colin supposedly left my house, so it looked like a wrong place, wrong time situation. Like he crossed paths with a robber making his getaway.

"After Tristan left, I went home. Changed clothes and burned the bloody ones in the fireplace. I didn't go to the funeral. Didn't try to get into contact with Tristan at all. But about a week later, he showed up at my house while my parents weren't home. He wanted answers—particularly about why I'd been following Colin around in the first place. So we sat right here, and I told him the truth. And then . . ."

"That's when he beat the shit out of you."

Jackson winced. "Right. He might have killed me, if one of my neighbors hadn't been walking by and jumped in to pull him off." He hung his head. "It's probably what I would have deserved."

Roxie didn't bother to agree or disagree with that statement. She didn't have the brain space to comfort Jackson about his mistakes or even to make her own judgments about whether this had really all been his fault.

Because now she had to decide how to tell her sister that she'd accidentally murdered the love of her life.

And then there was Tristan. God, Tristan. She'd been helping her sister investigate him for weeks, lying to his face, snooping around behind his back—and ultimately, getting him arrested. All while he was doing everything he could to protect her sister from finding out the truth.

She needed to talk to him. She needed him to fill in the last gaps of the story. More than that, she needed to beg him to forgive her for turning her back on him.

And just then, her phone rang.

Roxie saw her sister's name on the screen. She didn't answer it—she wasn't ready to talk to her yet. But a few seconds later, the ringing started up again.

"Skylar?" she said, pressing the phone to her ear. "Are you okay?"

"They released Tristan," she said without preamble.

"How did you—"

"Suzanna's death was ruled a suicide—apparently she had a note in her pocket, written not long after Colin died. The cops didn't have sufficient evidence to charge Tristan for anything, so they couldn't hold him for more than forty-eight hours. They let the bastard go."

She could barely contain the rage in her voice.

Roxie took a deep breath. "Skylar, we need to talk—"

But her sister had already hung up.

Roxie shook her head, cursing. "Send me the video," she told Jackson.

Jackson glanced at her, his expression wary. "What are you going to do with it?"

"I have no fucking idea."

33

Roxie could see light glowing softly through a broken window as she approached Ward Manor.

She had a feeling Tristan wouldn't want to go back to his own house after he'd been released from jail, considering it was just yards away from the girls who had gotten him arrested in the first place.

He didn't look surprised when she came through the door. She was the one startled—the place looked like hell. There was a blanket of red Solo cups on the floor, torn-down bone streamers, cobwebs, and curtains, and sticky puddles of spilled drinks on just about every surface. She noticed a pile of discarded shoes, and someone had smashed a pumpkin right in the middle of the living room floor, its guts spread over the antique carpet. Another enthusiastic partygoer had gotten into her stash of fake blood and dumped it all over the sheet she'd used to cover the couch—at least, she sincerely hoped it was fake. One never knew in this house.

Tristan was sitting apart from the chaos. He'd managed to clear an area of the floor in front of the fireplace and was burning a bundle of branches. He huddled close to the warmth, though he was still shivering.

Without a word, Roxie went to a closet where she kept some supplies. She'd slept over here more than one night when she felt like sneaking out and playing with shadows, so she'd stashed away a couple of blankets over the years.

She brought one to him—a quilt her grandmother had made—and held it out between them. A peace offering.

"Jackson told me everything," she said.

Tristan cursed. Rubbed his hands over his face. "Of course he did. That goddamn rat."

He didn't take the quilt. But she draped it over his shoulders anyway. Then she knelt in front of him and looked at him until he raised his gaze to hers. "I'm so, so sorry, Tristan," she said. "I was all wrong. So completely, horribly wrong. I should have known you would never do anything to hurt anyone." She added, with a wry twist to her mouth, "Except that goddamn rat, Jackson."

He didn't smile back. Roxie noticed he was still wearing the same gray hoodie as the night he was arrested—some of her fang makeup was smeared on his shoulder. "You should have known me better than that, Rox."

She nodded. Hurt and betrayal and exhaustion all weighed heavily on his face. It looked like he'd aged ten years in just the past couple of days. And her chest ached, knowing it was her fault.

But Tristan sighed. Then he reached out and grabbed her hand. "I was hiding so much from you for so long. I can't exactly blame you for coming to the wrong conclusions when I refused to give you the right ones. You asked me point-blank if I did it, and I couldn't give you an answer."

She squeezed his fingers in hers. "You were protecting Skylar. It was the last thing your brother ever asked for."

He laughed without humor. "You make it sound a lot more noble than it is. If I'd been there for him more in the first place, maybe he never would have gotten into this mess."

"Colin made his own choices—that isn't your fault."

Tristan shook his head. "If he'd just robbed a couple of places, honestly, things probably still would have turned out okay. He might have gotten caught and gone to prison for a few years. But he'd still be alive. The real problems started when he went to Dad."

The wind gave a howl outside. A moment later, they heard the patter of rain on the roof.

"Colin went to him for advice while he was still in prison. I don't know what the hell they talked about—where to get the best ski mask? But I think maybe Colin was expecting Dad to talk him out of it. To say he could do more with his life than what his father and grandfather had done before him. But, obviously, that's not how the conversation went.

"I never talked much about Dad with Colin. He always had Suzanna to protect him. I'm the one who got dragged out of bed all the time to go bury a duffel bag of cash in the woods before the cops came looking for it, or ride my bike to somebody's house to deliver a package I wasn't allowed to look inside, or bring beers out to him and his buddies all night while they planned out their latest small-time burglary like they were the crew from *Ocean's Eleven*. I'm the one he beat the shit out of when a job didn't go his way. And I'm the one who tipped off the cops before his last armed burglary and got him arrested—something Suzanna never forgave me for."

Roxie remembered Suzanna's cold words from the funeral home. *It should have been you.* Not only was Tristan a daily reminder of her husband's affair, but she blamed him for breaking up their family, too. And once Colin was gone, she'd decided she had nothing left to live for.

"Why did you tell me you'd been talking to her all this time? Did you have any idea she was dead?"

Tristan shook his head. "No. I mean, I guess I should have suspected. I didn't hear from her a single time after she left. Then again, I wasn't really expecting to. But every time you asked me about it, I thought it would sound too pathetic if I told you the truth—that the only mom I'd ever known didn't want anything to do with me. And your grandma kept offering to waive the rent for me. If she really knew I was paying for it all on my own, she probably wouldn't have given me a choice, even though she can't afford to keep that house without a paying tenant. I didn't want anyone to worry about me. So I lied."

The rain had started to come down harder, misting through the windows and dripping through cracks in the ceiling. The fire was burning low. Roxie and Tristan both huddled closer together, throwing the quilt over their heads to stay dry.

"If I'd been more open with Colin about what Dad was really like, he never would have gotten involved with him," Tristan went on. "He would have known Dad's schemes always end in disaster. Luke has a way of bringing people into his orbit and convincing them that they can trust him. But then the second shit hits the fan, he cuts them loose and takes off."

Which was exactly what Luke had done when Tristan was arrested.

She was already pressed against his side, but in that moment, Roxie needed to be closer to him. She pulled herself into his lap and buried her face in the hollow of his neck. His arms came around her, and he pressed his cheek to the top of her head while the thunder rumbled outside. And she hoped the heat of her body against his spoke what she couldn't adequately convey out loud. *I won't abandon you again, the way he did. I should have known better. I'll know better from now on.*

"But I didn't tell Colin any of that," Tristan whispered. "So, when Dad got out of prison and wanted to do the next job with him, Colin thought it would be a good idea.

"He had already hit the gas station and the coffee shop without a problem. But Dad told him he'd been thinking too small—he wanted to go for the bank. Which Colin wasn't so sure about. But Dad convinced him by telling him that he would go in himself, and all Colin had to do was wait out in the getaway car and be ready to drive. They'd split the money fifty-fifty.

"But that's where it went wrong. Because Colin wasn't planning on Dad killing Mr. Patterson.

"Dad told me Colin freaked out after that. He blamed himself for what had happened. He didn't want anything to do with the money, and he didn't think Dad should have any of it either, after what he'd done to get it.

"But he wasn't ready to take it straight to the police. Because he knew that when he did, he'd go to jail. And he'd lose Skylar—the person that he'd done all this for in the first place, as idiotic as it was. So, instead, he hid the money for a few days. Wouldn't tell Dad where it was, which went over about as well as you would expect. First, he was just threatening Colin, hounding him every day, calling him, and showing up when I wasn't home. Until finally, he threatened to hurt Skylar if Colin didn't tell him what he'd done with the money.

"And that was the last push Colin needed. That's when he decided to get the money back and turn himself in.

"At least, I think that's what happened. Dad didn't know exactly why Colin went to the Emporium that night. He thought maybe it was because he wanted to rob it. I didn't think so—not after Mr. Patterson died. But I couldn't think of any other reason he would have been there. Not until the Halloween party, when you told me that he'd hidden the money in the mirror. And then it made more sense. He must have been planning to go to the cops and tell them everything. But he went to get the money first—I think because he wanted to make sure Dad never got his hands on it."

Roxie bit her lip before she asked, "But it's possible that Colin was going back to take the money for himself, isn't it? Maybe he was planning to leave town with it. We can't really know for sure, can we?"

She felt Tristan shift for a moment beneath her before he said, "You're right. We can't know for sure. But I do know Colin. And he'd fucked up plenty of times before, but he always made it right in the end."

Roxie nodded—he couldn't see her under the dark of the quilt, but she knew he could feel her move against his neck. That was the version of Colin that made the most sense to her, too.

"But then why do you think he waited until after the Emporium closed, when he thought it was empty?" she asked. "He could have gone in while Skylar was working and snuck out with it."

"I don't know," Tristan said. "But I have a feeling he thought that if he saw her, he wouldn't be able to go through with it."

Roxie felt her already battered heart break a little more at that. And even though she knew that it was his own choices that had led him to that point, she still said, "Poor Colin."

"I could tell something had been eating away at him those last few days." Tristan went on. "But I didn't know what because I'd had no idea he was behind the robberies. No idea Dad was even back in town. And then, while I was in Ohio to help my cousin with his roof, Colin called me out of nowhere. He started saying he was sorry. That he'd been so stupid and there was no undoing what he'd done. He said he loved me.

"I kept asking him what was wrong, but he wouldn't tell me. So I told him to sit tight—I was on my way. I took the shortcut through the woods to get there as fast as I could. But it wasn't fast enough. By the time I made it back to Whistler, he was already dead." He let out a deep breath, stirring Roxie's hair. "I should have known the second I saw Jackson Mowery in my driveway that it was about to be the worst night of my life. Even before I noticed the blood on his shirt."

He paused for a long moment, his whole body tensing with the memory. She waited for him to go on, her cheek pressed to the heat of his collarbone as more thunder cracked outside and the rain came down even harder.

"Jackson showed me the video," he said finally. "I heard my brother's dying wish—*Skylar can't find out*. And there was no time to think about it. I did what he wanted.

"The lies just started snowballing after that. Where I'd been that night, where Colin was supposed to be, why I got so pissed at Jackson I almost killed him. Why my dad was back in town and what he was so desperate for me to find. I couldn't just rat him out to the police because he said if I did, he would make sure Skylar knew the truth of how Colin died. So for months, I've been turning this whole town upside-down, looking for the money so I could give it to him and he'd leave me alone. All while trying to keep my brother's secrets and make enough money to pay rent."

He let out a deep, exhausted breath.

Roxie shook her head. "I can't believe you've been carrying all this around for a whole year. I can't believe you let yourself get *arrested*."

"It's what Colin wanted."

She sighed. "He had no way of knowing it would come to this. You should have just told the cops the truth."

"And what do you think would have happened once Skylar found out she'd accidentally killed Colin?"

Roxie opened her mouth, but the words lodged in her throat. She had no idea. Didn't even want to think about it.

"Look," she said finally, "I don't want her to find out either. Of course I don't. But the cops are going to keep looking into you, and if you keep lying to them, you might end up getting punished for something you didn't do."

"Roxie, I didn't do all this only because my brother asked me to. I didn't just do it to protect Skylar. I did it because I've lost a sibling, and I know that it's hell. A never-ending hell. And I don't want you to have to lose your sister, too. And that's what's going to happen if you don't let me take the fall for Colin's death."

"No," Roxie said, her breath hitching. "We'll figure something else out."

She squeezed him hard around the waist. She could feel him shaking against her, and she didn't think it was from the cold.

"You don't get it—you can save me, or you can save Skylar. You can't do both. I'm trying to make it easy for you. I'm telling you to pick her. Whether or not she goes back to Yale, she's got a hell of a lot more going for her than I do. She's got a life to hold on to. I've got nothing."

"Bullshit," Roxie said. "You've got me."

Tristan was silent at that.

"Is that nothing?" Roxie pressed.

"No," he said. "It's not."

Roxie lifted her head from his chest. Though it was still too dark to see him clearly, she knew his mouth was close to hers. She could feel his breath on her lips.

And then he closed the gap between them.

There were a lot of people who were afraid of Tristan, even before he became the suspect of a murder investigation. But Roxie had always known better—and she would never let herself forget it again. She wasn't surprised by the way he touched his lips to hers. Slow, tender, searching, reverent.

It was Roxie who dove right in, pulling him hard against her with her hands balled up in his shirt. Her tongue that parted his lips. Her hands that roved over the solid plane of his chest. He responded, mirroring her movements, letting her take the lead.

And there's no telling where she would have taken him. Because she froze when she heard a clicking noise.

The thunder still rumbled outside. But this was closer. And she had the unmistakable feeling that they were being watched.

When she threw off the blankets, she was staring down the barrel of a gun.

But then Skylar swung the gun to the right, away from her, and pointed it at Tristan.

34

Tristan and Roxie scrambled to their feet.

How long had she been there? How much had she heard?

"Skylar," Roxie said, trying to keep her voice level. "Put the gun down. We need to talk. He didn't kill Colin."

"Right." Skylar barked a laugh. "Of course he didn't. That was me, wasn't it?"

All of it. She'd heard all of it.

"You just believe every bullshit story you hear from him, don't you?"

"It's not a story, Skylar. I spoke to Jackson—"

"Jackson? He's *terrified* of Tristan. He could get him to say whatever he wanted."

"It's the truth this time."

"After all the lies he's told you—"

"He *had* to lie. He—

Just then, a crack of thunder sounded through the room, so loud and close that the house shook with it.

And, for all of Skylar's practice, all her attempts to feel comfortable with a weapon in her hand, she flinched at the sound.

The gun fired.

The next moment was a blur of motion and sound. Tristan fell to the floor. Roxie screamed. But he wasn't hit—the bullet had gone past him, to the right, ripping a hole in the wall.

When he managed to get on his feet again, he was running. Skylar was standing between him and the door, forcing him the other way, up the rickety staircase.

She started to run after him, but Roxie tackled her before she could. She winced when she heard her sister's head hit the ground. The gun clattered away in the dark.

Skylar shoved her off, feeling around on her hands and knees, but Roxie found it first, trapping it under her boot.

Skylar growled in frustration. But then she ran up the stairs without it.

She had nothing to hurt him with now but her bare hands. Though after a year of pain and loss and rage building inside of her, Roxie feared that maybe that would be enough. She took off after her—but not before she threw the gun outside, through one of the broken windows.

There were five bedrooms upstairs. Tristan had to be hiding in one of them. Skylar was slamming the doors open, yelling his name over more *booms* of thunder.

By the time Roxie made it to the top of the stairs, Skylar was inside one of the rooms, throwing open a closet door and then searching the bathroom. Not finding Tristan in either, she turned to storm back out. But Roxie blocked her way.

It was the room where Lucy Clark had slit her sister's throat. She knew it by the dark stain on the floor but also because it was the only room with its own balcony. In her research, Roxie had dug up the renovation plans Eleanor had made. It had been built just for her, so she could look out into the woods every morning and watch the sun rise through the trees.

The balcony doors had fallen off some time ago. Now rain slanted in through the opening, warping the floorboards, misting all over the room.

Skylar tried to push past her, but Roxie stood firm, her hands braced on both sides of the doorframe.

"Move," Skylar demanded.

When Roxie still didn't budge, Skylar took a step back. The room was almost completely black, but Roxie saw her face briefly when the lightning flashed through the windows. The rage and the hurt were etched so plainly on her face. There were tears shining on her cheeks.

It made Roxie want to lie to her—to conjure some version of events that would keep her from the truth, if only just a little longer, the same way Tristan and Jackson had been doing for over a year.

They'd both been trying so hard to protect her with a story. But that's what had brought them here. Skylar was still in pain and still desperate for answers, shedding more and more of herself every day. So maybe the truth was the only way to save her now.

"Don't you get it?" Skylar said, her voice breaking. "Nobody is going to pay for what happened to Colin unless I *make* them pay." She held a hand against her stomach, like all the hurt in her voice had become a physical thing, eating her up. "It won't end until I end it. It won't stop feeling like this until I *do* something."

"I understand you want someone to punish for what happened. But there is no one to punish. It was an accident."

Skylar shook her head, trying to force her way through again and again. "Get out of the way. He's going to escape. He's going to—"

"I will," Roxie said. "But you have to let me show you something first."

And then she handed Skylar her phone.

35

Over the past eighteen years, Roxie had thought she'd seen Skylar's face in all its iterations, a thousand times over. She knew exactly how her features arranged themselves when she was frustrated with a problem she couldn't solve. Or when she had an idea, her lips spreading into a very particular type of smile, like this big, genius breakthrough was sitting right in front of her, entirely separate from her, and she'd never seen anything so beautiful. Roxie was painfully aware of the signs her sister was annoyed—rolling her eyes or pursing her lips. She knew how Skylar looked when she was grieving, like an ocean dried up, nothing but salt and grit and death left behind. Roxie knew what Skylar looked like when hope started to come back to her, a candle flickering, fighting back the dark.

But she had never seen the look frozen on her face now as she finished watching the video that Jackson had taken the night Colin died. And it terrified Roxie, not knowing precisely what Skylar's expression meant.

Her eyes were wide and blank. Jaw clenched hard. She was shaking all over.

And Roxie decided that, while they were telling hard truths, it was best to get it all over with at once.

"Grandma is the one who gave Tristan the stationery. She gave some to Colin, too, when he found out you were going away to Yale. He had some before he died. When you showed me the breakup note for the first time, I couldn't think of any reason why he would do that to you. But once I learned he was behind the robberies, it finally made sense. Because the only reason he would break your heart is if he thought staying with you would hurt you even more. He was about to turn himself in to the police for what he'd done, and he didn't want there to be any chance you might try to wait out his sentence for him. He wanted you to move on and live your life. Which is the same reason he begged Jackson to keep his secret. Because Colin loved you. The last thing he wanted was to hold you back.

"He made some really shitty choices, but he was going to do the right thing in the end. Because he was still the good person you knew. That's why he went to the Emporium that night—to grab the money from where he'd hidden it in the mirror and take it to the police."

Skylar was still silent. Still staring at the screen, long after the video had ended.

"You didn't know it was him," Roxie pressed on. "You had every reason to believe he was dangerous. To protect yourself. The ricocheting bullet was a freak accident. Nothing you could control. It was Colin who put himself in that spot in the first place. He didn't blame you, and you shouldn't blame yourself either."

The storm had become a pitter-patter of rain on the rooftop, suddenly soft.

And then, Skylar took a step. Not toward Roxie but in the direction of the balcony.

Maybe she just needed air. To feel rain on her face and clear her head so she could make sense of it all.

Or maybe not. Maybe she thought the weight of this new tragedy was too much for her to live with. Maybe she had decided she wasn't going to.

Whatever the reason, Roxie refused to find out.

She rushed forward, wrapping her sister tight in her arms. Holding her in place.

Skylar's whole body was quaking. She kept her arms at her sides, the phone still clutched tight in one hand.

"I know it's easy to feel like we're cursed," Roxie said. "But Grandma told me that it isn't true. No matter how many horrible things happen to us, we still get to decide for ourselves what it means to be a Clark. And I've decided it means that we don't give up on each other. Ever. I know this is a lot for you to face, and you're going to be facing it for a long time. But you won't be facing it alone."

"She's right."

Roxie turned her head to find Grandma standing in the doorway. Tristan must have called her—she could see his shadow hovering anxiously in the hallway behind Gertie's shoulder.

There were tears in her eyes. But she didn't seem the least

bit surprised by what she was seeing. Tristan had probably briefed her as well as he could. Even then, it must have been a lot to process so quickly.

But Gertie Clark had been through it all. And she wasn't afraid of pain or guilt or grief anymore.

Skylar hardly seemed to register her presence. But her grandmother still stepped into the room and put her arms around both girls.

She didn't say, *It'll all be okay.* Because sometimes, it wouldn't be.

She didn't say, *Everything happens for a reason*, because there was no good reason for Colin to be gone.

She didn't tell them, *Let's be thankful for the years we had with him*, because she knew it hadn't been enough. It would never, ever be enough.

Instead, she rocked them back and forth in her arms, just like the day their aunt Violet had died, and she whispered the same thing to them now as she had then, chanting it like a song to sing to themselves on the hardest nights: "I'm here. I'm here. I'm here. I'm here. I'm here."

Until finally, Roxie felt Skylar's arms squeeze them back.

And the last Clark women alive kept holding on to each other.

36

Three months later

"What do you think?"

Roxie stood with her hands on her hips, looking over her ghost-tour bus while Tristan watched her face to gauge her reaction.

She kept her expression carefully blank as she circled around the front, where most of the destruction had been. She examined the new windshield and the repairs to the front axle. There had been extensive damage to the frame where it had been crushed against the tree, but that was nothing but a bad memory now. The hood was propped open, and Tristan pointed out a few things—something about a radiator and an alternator and a power steering reservoir, all of which made zero sense to her, but she nodded along anyway like she completely understood.

"I had Nick triple-check the brake lines. Quadruple-check, actually." He rubbed sheepishly at the back of his neck.

Nick at a repair shop across town had done all the work.

Tristan wouldn't trust himself this time around, enlisting the help of a more experienced mechanic. He'd also wanted to pay for the repairs, saying the wreck had been his fault in the first place, but Roxie wouldn't let him—she knew he couldn't afford it anyhow.

She'd been saving up for a bus or a van before he'd given her this one, so she'd put that nest egg to good use. It hadn't been cheap, and he'd told her it probably would have been a better idea to use the money to buy a different vehicle altogether, but she refused. For better or worse, this one was hers.

She did one last walk-around, admiring the new paint job—jet-black with white stenciling, just like before. Then she stepped inside, Tristan trailing behind her while she assessed the interior. It looked like it had been ransacked by wolves—but that was in keeping with her original design plan, so nothing out of place there. The driver's seat had been replaced where the old one had been impaled by the tree branch. And behind it, sitting in the first row, her lovely skeleton assistant, Frannie Phantom, was already in place.

Roxie plopped down in the driver's seat before gripping the steering wheel. Then she looked up at Tristan, and her face broke into a grin. He smiled back, tilting her chin up to give her a long, deep kiss.

She blinked, dazed for a few moments afterward. She still hadn't gotten quite used to that. And she hoped she never would.

She snapped out of it when her phone buzzed in her pocket with a text message.

She glanced over her shoulder at Tristan as he settled into place on the seat beside Frannie Phantom. "Grandma says

Skylar isn't home yet," Roxie told him. "She wants me to go check on her."

"Do you know where to find her?"

"I think so," she said.

Tristan nodded. He had the same idea. "I'll ride over with you," he said. "It's close enough for me to walk home." Then he made a show of hunkering down in his seat, gripping the edges with white knuckles. "Now take it easy, would you?"

"Don't I always?" she said, winking back.

Then she revved the engine, making the bus rumble to life around them.

She ran her hand over the dashboard, and she whispered, "Welcome back from the dead, my friend," before she sped out of the garage and into the night.

☽

"How has she been?" Tristan asked.

Roxie frowned at the question. She didn't quite know how to answer it.

They were standing at the edge of Rose Hill Cemetery, looking at Skylar through the rungs of the wrought iron gate. It had snowed the night before, but Skylar didn't seem to mind. She was lying down on it as though it were a bed of soft grass, her wool hat cushioning her skull at the base of Colin's headstone while she stared up at the starry sky.

It had taken her a long time to visit Colin's grave. She hadn't come at all before the investigation because it was too sad. After the investigation, when the truth came out, she was too angry for a while.

It was a complicated anger, sometimes directed at him for

what he'd done, sometimes at herself for what she'd accidentally done. Sometimes it was an anger she could live with, burning just under the surface, barely even perceptible. But sometimes, it was a desperate, wrenching thing that made her want to scream or cry, or both, like someone was holding a blowtorch to her skin and she just needed to make it all *stop*.

Therapy had helped. A lot of it.

Still, there were some days when Skylar would be as unreachable as ever, and Roxie would feel the fear that she would never come back grip tight around her heart. Though she'd decided that no matter what happened, she'd never stop reaching for Skylar. And so far, Skylar had always let herself be reached.

The polite response Roxie gave to people in town when they asked how her sister was doing was simply, *She's much better, thank you.*

But because it was Tristan, she told him the truth. "Sometimes she's good. Sometimes she's really bad. We're taking it a day at a time."

He nodded, like he understood. And if anyone did, it was him.

Skylar had apologized to him. At length. He assured her over and over again that he wasn't upset with her. Which Roxie thought was pretty damn generous of him, considering she'd pointed a gun at his head.

Skylar wasn't exactly on track toward being his best friend. It was more of a *let's try our best not to be awkward now that you're my sister's boyfriend* kind of relationship.

Roxie appreciated the effort.

A gust swept through the graveyard, making her shiver; Tristan pulled her in close, a moment's refuge from the cold.

"Please don't freeze to death out here."

"You aren't the boss of me, Riley."

"Fair enough," he said, pressing a kiss to the top of her head before he let her go. "But I would appreciate it if you'd take my request into consideration."

Roxie gave a nod. "Consider it considered."

He tucked his hands into his jacket pockets. He took one last glance at Skylar and his brother's grave. Then he told Roxie, "I'll leave you to it."

As he turned to walk away from her, he said over his shoulder, "If you don't make it, don't forget to haunt me."

"Stop being so romantic, or I'll start right now," she said, kicking snow after him.

She watched him go, following the streetlights home, before she entered the cemetery.

Roxie approached Colin's headstone. Skylar was lying so still, Roxie thought she might have fallen asleep. But when she stood directly over her sister, she saw her eyes were open.

Skylar didn't acknowledge her. So Roxie lay down beside her in the snow. And they were both quiet for a long time.

"It really hurts today," Skylar said finally.

The words made Roxie's heart ache, but she didn't say anything back. She just reached out and grabbed her sister's hand, gripping it hard through their mittens.

It had taken a long time for her to learn how to be there for Skylar. Right after Colin had died, she'd mostly avoided

Skylar's grief—not because she didn't care, but because she had no idea what to say. Then, she'd tried to fix it, desperate for a quick solution to her sister's sadness. And that had nearly ended in disaster.

Roxie still didn't always get it right. But she'd learned the best way she could be there for Skylar was to listen. So she waited.

Finally, Skylar said, "You told me that telling ghost stories helps you feel more connected to the women in our family who are gone."

Roxie nodded, though it hadn't been a question.

"I want you to tell me a story about Colin."

That took her off guard. She thought about it for a few moments. "I don't think I have any you don't already know."

"Then tell me one I already know. Help me remember."

"All right," Roxie said. Considering for a few moments, she asked, "What about when he got the tattoo?"

She looked over at her sister, who had already started smiling, and she knew it had been the right choice.

"It was a dark and stormy night when Colin Riley decided he needed permanent ink," Roxie began, using the same voice she did on her tours, adding a veneer of legend to the boy they had known.

Truthfully, Roxie thought he'd only come to the decision because he didn't want the fake ID he'd paid a hundred bucks for to be a total waste. He'd attempted to use it a few times to get into the bars downtown, but he'd been foiled at every turn— not one bouncer believed the kid with the springy curls and baby face was even close to twenty-one. But he just needed to convince someone he was eighteen to get a tattoo, which was only a lie by eight months.

"He wanted witnesses," Roxie went on. "So we all piled in the car—you, me, and Tristan—and he whisked us off into the night."

There had been no plan, of course. He didn't have the slightest idea when he walked into the tattoo parlor what he wanted to have on his body for the rest of his life.

"We flipped through all the binders of sample artwork. Tristan wanted him to get donuts around his nipples. I was really pushing hard for a Minnie Mouse portrait on his ass. You wouldn't give any suggestions at all—just stood in the corner like this."

Roxie did her best Skylar impression, crossing her arms over her chest and rolling her eyes so hard, it hurt.

Skylar elbowed her. "Worst dramatized reenactment I've ever seen, but continue."

"So you're busy looking disapproving, I'm holding the binder against my butt to give everyone a visual of my Minnie Mouse idea, and Tristan keeps saying, *Man, donuts are timeless.*

"In the end, he ignored all of us and went with a tree design on his chest. But he didn't pick one out from the sample binders. Instead, he pulled a picture up on his phone, handed it to the artist, and hopped on the table."

"It was the sugar maple behind our house," Skylar jumped in, her voice soft. "The one we used to sit under in the summer."

Roxie remembered. Skylar and Colin would be out there for

hours sometimes, eating lunch on a picnic blanket, or watching a movie on her laptop, or just lying together, Skylar's head pillowed on his stomach while they talked and watched the clouds go by.

"I tried to pretend I still thought the tattoo was a bad idea," Skylar said. "But I think he caught me smiling when I saw what he picked."

"And then you held his hand the whole time while he pretended it didn't hurt like hell," Roxie said.

"I told him he got bonus points if he cried," Skylar said. "He asked me what *bonus points* meant, and I told him he'd have to give me a tear to find out. And out of nowhere, he manages to squeeze one out. Just this single tear going down his cheek." Skylar laughed, pressing her mittened hands to her stomach. "He was such a little shit."

They both went quiet after that, listening to the frigid breeze whistling through the headstones.

"Remember when he released those chickens down the hallway for the senior prank?" Skylar said.

"Now *that* was legendary."

"He wasn't even a senior."

"He didn't let labels define him! I really respected that."

They lay there for a while longer, telling stories back and forth. Like when he'd decided to take up track and knocked over every single hurdle but still decided to run a victory lap at the end. Or the time he'd played Joseph in the town nativity play, only to have his robe catch on the manger so he ended up mooning the entire town (which he swore up and down was an accident but never could explain why he hadn't been wearing underwear). Roxie had a history class with him once where he'd improvised an entire speech about Abraham Lincoln on the spot because he'd completely forgotten the assignment. The presentation was so factually inaccurate, he should have failed anyway, but the teacher was so impressed by the top hat he'd managed to make out of a coffee can and construction paper that she gave him a passing grade.

The whole time, Skylar was toying with her daisy necklace, which she still wore every day—on the good ones and the bad ones, and all the ones in between.

Finally, when they'd been there for so long that their lips started to go numb, they decided to have mercy on Grandma Gertie. She'd been blowing up their phones with *where are you* texts for the past half hour.

They pushed themselves to their feet, brushed the snow off their clothes, and walked home down the quiet, snowy streets. Not another person in sight. Though Roxie never felt completely alone in Whistler.

That's what she liked so much about this town—how the past and the present seemed to rub against each other. It was like a closet stuffed full of clothes, the new in the front and the old shoved to the back, forgotten about but still there whenever you were ready to take them out again. And Roxie loved nothing more than to shake the dust off the old things and wear them around for a while, letting them breathe.

You didn't have to live in Whistler to know what she meant. All you had to do was walk down any street in town, at any time of day. She had been to plenty of other places, but none of them felt quite like this one.

Ask, and she'd tell you what she told everyone—that it was just something you had to come and experience for yourself.

And if you need a guide, come find me.

Acknowledgments

It was my dream for many years to publish a book. *Two* books sounded too good to be true. But here it is, my sophomore novel! I hope you enjoyed it. I know I enjoyed working on it. It's a mash-up of all the things I love—ghost stories, family sagas, gallows humor, sisterhood, and small-town secrets.

There are so many people I have to thank for getting it into your hands.

Victoria Doherty-Munro, I've been so incredibly lucky to have you in my corner from the beginning of my publishing journey. Your steady guidance and expertise have been invaluable.

Camille Kellogg, I'm grateful for the way you stepped in to champion this story. Your immediate enthusiasm gave me a fresh surge of confidence when I needed it, and also assured me that Roxie was in good hands.

Allison Moore, one moment I was standing in an NYC

Starbucks feeling self-conscious and out of place, and the next I got an email saying you were interested in acquiring my first book, and my hands started shaking for a completely different reason. It will forever be one of the highlights of my life. *The Hollow Inside* and *After Dark with Roxie Clark* wouldn't be what they are without you.

Thank you to the team at Bloomsbury for all you've done to bring Roxie's story to life, specifically Diane Aronson, Laura Phillips, Nicholas Church, Yelena Safronova, Donna Mark, Sarah Shumway, Phoebe Dyer, Ariana Abad, Briana Williams, Faye Bi, Erica Barmash, Beth Eller, Valentina Rice, and Alona Fryman.

Dana Ledl, I could not have asked for a better cover. It captures Roxie and this story so perfectly, I kept it pulled up beside my Word document for inspiration while I worked on the final draft. I hope this book is even half as cool as your illustration for it.

To all my friends at Carmichael's Bookstore (especially Maggie Henriksen!). I moved to Louisville a month before COVID shutdowns and being in a new city where I knew almost no one felt especially isolating. Working at Carmichael's changed all that. Suddenly, I was surrounded by a group of wonderful, book-loving people who made me feel at home for the first time in months.

Thank you to Lilly for taking all those brainstorming walks with me, and Merlin, who checked on me the nights I stayed up until sunrise to finish the last big revision.

Patty Byard, every time I took a trip to visit you, I had an important breakthrough in plotting this story. I'm pretty sure I owe that to your home full of good books, great company, and amazing food. (I think I had approximately one thousand handfuls of party mix the last time I was there.)

Mom and Dad, I'm constantly in awe of how far you're willing to go for your kids. I know I tell you all the time, but I really can't thank you enough for all the miles driven, the billion trips to Lowe's, the reassuring phone calls, and all the other things you do to keep us going. I owe you the world, but I suspect you would just hand it back to me.

Quinton, you teach me more about love every day. You give me pep talks over breakfast and dream with me while we sip coffee. You ground me when fear and restless thoughts make it hard to breathe. You make my work better. You make my life better.

Weston, Afton, and Aubri, you taught me what it means to be a sister. In the words of Roxie Clark—*we don't give up on each other. Ever.*

And most of all, I want to thank you—my readers—for continuing to breathe life into this dream.